REVISITING
SUMMER NIGHTS

What Reviewers Say About Ashley Bartlett's Work

Cash Braddock

"There were moments I laughed out loud, pop culture references that I adored and parts I cringed because I'm a good girl and Cash is kind of bad. I relished the moments that Laurel and Cash spent alone. These two are really a good match and their chemistry just jumps off the page. Playful, serious and sarcastic all rolled into one harmonious pairing. The story is great, the characters are fantastic and the twist, well, I never saw it coming."—*Romantic Reader*

"This book was amazing; Bartlett has a knack for being able to create characters that just jump off the page and immerse themselves into your heart."—*Fantastic Book Reviews*

"Ashley Bartlett was able to leave me hanging on every word and then at the end just like a junkie from the book… I was hooked and craving more!"—*Les Rêveur*

The Price of Cash

"The chemistry between Cash and Laurel is fantastic. This match has tension, heartache that pulls you deep into their dilemma. You want them to go for it and damn the consequences. It is so good! The whole book is fantastic, the love story, the crime, supporting cast, really top notch. Ashley Bartlett has written a fabulous follow-up. I cannot say enough good things about this one. I am absolutely hooked on this series!"—*Romantic Reader Blog*

"This series is like nothing else I have ever read in this genre and it just keeps getting better. It's a solid storyline that keeps me guessing as to what will happen next. Cash and Laurel's emotions are highly charged and you can feel the chemistry brewing between them. I was hooked and kept praying they would just launch themselves at each other. 5 stars"—*Les Rêveur*

Cash and the Sorority Girl

"I live for this series. Live. For. It! I love the paradox that is Cash. This amazing human being with her genuine spirit just pulls to me. On the flip side, she's a drug dealer so there is the conundrum you find yourself, as the reader, in. It's glorious."—*Romantic Reader Blog*

"Bartlett writes really well. I especially love her dialogue writing skills. Anyone who has taken a creative writing class knows dialogue is not easy to write. Bartlett crushes it and is able to make a morally grey character extremely likeable. I actually think Cash would make my top ten list of favorite lesfic characters. Her sense of humor, her sarcasm and wit, the way she cares about people and communicates, makes a character that I want to read about."—*LezReviewBooks*

"Be prepared for an emotional rollercoaster. Because in reading this book, there are a few things I can guarantee. 1. You are going to laugh. A lot. 2. The sarcasm is phenomenal, and one of the main reasons I adore this series. And 3. Be prepared to feel emotionally destroyed afterwards because honestly, this book is all heart, but there are some hard to read moments. Is it worth it? F*ck yes!!!"—*Les Rêveur*

Journey to Cash

"This series is tons of fun to read; it's witty, well-written and completely entertaining. With every book readers get great characters, fantastic dialogue, and well-plotted stories. ...It's probably one of the most engaging contemporary lesfic series to come along."—*Lesbian Book Blog*

"*Journey to Cash* by Ashley Bartlett, one of my most favorite books of the year. I absolutely love the Cash Braddock series. There is nothing like this series in all of lesfic. It's creative, dynamic, and smart. Time after time, Ashley Bartlett has delivered exceptional writing. Every single book in this series deserves praise because it is absolutely outstanding. If you have not read this series I cannot recommend it enough. 4 books, all 5+ stars."—*Romantic Reader Blog*

"There isn't really anything else like this out there in queer fiction at the moment that I'm aware of and I love how much it stands out. It hit me whilst I was reading the third book in the series—*Cash and the Sorority Girl*—that one of the reasons I love this series so much is its inherent queerness. The discussions of the patriarchy and heteronormativity in an everyday manner and how it flows through the whole series are fantastic."—*LGBTQ+ Reader*

"This series is clever, witty, funny, heartfelt, angsty, and exciting. Each book in the series got better and better (with book 3 being my absolute favorite) and this is a series I will happily reread again and again."—*LezReviewBooks*

Dirty Sex

"A young, new author, Ashley Bartlett definitely should be on your radar. She's a really fresh, unique voice in a sea of good authors. …I found [*Dirty Sex*] to be flawless. The characters are deep and the action fast-paced. The romance feels real, not contrived. There are no fat, padded scenes, but no skimpy ones either. It's told in a strong first-person voice that speaks of the author's and her character's youth, but serves up surprisingly mature revelations."—*Out in Print*

Dirty Money

"Bartlett has exquisite taste when it comes to selecting the right detail. And no matter how much plot she has to get through, she never rushes the game. Her writing is so well-paced and so self-assured, she should be twice as old as she really is. That self-assuredness also mirrors through to her characters, who are fully realized and totally believable."—*Out in Print*

"Bartlett has succeeded in giving us a mad-cap story that will keep the reader turning page after page to see what happens next."—*Lambda Literary*

Dirty Power

"Bartlett's talents are many. She knows her way around an action scene, she writes *memorably* hot sex, her plots are seamless, and her characters are true and deep. And if that wasn't enough, Coop's voice is so genuine, so world-weary, jaded, and outrageously sarcastic that if Bartlett had none of the aforementioned attributes, the read would still be entertaining enough to stretch over three books."
—*Out in Print*

"Here we have some rough and tumble action with some felons on the run! A big plus is the main characters were very engaging right from the start. ...If you like your books super chocked full of all manner of things, this will be a winner. I definitely ended up enjoying this wild and woolly whoosh through the world of hardcore criminals and those who track them. Give it a try!"—*Rainbow Book Reviews*

Visit us at www.boldstrokesbooks.com

By the Author

Sex & Skateboards

Revisiting Summer Nights

Dirty Trilogy

Dirty Sex

Dirty Money

Dirty Power

Cash Braddock Series

Cash Braddock

The Price of Cash

Cash and the Sorority Girl

Journey to Cash

REVISITING SUMMER NIGHTS

by

Ashley Bartlett

2024

ISBN 13: 978-1-63679-551-5

THIS TRADE PAPERBACK ORIGINAL IS PUBLISHED BY
BOLD STROKES BOOKS, INC.
P.O. BOX 249
VALLEY FALLS, NY 12185

FIRST EDITION: APRIL 2024

CREDITS
EDITOR: CINDY CRESAP
PRODUCTION DESIGN: SUSAN RAMUNDO
COVER DESIGN BY INKSPIRAL DESIGN

Acknowledgments

Slasher movies are fucking great. They are a wonderful vehicle for moral quandaries and nihilism and also hot people running around bloody, which, let's be honest, makes them hotter. Slasher flicks can be as surface or as deep as you like. They are in constant communication with all of their predecessors and yet, they remain self-contained stories. They also exist under the auspices of their studios, which layers in this whole element of patriarchal control. Control of bodies and stories and characters who come from the minds of writers and are then twisted into thinly veiled excuses for consumerism and sex. What I'm saying is that I'm super fun to get stuck talking to at parties. But I'm also saying that slasher movies would be greatly improved by the addition of lots and lots of queers. So I thought I'd do that.

Writing is a solitary experience, but being a writer is very much not. Whitney, you were even more brilliant than I hoped. Your notes made this thing comprehensible, but also gave me the motivation to continue when I really didn't wanna. T, you taught me so much about making movies. You made this film set come alive. Thank you for helping me find the places where the machinations of filmmaking intersected with my plot and also for letting me believe I was doing something new even when I wasn't.

Bold Strokes is the best home. I feel privileged to have a seat at this table. Rad, Sandy, I'm so glad you like me even when I'm not likable. Cindy, you're a butthole for making me write a one-book story. It wasn't as hard as I thought it would be and I think I might have learned stuff. It sucked.

Finally, thank you to my readers. This novel is a bit of a departure for me (the protagonist doesn't commit crimes?) but there's still plenty to like (metaphorical kicking of the patriarchy). I sure do hope you like it.

Dedication

For my wife

PROLOGUE

Taylor Henderson squeezed her eyes closed as if committing to the act would make her more invisible. Blood was streaked across her strong jaw. Tears and sweat mingled, melting the blood until a drop trembled and fell from her chin. Grace was dead. Taylor had seen her go down in a lethal spray of blood. Their summer romance had been cut short in the very hayloft where they'd shared their first kiss.

The killer was approaching. His cowboy-booted footsteps were muted by the dirt and hay littering the barn floor. Taylor readied herself. She was the final girl, after all.

With a deep, steadying breath, Taylor stilled. Her fingers tightened on the rusted hoof pick, her only weapon. The killer's boots came into view between the slats of the horse stall door. She moved fast, digging the pick into his calf and dragging it through denim and flesh. She burst out of the stall and sprinted; his screams of pain and impotent rage followed her. She ran out to the pasture and the wide barn doors clattered and bounced shut behind her. Dust motes from the old wood floated in the moonlight.

The camera panned wide overhead, showing the trees surrounding the meadow, then turned and zoomed into Taylor's face. We saw her moment of desperate elation when she thought she'd escaped him. Then, suddenly, his shadowed silhouette came into view behind her. The worn, dark cowboy hat that shadowed his face, the baggy plaid shirt that whipped open in the summer breeze to show a white ribbed undershirt, the Wranglers and boots now soaked in his blood.

He tackled her. They grappled on the ground until she was trapped beneath him. There was no hope for Taylor. Her arms were pinned. Her wounds and soul-deep exhaustion robbed her of any remaining fight.

Black Hat raised the Bowie knife, held tightly between his hands. The silver tooling on the blade glistened red in the moonlight. Taylor was sobbing in fear. And then it happened. The pitchfork burst through his thick neck. Blood spurted from his severed carotid. The pitchfork was pulled out and Black Hat fell to the side. Grace stood perfectly framed behind him. She tossed aside the bloody pitchfork and extended her hands to Taylor. Grace's blond hair was matted with blood on one side. She was battered and dirty, but she was alive.

"I told you the barn was dangerous," Grace said. Her blue eyes glinted with that hint of flirtatious teasing that had so enraptured Taylor and the audience for the last ninety minutes.

Taylor smiled. "Summer nights are made for danger."

The camera panned up again, completing the same route as before, but this time it stopped and swirled overhead. The music swelled as the local sheriff in his beat-up SUV arrived. The brown Bronco bumped over the overgrown pasture. A cruiser joined them. Then another and an ambulance. Red and blue lights bathed the darkened evergreens all around them.

In the next shot, Grace was sitting on the bumper of the ambulance. An EMT stepped away so Taylor could step in. Taylor and Grace kissed and kissed and kissed. Destruction and danger surrounded them, but our final girls could only see each other.

When we filmed it, none of us knew it would be important. Even then, sitting at the premiere, holding Wylie's hand in the darkened theater, we thought it only mattered to us. We didn't know about the coming months and the crying girls and women who would line up to see it, to see themselves. We didn't know how history would shift. All I knew was that Wy and I were strangers who had been cast to play teenage girls who fell in love. Our agents hadn't told us not to fall in love for real. That was on them.

The movie wasn't great. We definitely knew that when we were filming. The plot was a little thin. The gore and sex were a little graphic. It was a mid-budget feature that banked on a couple of quotable lines and up-and-coming actors who were pretty. And damn we were—even though we didn't know it then. So I sat and watched myself kiss my real-life girlfriend on screen.

Wylie raised our joined hands and kissed my knuckle. We'd been scolded plenty by the studio. No kissing in front of the press. We could be in love in public. We could kiss on screen. We could not muddle the two.

"You're going to get us yelled at again," I whispered.

She leaned close. "What are they going to do? The movie's done."

I was well aware of what they could do. My agency and a team of suits had explained in painful detail. But right then I didn't care. So I kissed her. She smelled like fresh honey and bright citrus. Her lips were warm and soft and seductive. I wanted this event to be over already. I wanted to be back in a hotel suite we wouldn't notice, finding new ways to make her squirm and moan. But she wanted to watch the movie. It was her first feature and the novelty felt fresh and new.

"Can we get out of here yet?" I asked.

She laughed softly. "Soon." She pulled me to my feet.

Outside the theater, our co-stars milled about, waiting for us to pile into a limo with them. I had a feeling we'd be partying until dawn. Wy squeezed my hand and I didn't mind the wait. When we emerged, the paparazzi collectively turned and descended on us. They shouted our names and asked for pictures. We smiled and posed and tried to rush past.

"PJ, Wylie, come." Sean waved us toward himself. He'd already gathered Taryn and Jeffrey for another photo in front of the wide Oath Entertainment backdrop.

"I told you we should have snuck out earlier," I whispered.

"I thought he left," Wy whispered back.

Jeffrey stood between Taryn and Sean, his arm possessively around Taryn's waist. The press assumed they were a couple and they let the assumption stand. Jeffrey's agents were working overtime to sell his pretty boy muscles and charming smile as purely heterosexual. According to the studio, it just wouldn't do for three of the five stars to be queer. Wylie and I were already too much.

By the time we'd crossed the sidewalk to Sean, he'd wrangled Kaleb as well. With a subtle nod and a flick of his wrist, he sent the boys to the outer edges of our group and gathered me and Wy on one side, Taryn on the other. Director's privilege never ended. Jeffrey shot Taryn a look. Years later, that look would be Sean's damnation, but for tonight, he was king.

Sean put his arms around my waist and Taryn's. His fingers were hot, pressing into the thin material of my dress. He smelled like bourbon-soaked tobacco—an ironic scent for a man who notoriously didn't smoke or drink hard liquor. We all smiled for the cameras. Moments later, Jeffrey made a production of seeing our waiting limo. In the ensuing shuffle, Kaleb slid his arms around me and Wylie, holding us obnoxiously close and separating me from Sean. I rolled my eyes at him, playing it up like the siblings we portrayed on screen.

The photographers called for me and Wylie to give them photos. We held hands and waved before tumbling into the limo behind everyone. The photos were immediately posted with headlines like "Final Girl's Final Frontier." The implication was that two of us survived. They didn't say the queer part out loud.

Dangerous Summer Nights was a horror flick. No one expected it to actually be successful. But our real-life romance sold the movie. And who wouldn't love two young starlets who crashed the genre and made it something new? As if we had any choice in the matter.

CHAPTER ONE

There was nothing I wanted more than my bed. I knew my flight would be bad. I was too annoyed and exhausted for it not to be, but I couldn't have foreseen exactly how bad. From sitting on the tarmac at JFK for over an hour to an impromptu diversion for fuel, my five-hour flight had somehow taken eight hours.

I'd been up for twenty hours. Twenty hours of talking, which made it feel like forty. I was reasonably certain I'd spoken to every journalist in the tristate area about the film I'd just finished directing. I had not spoken to my agent, which was why I made the mistake of turning off airplane mode once I was in the car being driven to my wonderful bungalow with my wonderful bed. Paulie had called seven times, left as many voicemails, and sent twice as many texts. His assistant had also called and texted. Two things became rapidly clear: Paulie did not want me to go on socials and he wanted me to call the second I landed. I probably would have ignored him, but my assistant, Russell, had also texted that I needed to talk to Paulie—her I trusted.

I was never going to see my bed. I called Paulie's office.

"Voss Talent Agency, Paulie Schaefer's office. How may I direct you?" Paulie's assistant answered.

"Hey, it's PJ," I said.

"Oh thank God. I'll put you through. Hold please."

There was a single ring before Paulie picked up. "Addy. Are you back?"

"I just landed. I'm headed home now."

"Great. Tell your driver to bring you here instead." Paulie generally had the habit of telling rather than asking. I generally had the habit of ignoring that cute little flaw.

"No. I'm going home and I'm going to bed. I'll call you in about eighteen hours," I said. Paulie knew better than most how much I needed to decompress after a press tour. Hell, I needed to decompress after ordering a coffee. Interviews required at least a week without human contact. I probably should have seen his request for the red flag it was.

"Okay, I know you're exhausted. I get that. I sympathize. I empathize. But I need you to hear this from me."

"You're being very dramatic," I said. It was another of his adorable little quirks.

"Sean Murray was arrested in New York this morning," he said.

My stomach twisted. I swallowed my nausea and sudden dizziness. "What?"

"Two hours ago. It just hit the press."

I ran through all of my questions, but they all seemed too big and too obvious. I knew without asking that he'd been arrested for sexual assault. I also knew it wasn't for the sexual assault I'd been privy to. So I pivoted. "What does this mean for the movie?"

"I don't know yet. I've been trying to get Danny and Mick on the phone all morning. I mean, they only gave Sean EP to placate him, but the media is all over Oath right now."

"Maybe Danny shouldn't have blown us off when we asked him not to include a rapist on the project." Maybe I shouldn't have signed on to the damn movie in the first place.

"Yes, yes. You were right and they were wrong. Do you feel better now?"

"About agreeing to work with a guy who assaulted my costar ten years ago only to have him arrested a month after my contract has been signed? No, Paulie, I don't feel better." Not that I had anyone to blame but myself. Well, myself and Paulie, who had assured me Sean would be banned from set the days I was filming. "Fuck. Shit. Taryn. How is she?"

Paulie's sigh was loud enough to carry through the phone. "She's as well as can be expected. Cary is writing a statement with her right now. That's the other reason I'm calling. The agency would like it if we released at the same time."

"Dammit." I set the phone down and leaned forward. "I'm sorry. I need to go downtown instead."

The driver looked at me in the rearview mirror. "Yes, Ms. Addison. Where are we headed?"

"VTA. Thanks." I put the phone back to my ear. "I'm headed to you."

"I love you."

"I'm going to need my weight in coffee."

"Yes. You got it. I've already got a statement drafted."

"Bye."

There was a faint "See you" as he hung up.

I let my head drop against the seat. A puff of cool, leather-smelling air enveloped me. It was better than smelling myself. My skin felt itchy from dried sweat and my deodorant was a distant memory. I was too exhausted to clean the smears off my glasses. My once dashing and fluffy coif had fallen so the waves were brushing my eye. I'd been sitting long enough that wrinkles were appearing between the patterned windowpanes on my pants. I hadn't even realized wool could wrinkle. That was how long I'd been wearing this damn outfit. I was rumpled and grumpy and I did not want to spend my day talking about Sean Murray.

This was going to be a shitshow. Sean had been impenetrable for years. The rumors had started before we filmed *Dangerous Summer Nights* and only escalated from there. Though in all fairness, the cast had been responsible for spreading most of those rumors. There's nothing like a misogynistic director sexually assaulting your costar to bond a group of twenty-somethings.

Fifteen minutes later, I was sipping an exquisite Guatemalan roast and trying not to doze off in Paulie's office. I'd pushed my hair up, but it was already falling onto my forehead again.

Paulie burst through the door. "Sorry. I'm sorry I made you come down here, then made you wait." His normally perfect hair was askew, and he was wearing trendy eyeglasses. The glasses meant he'd gotten up before dawn. Never a good sign.

I took a deep breath. "It's fine. What have you got for me?"

He handed me an iPad with a document open. "Legal went through my statement. This is what they cleared us to say."

I read the four bland sentences on the screen. "Please tell me you're fucking kidding."

"You know I'm not." He sat next to me on his beautifully uncomfortable couch. "I started with what we wrote when that *Vanity Fair* article was being vetted." Ah, yes. The meticulously researched article that was killed hours before release. "But without that article to establish a baseline and without any idea of the veracity of the charges, legal won't let us say anything that will get you or us sued."

"Paulie." I sighed. I didn't really have a follow-up.

"I know."

"I can't sign off on that," I said.

He blanched. "We have to say something."

"Not if that is the something." I grabbed the iPad and read again. "No way. I'm sorry."

"Come on. If we say nothing, they'll hound us."

"Talk to legal. That's not my problem."

"They'll hound you." He paused then went for the jugular. "They'll hound Taryn."

I stared at him. Turned that over in my head. He was right. They would go after Taryn. They would go after every cis woman Sean had ever worked with, but they would focus on his rumored victims. Rather than speculating on what form that would take, I decided to ask her. I stood.

"What are you doing?" he asked.

"Is she here?"

"Who?"

"Taryn. You dragged my ass in here. I bet Cary dragged her in too." I marched out and down the hall to the opposite corner office. The door was closed, but I bypassed Cary's assistant and let myself in after a brief knock.

Taryn was curled up in a massive club chair. Her hair was longer and redder than the last time I'd seen her. Her eyes were puffy. She wasn't crying at the moment, but the rich brown swam like melted chocolate. She was gorgeous. Cary was perched on the coffee table talking to her in low, soothing tones. He was almost as pretty as her. His black hair was slicked and combed with a rigid part. He was cradling Taryn's hand, his dark complexion making her pale skin look even more translucent. They looked up when I opened the door.

Taryn heaved a long-suffering sigh and got up. "What are you doing here?" Her voice had a hint of a whine in it. Like she was already apologizing.

"Same as you. Reviewing bullshit statements for this Sean debacle."

"Babe." She stepped over Cary and came toward me.

"Babe." I pulled her in for a long hug.

"Cary says we have to say something," she said.

"I'm not saying anything if it's that bland shit from legal. Is yours bland? I bet it is." I reached for the stapled packet Cary was holding. His statements were all red-penned. I skimmed the lines. "I think this might be worse than mine."

Taryn turned to Cary. "I told you."

"We don't want to put you at risk of litigation," he said.

Paulie joined the party. "Sorry, Cary."

Cary waved a manicured hand. "It's fine."

"How is saying nothing worse than this?" Taryn pointed at the thin packet I was holding.

"Because you're going to be inundated with media requests," Cary said.

I watched Taryn's beautiful face fall. It pissed me off. I hadn't seen her much the last few years, but she had done so much emotional work. She was happy in a way she hadn't been since she was twenty-two. And now Sean Murray was going to come and take that peace away again. Fuck that.

"Or." I tossed the packet onto the coffee table. "We make a different kind of statement. Come over to my place tonight. We'll have a couple of drinks and post some photos. That will send an ambiguous message, but clearly one of support. If people want to read it as a fuck you to Sean, that's fair. If they want to read it as relief or silence or whatever, that's fine. It'll say he's so unimportant, he's not worth a statement."

"Babe. I love that."

"Well, I love you, babe." I grinned at her. She was one of my oldest friends and I didn't see her enough. Even if she did get me to compulsively say babe.

"You guys okay with this?" Taryn asked our agents.

They exchanged a look and a shrug. "Yeah," Paulie said.

"Fine by me." Cary nodded.

"We still need to release a statement from VTA, but I think—" Paulie turned to me. "What did you call it? Bland?" he asked. I nodded. "Yeah, bland is fine for the agency."

"Excellent. I haven't slept in days. I'm going home." I looked at Taryn. "Seven?"

"Perfect. Love you." She blew a kiss at me.

"Love you, babe."

I made it to the elevators before Taryn called out, "Babe. Wait." She was leaning halfway out of Cary's office with her phone pressed to her shoulder.

"What's up?" I hit the elevator button.

"Jeffery too?"

"Sure. Let's make it a full-blown reunion," I said.

She put the phone back to her ear. "Yeah. We're going *DSN* reunion." She paused, then pulled the phone away again. "The husband too?" she called.

"Yeah. I haven't met him yet. And the more pretty people, the bigger the show of support." The elevator door opened. I blew her a kiss. "Seven."

"Seven!"

❖

Taryn was the first to arrive. Her face was made up to look like it wasn't. Perfect for casual photos. She handed me a bottle of wine, kissed my cheek, then handed me a second bottle.

"I was going to get flowers because flowers are pretty. And then I remembered you throwing that vase with the gorgeous bouquet and decided that you don't get flowers," she said.

I rolled my eyes. "You throw one tiny tantrum and one moderately-sized flower vase and suddenly everyone thinks you're difficult." In my defense, I had been on a press tour with my first serious girlfriend and the press kept calling our love fated and asking invasive questions. Plus, I was twenty-six and immature and hungover.

Taryn held back a laugh. "Sure, babe."

"Have you seen the house? I don't think you have." I didn't give her time to answer. "This is it." I waved a hand behind us like I hadn't spent years searching for the perfect mid-century modern sideboard to really make the foyer come alive. "Now come outside."

When we walked outside, Taryn groaned. "You've got to be kidding me. This is fucking amazing." She reached up and brushed one of the low-hanging palm fronds that shaded the yard.

"What's the point of making movies if you can't make your own paradise?"

"And I just thought you were vain." She fell onto the bamboo-framed sofa and stared at the sunset over LA.

I set the bottles of wine she'd brought on the outdoor bar. "My mother is the vain one. Child star, remember?" I grabbed a couple of glasses and the pitcher of sangria my assistant had left for us.

Taryn waved her hand at me. "You loved it." She took one of the glasses from me and sipped her drink.

The doorbell rang again. "That'll be Jeffrey and—shit, what's the husband's name again?" I asked.

"Florian."

"Wow. Okay. But we like him?"

"We like him." Taryn nodded.

"Back in a sec."

She ignored me, seemingly preoccupied with her drink and her view. Which was exactly what I wanted her to be preoccupied by.

I opened the door. It was not Jeffrey and Florian.

Wylie Parsons handed me a slender bouquet of orchids and smiled. She was wearing a baggy Hawaiian shirt with exactly two buttons fastened, leaving her exquisitely tanned body on display. She'd gained a few faint laugh lines, but that pretty twenty-four-year-old had grown into a stunning thirty-four-year-old. "Hey, stranger," she said. "Damn, you look good."

CHAPTER TWO

Wylie crossed the threshold and kissed my cheek. "I brought you orchids. You know I'm required to until the end of time."

"Did you and Taryn plan this?" I asked.

"No, Jeffrey invited me. Is that okay?" A flash of old insecurity crossed her eyes. "He said we were doing a reunion to support Taryn."

"No. I mean, yes, it's fine. I was talking about the flowers. She was just teasing me about it." I waved her inside. "I'm glad you came. Taryn's already out back."

Wylie brushed her fingers down my forearm. The whisper of contact was familiar and foreign. "How is she?"

"She seems to be taking it in stride. He's an inconvenience more than anything."

"Good. What about you?"

I shrugged. "I'm fine. You?"

She mirrored my shrug and added a wry smile. "Same."

What were we supposed to say? The handsy director who took credit for as much of our success as he could and probably outed us after we wouldn't fuck him was an asshole? And the reminder of his looming, disgusting presence was bad? It was fine. Or it was no less fine than it had been the day before or the week before.

"Go through there." I pointed to the hallway that led out back. "I'm going to grab a vase."

She followed my instructions but stopped halfway down. "You have the Winifred Cal piece?" she called.

"Yes. I got it like eight years ago? It's been sitting in storage though." I grabbed a vase and started filling it.

Wylie followed me into the kitchen. "You asshole."

I looked up in a decent imitation of surprise. "What did I do?"

"You outbid me."

I bit back a grin. "I didn't know I was bidding against you."

Her jaw dropped in intentional outrage. "You did. My God, that makes you an even bigger asshole."

"I didn't know it was you." I pulled away the paper wrapped around the flowers and put them in water. "Okay, I suspected it was you, but I didn't know for sure."

"It was an anonymous auction. You could have asked me. I hate you."

"Oh no. I'll never recover." I ushered her outside.

"You are the worst," Wylie said.

Taryn looked up when we came outside. "Babe!"

"Babe." Wylie leaned over to hug Taryn.

"Why is Addy the worst?" Taryn asked.

"She outbid me at auction."

"When? What auction?" Taryn asked.

"A Winifred Cal auction almost a decade ago," I said. I pointed at the sangria pitcher with an empty glass. Wylie nodded.

"And we're just mad about this now?" Taryn asked.

Wylie draped herself dramatically over the side of the sofa Taryn wasn't dramatically draped over. "Well, I didn't know until right now when I saw the piece hanging in the hallway."

"Sure. Sure." Taryn nodded indulgently.

"I don't spend a lot of time at my ex-girlfriend's house," Wylie said.

"And why would you?"

The doorbell rang again. "You didn't invite anyone else, right?" I asked Taryn.

"I only invited the boys. They're the ones who invited your ex," Taryn said.

"Excellent."

It was the boys. Florian handed me wine. Jeffrey handed me a second bouquet of orchids. The media had mostly forgotten my fit of pique, but my old friends apparently never would.

"Jeffrey, babe." Taryn actually stood to hug Jeffrey. Florian kissed her cheeks.

"Introductions," Jeffrey said. "My husband, Florian." He placed a hand on Florian's shoulder in such a way that his wide, diamond-studded wedding band was displayed. "You know Taryn. Wylie Parsons, the queer Casanova of late aughts Hollywood. And PJ Addison, our host and Wylie's first conquest."

"Hey," I said. I let the full weight of my annoyance show.

"Hey!" Wylie shouted.

"I was not a conquest," I said.

"I am no Casanova," Wylie said.

"Wylie, babe, where's wife number three?" Taryn asked pointedly.

"Could you please not call her that?" Wylie asked.

"Sure. Sure. But where is she?" Taryn asked.

Wylie sighed. "Ojai, I think."

"You don't know?" Florian asked.

"She's on a meditation retreat. We don't share everything."

"Yes. The sign of a successful lesbian marriage," Jeffrey said.

"God, I hate all of you." Wylie saluted us with her glass.

"My husband undersold all of you and I am delighted," Florian said.

"You mean you never saw our early press tours?" Taryn asked. "We were hellions."

"Oh, I did. I just thought you would mellow with age." Florian smiled. He was absolutely beautiful and he knew it. Dark, thick curls haloed his face. His eyes were bright and warm.

"To be fair, we did mellow. We just bring out the adolescence in each other," I said.

"It's true. Addy is always serious until she gets around us. And then she gets mildly less serious," Jeffrey said.

"Please. I am not that serious."

They all roared with laughter which did nothing for my point.

"This explains why she went into production," Florian said.

Wylie rolled her eyes. "Child abuse explains why she went into production."

Taryn nodded too enthusiastically. "Always in control that one." They clinked their glasses together.

Jeffrey laughed. Florian looked a little uncomfortable with jokes about my childhood trauma. He clearly hadn't been in Hollywood long. Or maybe we were all just irreparably broken.

"So is it going to be weird directing yourself?" Florian asked. "You've never done that before, right?"

"No?" I didn't follow his question. "I don't really act anymore though so it's never an issue."

"But you're in the reboot, right?"

Wylie and I looked at each other. "Well, we did sign off on it, but we don't know what will happen to production now," I said.

"The movie will probably happen, but I'm sure Oath will push it back. They'll want to see how this plays out," Wylie said.

"But aren't you directing the reboot?" Florian asked me.

"What? No. God, no," I said.

Wylie started laughing. "Can you imagine? It'll be enough to play married final girls again. If you were directing us, I don't think we'd make it through production."

"It sounds like a nightmare." I wasn't remotely offended by my ex being horrified at the idea of me directing her. We'd been friends longer than we ever dated. She'd destroyed me once, but playing an iconic queer couple every few years in endless sequels took the sting out of the heartbreak.

"Seriously?" Florian asked.

"Yeah. Why?"

"It's all over socials." He dug out his phone. "You're trending."

I glanced at his screen. I was, in fact, trending. "Shit."

"What? Let me see." Wylie leaned forward. Her shirt billowed open. "Oh, God." She started reading. "PJ Addison slated to direct failing Oath Entertainment's *Dangerous Summer Nights: Redux*. The film is Oath's last grasp at relevance in a post #MeToo world after continually employing serial abuser Sean Murray. Can the out queer director undo the damage done by her predecessor?"

"What the fuck?" I patted my pockets, but I knew my phone was inside. I'd intentionally left it there to avoid the inevitable media requests. "Paulie must have called." I stood to go inside.

"You know what? No." Wylie put a hand on my arm and directed me to sit back down. "We met up to support Taryn and each other."

She squeezed Taryn's thigh. "We're going to drink this sangria that I can't believe your assistant still makes because it's damn good. She should market this shit. And we're going to take gorgeous pictures with this gorgeous sunset. We're not doing work, dammit."

"You're so right," I said.

"I know."

Taryn scooted closer to Wylie. "Get over here, Addy," Taryn said. I sat on her other side. "Jeffrey." Taryn patted my knee.

We laughed as Jeffrey sprawled across our laps. We were all firmly in our thirties and re-creating photos we took when we were young heartthrobs. Florian settled into his role as photographer and directed us through a series of shots. Me and Wylie kissing Taryn. Taryn reclined against my chest with her bare feet on Wylie's lap. Jeffrey and Taryn snuggling. How anyone ever bought them as a couple was beyond me.

The sun dropped low enough that we lost our golden lighting. So we opted to continue drinking and not talking about Sean Murray.

"Wait. Wait. So you were her wife's best man?" Florian asked. He pointed back and forth between me and Wylie who was sitting on the ground, leaning back against my leg.

"Oh yeah. It was a bet gone very wrong," I said. "Bubba's actual best man was her brother. But he got stuck in Japan and couldn't get to Napa in time for the wedding. So Bubba shows up at my hotel room two hours before the ceremony with a tailor and a tux."

"How is that a bet?" Florian asked.

"Yeah, I never understood that," Jeffrey said.

I felt my face getting red. Wylie burst out laughing.

"I don't remember," I said. My face got hotter. "Apparently, at the bachelor party, I was losing at poker and I didn't have anything else to put in the pot. Bubba made me promise to stand up with her if her brother didn't show up."

Wy was on the floor, laughing. "There was a video. Terrible quality. We're talking early gen iPhone. No lighting. But there's a distinctly drunk PJ Addison swearing fealty to my fiancée. It was hilarious. Bowing was involved." She did a flourish with her hand.

"There's no hangover like finding out you're going to be in your ex-girlfriend's wedding, standing up for her soon-to-be wife." I shook my head.

Wy kept laughing. She dropped her head back on my thigh. "That was a fun wedding."

"You would know," I said.

"Oh, shut up, asshole."

"You sort of deserve that one," Taryn said.

"Three marriages is not that many," Wy said.

"Sure, babe," Jeffrey said.

"Yeah, sure, babe," I said.

"Sure, babe," Taryn added, giggling.

"Am I allowed to ask why the first two ended?" Florian asked.

"Bubba proved that Wylie was not, in fact, the only queer Casanova of aughts Hollywood," I said.

"I don't appreciate the comparison. Bubba was a two-timing cad who slept with half the makeup girls in LA," Wylie said.

"Sorry." I took Wy's hand and kissed her knuckles. "Wylie was just a cad who flirted with makeup girls."

Wylie tugged her hand out of my grip. "How did we end up discussing my failed relationships? We only get together once every few years. Can't you people be normal?"

"That's a hard no," Jeffrey said.

"Sorry, babe. We are who we are," Taryn said.

"If it helps, my mother loves to bring up the fact that you've been married three times and I," I pitched my voice higher in a decent imitation of my mother, "can't make a relationship last longer than a month."

"Oh, Geraldine. She's a real one." Wy leaned back and grinned wide at me.

"She's still convinced you're the one who got away," I said.

"I know Gerri is a handful, but that bitch is awesome," Taryn said.

"She certainly is a handful," I said.

"Aww. Still not getting along with Mom?" Wy pouted at me.

"We get along great. As long as we talk about you. Or sea turtles or whatever the hell she's protecting this week."

"Can she protect me this week?" Taryn asked.

"Of course, babe. You know if I call her, she'll be at your place in the morning, right?" I was absolutely serious and Taryn knew it.

Gerri had happily been the stage mom to my child star, but she hadn't given it up when I turned eighteen. During *DSN*, she'd adopted most of the cast. She didn't stop showing up on my sets until I stopped acting in my late twenties. It wasn't a small part of why I quit.

"Oh, I know. I'll keep her in reserve," Taryn said.

"I'm honestly surprised she's not already here for Taryn," Jeffrey said.

"She's probably sitting on your doorstep right now, lounging in white sunglasses, reading whatever the trendiest book is this week." Wy turned up her chin and fanned herself in a classic Geraldine pose.

"I'd better get home then." Taryn feigned standing.

Wy playfully pushed her back down. "You can't leave us yet. I haven't seen my wife in three days, and I have no idea when she's coming back. I can't go home to that empty place."

Taryn laughed. "Babe, you know you're just setting yourself up here."

Wy rolled her eyes. "I'll be making out with PJ on screen again soon enough. And then I'll get to have the sexual chemistry discussion. Again. Marriage three isn't long for this world." It wasn't clear if she was being serious or not.

"No, no. I'm not carrying your failed marriages. I can't help that we look good when we make out." I shoved her so she wasn't leaning against my leg anymore and shifted my feet to the other side of the chair.

Wy laughed. "See? If my wives just saw this side of you, they'd know we're not getting back together."

Jeffrey leaned over and loudly whispered to Florian, "That's what killed marriage number two."

"In all fairness, they do look stunning together," Florian said.

"Please, I look stunning with everyone," Wy said.

"It's true. I'm just a prop," I said.

Florian gave us a look stuck between pity and mockery. He pulled out his phone. "I'm not sure that's true." He handed over the phone with a photo from earlier.

We leaned close to study the photo. In it, I was stretched out with my feet up. Wy was on the ground, her head resting on my thigh, blond curls cascading over me. She was laughing in that way she had, where the whole world was funny. Her smile was wide, the lines framing her mouth were deeper than I remembered—joy given form. My ears were pink with embarrassment. The soft gray starting at my right temple gave my embarrassment a distinguished edge. I didn't look like a gawky teenager anymore and I didn't know when that shift had happened. Somewhere in my thirties, I guess.

"My God, you two are gorgeous." Taryn leaned over. Her auburn hair fell to cover the screen and she pushed it behind her ears. "That's going in the photo drop."

I shrugged, aiming for nonchalance. For a professional, I was a terrible liar. "With any luck, wife three will comment something snarky and keep our clickbait media cycle going."

"Please. She's not the jealous type." Wy handed the phone back to Florian.

"You're literally holding hands, babe," Jeffrey said.

"No, we're not," Wylie said.

She and I leaned forward and looked at the screen again. We weren't holding hands. Technically. Our fingers were entwined and looked nearly pornographic. Wy's index finger was extended and tucked under the edge of my shirt.

"It's habit," I said.

"Our careers are built on looking pretty together," Wy said.

"Yeah. That," I said.

Jeffrey angled his head to Florian and whispered, "Save that. We'll frame it for their wedding."

I scowled. "You're not invited to our wedding."

"Yeah, it'll be a small affair. Us and Gerri." Wy grabbed my hand and kissed it. "We're very private, you understand."

"That much is clear, babe," Jeffrey said.

CHAPTER THREE

I had made a poor choice. Well, I had made a series of poor choices and they led me to reading the recent pages for the script we were starting to film in a matter of hours. Rather than push it back, Oath had decided to dramatically move up the timetable. They barely had a cast. They had a handful of locations. They didn't have a finished script. They did have the scene I was currently reading where Taylor Henderson and Grace Durant got sexy. As written, it violated at least six clauses in our contracts. Each.

They also had an idiot director who had let her agent talk her into this shitshow. Granted, they had agreed to every single one of my demands and they were paying me a stupid amount of money. But in exchange, it was possible I'd given them my soul.

There was a knock at my trailer door. "Ms. Addison, half hour warning."

I opened the door. A very nervous PA was waiting. "Baird, I asked you not to call me that."

"Yes, I know. It's just—it seemed respectful." Baird was young. I'd be shocked if he could legally drink. He had to be a nepotism hire, but I was very carefully not asking who he was related to. None of my business. But he did have a two-hundred-dollar buzz cut and he was wearing Japanese denim that cost more than my first modeling paycheck when I was six.

I nodded. "Noted. But it's arguably disrespectful to call me something other than what I asked you to call me."

His mouth formed a small, shocked O. "Right. Sorry, ma'am. Do you prefer PJ or Addy?"

"Either is fine."

"Okay. Got it. Half hour warning, Addy."

"Thanks, Baird," I said. Russ approached from behind him. "Oh, I don't know if you've met my assistant, Chloe Russell. If you can't find me, she will know my location."

"Hi." Russ put her hand out. "I saw you in passing yesterday."

"Right, yes." Baird shook her hand. He looked nervous making eye contact with her too. Maybe it wasn't only me. Maybe he was just a nervous guy.

Russ nodded and let Baird dismiss himself. He walked off at double speed. "You wanted me to get you when Lenny got on set," Russ said.

"Great. Thanks." I grabbed my coffee.

I followed Russ across the lot. The sun was up and burning away the fog. Maybe we would actually be able to start shooting on time. That would be novel. I reached for my sunglasses on my shirt, but they weren't there so I pulled off my backward baseball cap and turned it around. I pushed back my eyeglasses with a knuckle. Once hair and makeup got ahold of me, they would fix whatever abuse my hair was suffering under the cap.

It was just after six in the morning, but you wouldn't know it from the movement on set. We were stopped by my script supervisor, flagged down by a wardrobe assistant, and spoke to two more PAs before we found Lenny locked in what looked like a heated conversation with one of the executives. Everyone around them was giving them a wide berth, but their voices still carried. We hustled toward them. One of my young actors approached me, but Russ intercepted her.

"Lenny, Mick, let's move this somewhere more private," I said.

Mick turned to me, his hackles already in the stratosphere. "You deal with him. He likes you."

"I'm very likable." I smiled in what I hoped was a disarming way. It worked better when I was twenty-two and presented as femme.

"Or he's an ornery bastard who doesn't get along with anyone," Mick said.

Lanny scowled, but I knew he was taking that as a compliment. "Just not studio dicks."

Leonard Pace had written every single *Dangerous Summer Nights* movie in the primary franchise. He was also responsible for the *Slaughterhouse Ranch* films, the ensuing spin-off TV show, and a slew of teenage rom-coms that could only be described as paragons of aughts culture. The man was an icon. Mick was a white guy with money and a pinkie ring and an inflated sense of his own importance.

"Okay, let's take a walk." I put my hand on Lenny's shoulder and steered him away. We passed crafty. Too many people milling around eating breakfast. There was an open field off one of the barns. Two of the leads were sitting on a dilapidated picnic bench running lines, which was cute because they'd only been given like three scenes. Total. Someone from props appeared to scold them for sitting on a set piece.

"I think we're far enough away for you to yell," Lenny said.

I rolled my eyes and stopped walking. "I'm not planning on yelling. But if Mick asks, tell him I did, okay?"

"You're a good kid." Lenny didn't mean to infantilize me. I'd been an adult in the industry long enough to tell the difference between men who remembered me as a starlet and gave me a pass because they used to want to fuck me and the ones who remembered me as a starlet and gave me a pass because they liked the adult I'd grown into.

"I read the pages you gave the studio," I said.

He sighed. "Jesus H. I've already got Danny and Mick crawling up my ass."

"That's real rough, pal. My condolences. But I'm shooting a fucking movie and I don't have a script."

"You have at least two-thirds of a script."

"I have forty decent pages and—" I flipped through to count. "Seven of them are me fucking. Do you have a thing for lesbians, Lenny?"

He gave me a withering look. "Addy." He sighed. I deserved the pointed sigh. I'd known the guy since I was fifteen. He very much did not have a thing for lesbians. Or women under the age of sixty. "We're all scrambling. I'll get you your pages. I'll even make them decent and maybe funny and scary. But you need to keep the guys off my back."

"I will. But please give me something I can actually shoot," I said.

"I only gave those pages to Mick so he'd piss off." He shrugged. "He wanted sex. I gave him sex."

"And I love that. I'm all for this *Wild Things* give the audience what sells even if it kills them thing you've got going. I'm just not for it when the actors didn't sign up for it."

"I got it. I got it." He put his hands up like a surrender. Then he pointed at me, an impish grin on his grizzled face. "But that sounds fun. Let's do that film next."

I started walking away. "They already made a *Wild Things* sequel."

"They made two," he called.

I waved him off. Russ fell in line next to me. The young actor she'd been talking to was nowhere to be seen. "What did Emily want?" I asked.

"Emma. And she wants to talk to you about her character's sartorial choices. I told her you were speaking with wardrobe this afternoon and she would want to wait until after that." She was scribbling fiercely in a small, cheap notebook with an expensive fountain pen as she spoke. The ink bled, but it didn't impede her large, loping script. I'd tried to give her nice notebooks over the years, but she was a creature of habit.

"I didn't know I had a meeting with wardrobe today," I said.

"I'm sure you'll talk to someone in wardrobe. That's a meeting." She smiled at me briefly and made another notation.

"Remind me to give you a bonus after this movie."

"You give me a bonus after every movie," Russ said.

"Yeah, but don't let me forget."

"Sure thing." She tucked away the notebook. "Hannah is waiting at your trailer. She wants to review the setup for the last scene of the day. There's some issue with the tracking equipment. It'll be resolved by then, but she needs to know what your plan is."

Hannah was my first assistant director. Another one of Oath's concessions. I asked for my usual reliable crew—AD, editor, assistant, cinematographer. Normally, they would have pushed back in negotiations, but since someone's assistant leaked my name to the press before they bothered to ask me to direct, it forced their hand. I'd taken full advantage of my leverage.

"Is that the scene with Benny and Sadie?" I asked.

"Yeah. The characters' first meeting."

I'd almost made it back to my trailer when a different trailer door flung open. Wylie stood in the open doorway. She was wearing a light cotton button up but hadn't bothered to do any of the buttons. The only thing keeping her from flashing the entire set was the lack of a breeze and possibly magic. I made a conscious effort to look up from the wide strip of skin. Wy's hair was wet and slicked back from her face. She was annoyingly sexy. This movie was going to be hell.

"PJ, got a minute?" she called.

"No."

She gave me a withering look and stepped down to walk with me. She did one button as she walked. Just one. "Have you read these pages?"

"Yeah, but I just talked to Lenny. He's rewriting them."

"Thank God." She put her hand on my arm. "I love you but I'd rather not record loving you on screen, you know?"

"Believe me. I know." I settled into my indifference. It was the best shield in my arsenal.

Ahead of us, Danny stepped out of his trailer, saw us, and took off in the opposite direction.

"That man is spineless," Wy said softly.

"No shit."

"Love, I need a moment," a distinctly Californian voice said. The British nickname sounded particularly strange on her tongue.

Wy turned to the blonde with a pixie cut leaning out of her trailer. "We'll only be a minute."

"Oh my, you're PJ Addison." The blond stepped down and came toward me with her arms extended. "I'm Jocelyn Parsons." She came right in for the hug.

I hugged her back purely out of instinct. "Nice to meet you," I said.

"I've seen a ton of your films. At least the ones with Wylie." Jocelyn winked at Wy. "But my word, you are gorgeous in person."

I forced a smile. I'd only consumed two of my sixteen cups of coffee. It was an ungodly hour. I was on a film set that I was supposed to be running when I had absolutely no resources aside from money and overeager first-time actors. And my ex-girlfriend's third wife was telling me how good-looking I was.

"You're sweet," I said.

"I'm sorry, Addy, I don't mean to be rude." Russ looked at her watch, then my trailer. "But we really need to go."

"It's fine. It was nice to meet you, Jocelyn." I turned to Wy. "Did you need to talk about anything other than that scene?"

"Yes, but I'll catch you later." She took Jocelyn's hand and backed away.

"Wait," Jocelyn said. "I'm only in town for a few days to get Wylie settled. Join us for dinner tonight?"

I glanced at Wy in time to see the smallest sigh of annoyance. "I can't tonight. I'll be on set."

"Oh. Of course!" Jocelyn gripped my forearm. "I'll be here until Tuesday. I'm sure you can make time one night." Somehow it sounded like a threat rather than an invitation.

"Sure. I'll text Wylie when I have a better idea of my schedule."

Russ directed me back to my trailer and followed me inside. "Sorry. She doesn't look anything like the photos I have."

"What?"

"Jocelyn. She must have just gotten that haircut. In all the pictures I've seen, she's got shoulder-length hair."

"Why are you looking at pictures of Jocelyn?" I asked.

"So I can run interference. Come on. I always keep track of your youthful costar slash ex-girlfriend's paramours. How else would I shield you from them?"

I laughed. "Well, when you say it that way."

She shrugged. "Okay, I'm going to find Hannah. She's supposed to be here."

Russ left and two minutes later, the door to my trailer flung open. I was expecting Hannah and Russ. Instead, Mick barged in.

"Did you get Pace back on track?" he shouted.

"I wasn't aware he was off track," I said.

"We don't have a completed script!"

"We would if you hadn't insisted we start shooting without one." I grabbed a water from the fridge and drained half of it. It was too cold and it hurt my teeth. But it was worth it to let Mick stew.

"He assured Danny and me that we would have a script on time," Mick said.

"And he will if you stop pestering him for updates. And you can't pick fights with him on set. You can't pick fights with anyone on my set."

"I'll do anything I damn well want on my film set." He got in my face and pointed at me. "Don't forget who is funding this shitshow."

"Yes, yes. Your money is very impressive."

"So is my influence. Don't forget who got your whole team in place for this project. I can pull them just as easily."

I rolled my eyes, but his point landed. Danny's negotiations involved money. Mick was the only executive willing to give me the bodies I asked for. "I appreciate that. But you need to stop antagonizing my screenwriter."

Hannah and Russ opened the door in time to catch what I said. Hannah stopped just inside the door, crossed her arms, and glared at Mick.

Mick looked furtively between me and Hannah. "Fine."

"Good," I said.

"Great." Mick stomped to the door. He slammed it shut as he left.

"What the fuck was that?" Hannah asked.

"Usual tantrum. Mick being a dick."

"Mick's always a dick," Hannah said.

"Yeah, that's why everyone says 'Mick is a dick,'" I said.

Hannah laughed. "His parents kind of fucked up naming him."

Russ rolled her eyes. "His parents fucked up a lot with him."

Hannah bit back a grin. "Will you go find Claude? He needs to get Mick under control."

"On it." Russ took off to find our producer.

Baird caught the door before it could shut. "There you two are. You ready?"

Hannah turned and grinned at me. "What do you say, boss?"

"Let's go make a movie," I said.

Chapter Four

I'd managed to avoid Jocelyn for all of thirty-six hours before she cornered me and made me promise that I'd meet them for dinner. Production was stalled for the evening anyway, but Russ could only field my calls for so long.

So I was sitting in a trendy restaurant decorated entirely with concrete and wood, drinking a gin and tonic made with good gin and too much tonic. Given my choice, we would be at Jed's, the dive burger joint just off Thackerton's main street. When we'd filmed the first *DSN* here, Wy and I had found Jed's in the first week and practically lived there until filming was finished. The rest of the cast slowly joined us as the weeks went by. It became our refuge. The staff didn't give a shit that we were famous or pretty. They just served the best goddamn french fries and let us play pool until closing. It hadn't been updated since Jed bought it in 1974 and I would bet my contract that it still hadn't.

The rest of Thackerton hadn't been so resistant to evolution. The kitschy shops that hadn't changed since the nineteen eighties—inexplicably housed in buildings from the eighteen eighties—had shifted into Instagram-worthy local color. There was a Victorian-looking barber shop, a soda and candy shop that had been transplanted from the forties, and a slew of antique stores that carried only perfectly restored items for a premium price. It was cute. It was dripping with money and had lost most of its charm in the process, but it was cute.

If I remembered correctly, the restaurant I was sitting in had been a pool supply store. Which was ironic considering the lack of pools in

Thackerton. But that was probably why they went under. This high in Northern California never really achieved pool weather. Instead the concrete blocks made for displaying pool vacuums were repurposed into the worst barstools I'd ever sat on. Or maybe that was just the discomfort of waiting at the bar for two people who had insisted on meeting for dinner only to be twenty minutes late. I wanted to be alone in private, not alone in public. The latter required far too much effort.

A hand dropped on my shoulder. I turned around in time to catch Jocelyn launching herself into my arms. I got lost in layers of the exquisite cream silk draped around her. I hated people who assumed hugs were the norm. More so when they enveloped me in vanilla-scented soft fabric. Maybe it was a problem that I was deeply uncomfortable with textures and scents other people considered comforting, but that was an issue for my therapist.

"Oh my God. Hi." She gripped my shoulders and studied my face. "How do you look this good after working for two days straight? Wylie says you never leave set." She stroked the linen collar of my shirt.

"I pay people lots of money." I grinned so she would think I was joking, but I wasn't.

Jocelyn laughed. And laughed. "They're earning their keep."

"Where's Wylie?"

"Grabbing our table." She pointed into the dining area.

Wylie was being led to a table made out of—you guessed it—a concrete slab. She was dressed more casually than either Jocelyn or me. Her oversized white T-shirt probably came from a twenty-year-old designer out of Brooklyn and cost more than my entire lighting department.

"I wanted to come get you." Jocelyn slid her hand down and entwined her fingers with mine. We were hand-holding friends now. Neat.

We got to the table as the waiter was leaving. I set my drink down and disengaged my hand from Jocelyn so I could sit. Wylie caught my eye and apologized in a glance. I looked at Jocelyn but she hadn't seen. Or hadn't noticed.

"Oh, I'm so glad you were able to get away tonight." Jocelyn touched my wrist across the table.

"It was pure luck."

"Drew still cursing the generators?" Wy asked.

I bit back a smile. "When I left, he was on a whole generator maintenance soapbox."

Wylie laughed. "He knows his whole crew is trained for this stuff, right?"

"Oh, who is Drew?" Jocelyn asked. Her eyes were wide in what could only be a genuine desire to learn.

"He's the lighting director. We start night shoots tomorrow," I said.

"We worked with Drew on *DSN: Spring Break*," Wylie said.

"Oh, I love that one," Jocelyn said.

It was, frankly, another strike against Jocelyn. The *Spring Break* movies were a distinct departure from the original timeline. I'd never been able to watch one in its entirety—including the one I was in. But making it paid for my mother's Aspen house, which kept her in Colorado at least nine months out of the year. I'd make another *Spring Break* if it kept Gerri out of California.

The waiter returned with an old-fashioned for Wy and something sparkling for Jocelyn. He looked at my nearly empty glass. "Another?"

"Please."

"Are we ready to order?" he asked the table.

"Oh, we haven't even looked, but I read the charred octopus was divine. Could we start with that?" Jocelyn looked at us for approval.

"Actually—" I started.

"Sorry. That's a no on the octopus." Wy squeezed my hand briefly. "If we could just have a minute. Thanks."

The waiter nodded and went to retrieve what was hopefully a stronger drink.

Jocelyn looked back and forth between us in confusion. "Are you allergic or something? Oh, I didn't know. I'm so sorry."

"No, it's just one of my…" I was going to say pesky ethics, but one look at Wy and I toned it down. "Octopi are really smart. I won't eat them. Same with pigs."

"And she's judgmental as hell of other people who eat them."
Wy caught my eye and winked.

"Oh, wow. Oh, that's so neat. Wylie said you were super smart,
but I didn't know you had such conviction." Jocelyn beamed at me. I
honestly couldn't tell if Jocelyn was hitting on me or if her fawning
was genuine, but I was damn sure I didn't like it.

The waiter set a gin and tonic in front of me.

"Thanks." I counted to five before taking a sip. That was a
perfectly reasonable wait time.

"Oh, we didn't even look at the menu," Jocelyn said.

If this chick started one more sentence with "oh," I was going to
lose it. I glanced at Wy and read her irritation. It was layered. She was
irritated as hell that I was annoyed by Jocelyn. She might have been
a little peeved by Jocelyn, but, no, most of her ire was directed at me.

We managed to order food that wouldn't give me motivation
to lecture. I did my damndest to make conversation with Jocelyn. It
was a challenge because she spoke almost entirely in therapy-speak.
One could write that off to a result of her business, but I wasn't quite
so forgiving of the conversational drag. She ran a group of wellness
centers catering to wealthy clientele. Which sounded great for her.
She also made it a point to set up mental health centers at underfunded
high schools, which was super cool. She seemed lovely, genuine,
and kind. I couldn't stand her. I'd adored Wylie's first wife. I'd been
friendly with the second. I was trying with the third, but damn, it took
effort. I needed to text Taryn and find out if it was just me.

"I have to confess." Jocelyn shot a mischievous look at Wylie. "I
was obsessed with *Blackbirds* when I was a kid."

I nodded politely and finished my second drink. "Yeah? That's
nice to hear." I gave her one of my generic smiles. The same smile
that had presided over the *Blackbirds* title sequence.

"No, like it was my whole personality until the summer before
freshman year." Jocelyn beamed. She thought she was complimenting
me. I'd been on a teen TV show. She'd been a teen watching that TV
show. We were supposed to be bonded now.

I chuckled the way I was supposed to. "What changed the
summer before freshman year?"

She shrugged. "The show ended. I was devastated, of course."

"Right. Sure." I did some math. Wylie was about a decade older than Jocelyn. Watching my ex become a Hollywood cliché should have amused me. Or maybe disappointed me. Instead I just felt hollow.

"Oh, what was it like working with Neil Bernard? Is he as fun as he seems? Those early scripts are just hilarious."

"Sure. Bernard is great. A little obnoxious on set." I fell right into interview mode. I'd talked about *Blackbirds* enough that I could do it half-dead and drunk, which was how we'd done most of the early press.

"Oh, right. He's like a total prankster, isn't he?"

"Yep. Which is good when you're pulling fifteen-hour days. But it's not the best quality in a showrunner." I shot Wylie a look to save me from this utterly generic conversation.

Wy rolled her eyes. "Remember when Kaleb decided to be a prankster?"

"All five minutes are etched on my psyche," I said dramatically.

"Kaleb? Like Kaleb Holder?" Jocelyn asked. Wy nodded. "I didn't know he pranked you all on set?"

"Only the one time," I said.

"It didn't go over great." Wylie shook her head.

"Legal shut that shit down quick."

"What?" Jocelyn looked back and forth between us. "What did he do?"

"Oh, we can't tell you," I said very sincerely.

"What? Why not?" Jocelyn was eating this shit up.

"Nondisclosure agreements," Wylie said. I nodded. She nodded.

"Seriously? What could he have done that was that bad?"

"We'd love to tell you, but our hands are tied," I said.

"I'd rather not relive it, thanks," Wylie said.

"Then why'd you bring it up?" Jocelyn looked at her strangely and I witnessed the exact moment when Wy realized she'd overplayed her hand. "Oh. Oh, you butthole."

I did not react to Wylie's wife calling her a butthole, which should have earned me an Oscar.

"Sorry. Old habits. We used to see what rumors we could start with reporters," Wylie said.

"And how long it would take for them to ask one of our unsuspecting costars about said rumor," I said.

"No way. Like what?"

"Well, prankster Kaleb was one. And Jeffrey wearing a lucky, smelly jockstrap to film," Wylie said.

Jocelyn's jaw dropped. This woman was painfully over-the-top. "Wait. Jeffrey didn't wear a jockstrap?"

"No. But his agents encouraged the rumor," I said. "They thought it made him sound more manly and hetero."

"Because straight cis dudes are known for casually wearing jockstraps." Wylie laughed.

"Yeah, any appearance in gay porn is both rare and accidental."

"Oh my God. You two are hilarious together. It's good I'm not jealous." Jocelyn smiled. She seemed to be going for coy? "Or I'm just into it."

My watch lit up with a call from Russ. I was going to give that woman seventeen raises. "Sorry. It's Russ." Wylie nodded in resignation. Jocelyn looked confused. "My assistant."

"Oh, right. Of course." Jocelyn squeezed my hand.

"I'll be right back. I'm just going to step outside." I nodded at the wide, seventies aluminum-framed windows. By the time I got outside, Russ had hung up. I pulled out my phone and called her back.

"Hello. Addy?"

"Hey. What's up?"

"Sorry to interrupt. Are you still at dinner?" she asked.

"Yeah, I just stepped out to call you."

"Oh, cool. Then I'm not sorry. I just was calling to give you an out. You've been there for about ninety minutes. That's long enough so you can politely leave if you want."

"I adore you."

"You better. I'm a very good assistant."

I laughed. "Thanks for the call."

"Sure thing. And if they ask, Lenny wants to speak with you. He doesn't, but he's in on the excuse," Russ said.

"You're right. You're an excellent assistant."

"I know. The car will be there in five minutes."

I went back inside and made my excuses. Jocelyn wrapped me in a cloying, saccharine cloud and kissed my cheek and called me love twice. I was going to have to shower twice to slough off the Warm Vanilla Sugar scent.

Wylie wrapped her arms around my shoulders. I slid mine around her waist. The expensive cotton of her T-shirt was a smooth whisper between my hands and the warmth of her skin. I was usually a one-arm hugger. If I went for two, I went one over the shoulder, one under. It allowed me to lead with shoulders and hold my body back. But Wylie had always touched me differently. Her torso pressed the length of mine. Cool heat seeped into me. I carefully didn't breathe her in as I stepped back.

"Stay up as late as you can," I said in parting.

"Please. I'm not the one who falls asleep on night shoots." Wy winked. She and Taryn had covered for me sleeping on set more than once.

I laughed wryly. "I gave up the luxury of sleep with this gig."

In truth, this would be the last night I might get a full night's sleep. Our shooting schedule was largely dictated by the sun. Ideally, we would have waited until winter to start filming for the longer nights, but Oath wanted this film done yesterday. So tomorrow I would become nocturnal.

The drive back took ten minutes. Five to get out of town and five winding through towering trees on half-paved roads to get to my cabin. The studio had rented the same rustic resort as the first film. Everyone above the line had private cabins. Most of the non-local crew had rooms in the main lodge. I was in a cabin identical to the one I'd stayed in ten years previous. Danny offered me one of the two larger cabins—the same cabin Sean Murray had when he directed. But I couldn't stay in the same place where my friend had been assaulted. The strangeness of the compromise was not lost on me.

It was possible that they had updated the cabins in the last decade, but the overpowering smell of varnish suggested they had only refinished the floors and wood paneled walls. I'd had the loft windows open since I'd arrived, filling the second floor with cool mountain air and the scent of pine. The bedroom and small bathroom took up the entire top floor. The bed was positioned under the windows that jutted out from the sharp angle of the roof. A railing spanned the length of the cabin, allowing you to look across the living room below and out the wall of windows that made up the back of the cabin.

I climbed the stairs and stripped, heading straight to the bathroom. The water pressure was better than last time. I washed my hair, scrubbed at my skin, but I could still smell Jocelyn. There was nothing for it. I got out and pulled on boxer briefs with a worn Madras shirt. I hit the lights and went back downstairs. I grabbed a beer from the small, well-stocked kitchen. I'd already rearranged the living room furniture, shoving most of the contents to the far wall. A single Danish armchair was positioned in front of the windows. I dropped into it. My shirt fell open, but no one could see inside with the lights off. It was freeing. Just a moment to exist where I didn't have to embody PJ Addison. Isolation was a small price to pay for moments of honest privacy.

The darkened forest sprawled before me. I was at the top of a spectacular valley. There were stars here. Bright, shimmering stars. I sipped my beer. It was cold and sharp and smooth. There was plenty worth changing in my life, but right then, I was content.

CHAPTER FIVE

I handed my headset off. Jay took another swipe at my face. He was just doing his job, but it was annoying the shit out of me. Actually, I was just annoyed. Jay happened to be in front of me, so he was catching my ire.

"I'm good," I said.

"You're not." He set a hand on my shoulder. "You will be in two seconds if you just stop moving."

"You just did—"

"Stop harassing Jay," Wylie said from directly behind me. "If you touch your face, he has to fix it."

"I didn't touch my face."

Jay dropped the hand holding a sponge. "Oh my God, Addy. It will take two goddamn seconds." He stared at me and waited.

"Sorry." I took a deep breath and willed myself to hold still.

"On the set of the original movie, her mother attended all her hair and makeup sessions," Wylie said.

"Shut up." Jay stopped and looked at Wylie.

"We all thought Gerri was being overbearing until she wasn't on set one day. It was the funniest thing I've ever seen. Like a seven-year-old who's been given too many Popsicles."

I gritted my teeth and ignored the bait.

Jay pursed his lips and tried not to laugh. "Can we still get her mother on set?"

Wylie laughed. Jay laughed. I did not laugh.

"Can you stop undermining me on my own set?" I asked Wylie.

"Please. You're undermining yourself." Wylie cupped my elbow. "I need to steal her, Jay. Are you done?"

He booped my nose with a brush. "Yep."

"We've got to get back to filming." I tried to steer Wylie back to the wide front porch we were supposed to be sitting on. Our sunset was fading.

Wylie ignored me and kept walking until we were just out of earshot of the crew. "Is this working?"

I rolled my eyes and sighed, but it didn't change my answer. "No. You know it's not."

"You've never directed yourself," she said.

A tingle started at my scalp and raced down to my fingertips. It made my elbows and wrists itch. I shook out my hands and faced Wylie. My indignation dropped away. She wasn't challenging me. She was just stating a fact. I was filling in the very obvious conclusion that I couldn't direct myself.

"Does everyone know?" I asked. It made me feel vulnerable as hell, but it was better to ask her than literally anyone else.

"No. They all just think you're in a shit mood." She kept her voice low, which I appreciated.

"Great."

"It is. You're always on edge the first couple of days of shooting. They all just think it's normal irritability."

"Instead of me being terrible at my job." The tingles started again. I scratched my wrist and shook out my hands again.

"Listen." Wy grabbed my hands and squeezed. "We're going to figure this out. But right now we're losing the sunset, which we kind of need because Lenny was very insistent." She didn't need to show me the all caps SUNSET direction. "So can you just trust me?"

I tried to let go of my ego. When that didn't work, I took a deep breath and nodded anyway. "What do you have in mind?"

"The blocking isn't great. I should be looking at you, not the sunset."

"Okay."

"Just follow my lead. We've always been good scene partners." She was right.

I sighed. "Yeah, okay."

She tugged me back to the house. I sat on the top porch step and spread my legs wide enough for Wylie to sit between them. She settled onto the step below me. Instead of keeping her back to me, she turned halfway around and leaned back against my left thigh. She tucked one bent leg under my right knee.

Scottie, our DP, got in place. The crew scrambled to check lighting and timing and blocking. The marker snapped. Hannah called action. And then we were off to the races.

Wylie watched the sunset. I watched her. She turned, laced our fingers together. "We've been thinking about this place all wrong."

"How else are we supposed to think about it?"

Wylie's lip twitched, fighting the brilliant smile that made her famous. "It's where we fell in love."

The air between us felt warm. It was like foreplay. Wylie's bated breath. Lenny's vision. It all suddenly coalesced and unfurled. I stared into her eyes. Held the moment. And forgot my line. "Line?"

Wylie tried not to laugh, but immediately lost it. I lost it. Half the crew started laughing with us.

"Is that supposed to undo all the suffering?" the script supervisor called to me. She was laughing too.

"Thanks." I grinned at Wylie, trying to stay in the moment, but it was gone.

"Better?" Wy asked.

"Much."

"Back to one," Hannah called. Everyone shuffled back into place.

I closed my eyes and took a couple of deep breaths to center myself. I could feel Wy doing the same thing.

The marker snapped. I watched Wylie staring off in the distance. She turned and took my hand. Our fingertips entwined. The gentle pressure of her thumb created a dimple in my hand.

"We've been thinking about this place all wrong."

I stared down at our hands. "How else are we supposed to think about it?"

Wylie tugged lightly and I looked up in time to see the whisper of her smile. "It's where we fell in love."

I forced myself not to react. She was trying to draw it out of me. That kindness, that sweet sincerity, was designed to make me fall in love. But I wasn't going to go that easily. "Is that supposed to undo all the suffering?"

"No. No, of course not. But I'm not going to let what we lost taint what we gained."

I sighed. The kind of resigned sigh reserved for moments you've been outplayed. And you enjoyed it. "And that's why you want to start this place up again."

Wy unleashed the smile. "That's why I want to start this place up again."

I gripped her chin and kissed her. She angled back, then kissed me again, letting her bottom lip linger between mine. The slide of lipstick, the smell of setting spray, the crew standing on the edge of my awareness all let me know it wasn't real. And that was okay. Kissing on screen was far too clinical. To make it look good, you had to do it bad.

Wylie pulled away and faced the sunset. She settled back into my embrace. One hand curled around my forearm. The other snaked around my calf. I breathed her in. I could still smell the hairspray, the layers of makeup coating us. But under that, she smelled like citrus and sage. Her skin was faintly sweet with a suggestion of honey. She smelled like innocence and young love.

"Cut!" Hannah yelled.

Wylie grabbed me and pulled my face down to smack a kiss on my cheek. "Did you feel that? We're so damn good."

"We are damn good." I grinned at her. "Thanks."

She winked. "I got you."

We ran it through a few more times to make sure we had all the necessary angles. By the time we were done, our sunset was gone. It wasn't strictly necessary. We'd been shooting B-roll of the horizon the whole time.

The crew broke to move on to the next scene over in the barn. Jay stopped me before I could rush off. I needed to change shoes. I needed to remove my contacts. I needed to talk to Xavier and Benny to make sure they were prepped for the scene. I did not need to chat with Jay.

"Can you walk with me?" I asked. "I need to get to the barn."

"Hannah says the setup isn't finished. You've got fifteen minutes."

I changed direction and headed to my trailer. "I'm going to change. What's up?"

"You know what's up. I need to get that off your face. If I don't, you'll wear it all night, shower at four a.m., and break out by six."

"Gee, it's so nice to work with people who know me so well."

"I can't help that you're so sensitive." Jay followed me into the trailer. A wardrobe assistant and Russ crowded in after Jay. Russ disappeared into the back of the trailer.

"I'm not sensitive." I started unbuttoning my shirt.

Jay gripped my chin and started wiping, and he wasn't being gentle. "I meant your skin. Close your eyes." He pressed a wipe into the corner of my eye. It wasn't pleasant, but he knew exactly how much pressure to use for maximum makeup removal without hurting me.

When Jay pulled back to grab a new wipe, I took off the flannel and handed it to the wardrobe woman. I pulled off my T-shirt and caught the long sleeve tee Russ tossed at me. Jay cupped my face with his long fingers to keep me still as I tugged the shirt into place. He was really going to town on my eye.

"Are you done yet?" I tried to kick off my work boots, but Jay was making that difficult.

"Almost. You're such a baby. The other actors don't need this much handling. Close your eyes again," he said.

"Should I remind you I'm your director? And producer?"

"And I'm union, sweetie. You can open."

I opened my eyes to find him grinning at me. "I feel like my threats aren't very threatening."

"They're not. Do you really want to be threatening?"

"Yes. Very," I said.

"Okay. Sure. I'm terrified. Stay hydrated tonight. I want you glowing."

"How are we on time?" I called.

"You've still got ten," Russ said.

I pulled on my worn Chelsea boots. The work boots looked great on camera, but mine were actually comfortable.

"We about ready?" Russ asked.

"Almost." I looked up from adjusting my socks. Russ was holding out my watch in one hand and had her other cupped to catch my on-screen accessories. "Thanks." I unbuckled the watch and pulled off Taylor's wedding set. I dropped the lot in her hand and accepted my watch.

"Hey, Russ?" Jay asked.

"Yeah?"

"Make sure she stays hydrated tonight," Jay said.

"You got it." Russ popped open a contact case and I dropped in my contacts. She watched me blink. "You want drops?"

"No."

She sighed. "Addy."

"Thanks though." I started to stand.

Jay pulled me back and scrubbed below my ear. "Sorry, done now."

"Good night, Jay."

He winked. "Always a pleasure, ma'am."

"Russ, remind me to ruin Jay tomorrow," I said loudly as we left the trailer.

"I'll start brainstorming underhanded techniques right now." Russ touched my elbow to direct me to the barn.

Benny and Hannah were standing on the edge of the lights at the barn, waiting for me. Drew was in heaven. He was staring intently at the warm lights on Benny's face and muttering into a walkie. The man was a horror-lighting genius, and I was relieved he signed on. Lighting a barn in the dark while maintaining the darkness was a challenge on its own. On top of that, Teddy and Diego—the guys playing Benny and Xavier—weren't white. Conventional lighting practices would light them like white boys and lose half their facial features. I wanted to have my entire cast actually show up on film. Drew had been delighted by my direction.

It took five minutes to wrangle Xavier who had wandered off in the ninety seconds he'd been unattended and another ten to review blocking with the stunt coordinator and the boys' doubles. We spent the next couple of hours filming a single scene. Xavier was supposed to leap off a pile of hay and tackle Benny. They would then get in a semi-serious fight over the prank, which meant Xavier had to laugh for four hours and Benny needed to scowl. All while rolling around on the floor of the barn. There was nothing particularly challenging about it, but it was a slog nonetheless.

When the boys left set, we called in Rob. As our resident Black Hat actor, he was banished from visibility on set if any of the principal actors were present. He was already in his Wranglers and white ribbed undershirt. In a pre-production panic, I'd chosen a Tom Ford number for the tank. At the time, I didn't know if it was right, but decisions needed to be made. Watching him emerge from the shadows around the barn, I knew I'd made the right call. It fell and clung in all the right ways. His open plaid shirt flapped around him in the gentle breeze. He was the epitome of American masculinity—the darkest version. Deceptively beautiful, lurking, dangerous.

Drew did a quick lighting check. Making sure Rob's face never showed up on film was just as difficult as lighting everyone else's face. Mostly because we had to ignore every instinct we had about lighting. Drew had devised a system of lights angled from just above the brim of Rob's cowboy hat. The trick was to keep the shadow right at the edge of his chiseled chin.

We shot a ton of clips of Black Hat lurking about the barn. They would be interspersed with Benny and Xavier's wrestling match. The haunted silhouette would hover just out of easy range, taunting the audience, invisible to the boys.

Jay was wrong. I made it back to my cabin at the luxurious hour of three a.m. There was an envelope taped to my door. I grabbed it and stumbled upstairs. I tore it open as I ascended. It was tomorrow's call sheet. The *Teddy Finch "Benny"* and *PJ Addison "Taylor Henderson"* were circled in bright blue Sharpie and the rest of the sheet was illegible because of the message scrawled across it in Wylie's handwriting.

Breakfast and blocking at 9 xx Wy

CHAPTER SIX

I woke to the sound of someone moving in my kitchen. They were trying to be quiet, but I'd lived alone long enough that hearing someone in my space while I was still in bed was disconcerting.

"Wy, that better be you," I called.

"No, it's paparazzi," Wy called back.

I grabbed my phone. It was ten after nine. There weren't any dire texts from when I was asleep. Phil sent editing notes from the first round of dailies. He was already ensconced in his studio starting to cut together the film. Otherwise, email was standard. Nothing pressing. I scrolled Insta for a few minutes.

"Get off your phone and come down here." Wylie's voice sounded louder now. Like she'd moved out of the kitchen and was standing directly below the loft.

I groaned in response. My eyes felt gritty. The days when I could run on five hours of sleep were long past. I could rally and survive it, but not for weeks on end. Black Hat was for sure going to kill me this time.

I pulled on a shirt and hit the bathroom before going downstairs. Wy was leaning against the window frame, staring out at the mist and evergreens sprawled below us. She carved a slice from the apple she was holding. She held the slice between her thumb and the paring knife and slowly brought it to her lips.

"You know I hate when you do that," I said.

She cut another slice, carefully drawing the sharp knife edge toward her thumb. "I know."

"You're going to lose a finger."

"Just be happy I'm not slicing carrots." Wy ate another apple slice. She let the knife tip linger a moment too long on her bottom lip.

I shuddered. Not from her erotic knife display—and it was—but at the memory of her slicing carrots. My childhood was non-traditional, so I'd never gotten cooking lessons, but I refused to believe any normal person handled a knife the way Wylie did. She laughed at my reaction and cut another piece from her apple.

I grabbed a cup of coffee and my own apple. I leaned opposite Wy to stare out the window. "So what's your plan here, babe?"

Wy turned away from the window. "Nothing grand. Run through the scenes we're filming today. Just your scenes. Get a handle on what you need to do as an actor so you can be a director on set."

"And tomorrow?"

"Same thing. Tweak as necessary." She shrugged like she wasn't offering me a lifeline.

Theoretically, there were any number of people on set who could and would give me performance feedback. Hannah, Claude, they were in my corner. And it was their job. But I didn't know them like I did Wy. More importantly, they didn't know Taylor's character. Not like Wy and I did, at least.

"You don't mind?" I asked.

Her eyes softened. "No."

"Because I'm losing it here." I wouldn't have told anyone else that. Maybe my mom. But she wasn't around. Wylie was the reason I didn't trust anyone, but she was still the person who knew me best.

"I know." Wy grabbed my hand and squeezed. "This production is fucked. They're not giving you anything to work with. If Oath didn't need this so bad, I'd think they were setting you up to fail."

"They did agree to all my demands. I just didn't know I needed to demand a whole entire script and a full cast."

Wy laughed, then suddenly stopped. "Oh, shit. That reminds me. Are you the one who got me EP?"

I grinned. "Yeah."

"Ugh. I love you."

My pulse raced but I just kept smiling. "I'm tired of this patriarchal bullshit. If they can give rapey Sean EP to shut him up, then they damn well owe us for all the times they shut us up." We'd earned executive producer credits about ten times over. It was about damn time they acknowledged that.

"I love when you rant about the studio."

"Good. Ninety percent of my personality has been replaced with being pissed off at Oath," I said.

"No way. You've still got a solid thirty percent of personality left." She set her coffee on the counter and pointed at one of the chairs I'd shoved away from the windows. "Now help me move this back."

I huffed like it was an inconvenience but set my mug down and helped lift the chair. We set it at an angle by mine so she could see the view and still look at me. Wy refilled coffee while I gathered my script and notes.

"I've only got one scene today," I said.

"The one with Benny. The recruitment scene." Wy nodded. "Is this your first scene with him?"

I nodded. "It's practically my first conversation with him." I channeled my sudden panic into an eye roll. This production was doomed. The lack of a table read had paled in comparison to the rest of the roadblocks I was facing, but I was suddenly very aware of how much I could have used that experience. As an actor. As a director. As an executive producer.

"Your eyes just cycled through about ten levels of panic," Wy said.

"No, they didn't."

"You're a very bad liar."

"Can we just run the lines?" I asked.

Wylie grabbed her script. "Okay, page twenty-three. We're in Benny's office. I'm Benny, a twenty-something doctoral student dude. But like a sexy one with abs."

I nodded vigorously. "The abs are very important to the character. They were literally the only parameter the studio gave when casting Benny."

"Yes, I can feel them. I'm channeling abs." Wy winked. "Action."

I knocked on my armrest. "Excuse me, I'm looking for Benny?"

"You must be Ms. Henderson. From the Durant ranch?"

The first read-through, I didn't take notes. I just felt the scene. I stumbled over a couple of lines, but I still had a few hours to memorize them. When we were done, both of us stopped to write in the margins. Wy finished first, but she didn't rush me.

"Okay, so why are Grace and Taylor hiring PhD boy? What's with all the technical jargon?" Wy asked.

"Hell if I know. Lenny said he's twenty-first century Indiana Jones."

"So an archeologist?"

"Yeah."

"Then what's cultural resource management?"

"Fancy archeology?" I shrugged. "Apparently, they don't dig shit up anymore. They catalogue and put things back in the ground and tell people when they can't dig somewhere."

"So we're hiring him to tell us where we can't build on the cursed ranch?"

"Yep. And Lenny shoehorned in a dissertation on the history of the town and ranch to placate Danny."

"Why does Danny want a dissertation on a fictional town?" Wy asked.

"He doesn't. He wants the character to be writing a dissertation on the fictional town."

"Right, right. Okay. And why does he need abs for that?"

"Because Oath didn't see why we insisted on casting a Native American kid to play a Native American role. So they insisted on abs," I said. As if every single actor casting had sent up didn't have abs regardless of their race.

"Of course."

I flipped back to the start of the scene. "There's not much to block here. We're going to be sitting after the initial handshake."

"Yeah, but do we like him? Do we trust him? Did Lenny tell you who the killer is?"

"Benny is our resident dreamboat. Xavier—Diego's character—is the comedic relief. Benny—Teddy is the leading man. And, yes, I know who the killer is. And, no, I'm not going to tell you."

Wylie sighed. Then sighed again when I didn't react. "Benny has to do most of the work here. We're establishing him," she said.

"Yeah, but Taylor will give him legitimacy. If she thinks he's trustworthy, then he is," I said.

Wy nodded and wrote another note. "Cool. So open body language. Face him head on."

"And I'm doing warm lighting but not overly saturated. Comforting. Drew has all but guaranteed me natural light."

"Where are you shooting?" she asked.

"The library over in Miller's Port. It's all plaster walls and walnut-framed windows. Perfect for a pseudo university. "

"Which means you're going to run lines with Benny on the way there," she said.

"Yeah."

"Which means you don't need to run lines with me right now," she said.

"I don't know Benny. I don't know if I have chemistry with him." I tried to keep the whine out of my voice, but it was there.

"You have chemistry with walls, babe."

"Whatever."

"Page twenty-three?"

"Page twenty-three."

❖

Teddy and I had the back of the SUV to ourselves on the drive to Miller's Port. It seemed like a good opportunity to get to know the guy so I sent everyone else separately. Normally the drive took an hour, but chauffeuring the director apparently made our driver nervous so he was sticking strictly to the speed limit, which put us firmly fifteen minutes behind. Luckily, I didn't make Teddy nervous. He stopped halfway through our second read-through.

Teddy fixed me with a very serious stare. "Am I the killer?"

"What?"

"Because, listen, from what I know of Mr. Pace's work and yours, I just don't think you'd have an indigenous man be the killer. Plus, my agent assured me I wasn't playing a villain. And honestly, all of this seemed way more important when I wasn't riding in an SUV running lines with the PJ Addison." His tone suggested my name was an honorific. Which was flattering.

"I'm not sure that title is well placed, but you're right. Having you be the killer wouldn't fit my brand," I said.

"Okay. Cool. Because at this point I'd be fine with it, but I need to know how to play him." He leaned forward and pointed to his next line. "Like here. I can be academic or menacing or ambiguous and mysterious. What do you want?"

"Can you give me menacing?"

Teddy nodded and took a deep breath. He looked at me with a glower. "This land is old, Ms. Henderson. I'm not sure you want to know what's buried in it." He was right. Very menacing.

"Okay, good. Now ambiguous and mysterious," I said.

He closed his eyes for a moment. When he opened his eyes, there was the suggestion of mirth in them. "This land is old, Ms. Henderson." He paused just long enough. "I'm not sure you want to know what's buried in it."

"That was great. Can you combine them?"

"Yeah. Yeah, okay." Another deep breath and then he delivered it perfectly. "This land is old, Ms. Henderson." There was a hint of anger behind his eyes. My arms erupted in goose bumps. "I'm not sure you want to know what's buried in it." He dropped his voice to give the line some quiet mystery.

"That. Do exactly that." I held up my arm. "Goose bumps."

"Yeah?" He drew a slash between the two lines. "This is so wild. I can't believe I'm here. With you. Playing this character." He sat back and fixed me with a stare. "Can I just geek out for a sec?"

"Geek away."

"I loved *Mercédès Herrera*." His eyes got wide like he'd already said too much, but then the rest of his confession tumbled out. "I was at the Desert Fest premiere, and I saw your talk at the end. It was one of the most brilliant discussions of identity and film I've ever heard."

"You were at Desert Fest?"

He nodded vigorously. "I'd seen *Green Rowboats and Other Tales* and was obsessed so I begged my agent to get me in and it was so worth it. That audience was made for *Mercédès*. And you."

I smiled. "I got lucky with that audience."

"No. No. It was you. God, you were brilliant." He laughed. "Okay. I'm done. I'm not a stalker. I just think you're an amazing filmmaker."

I laughed with him. "I don't hate it. You're good for my ego. But I had a fantastic crew. And Lindsey and Isabel are wonderful screenwriters. I'd wanted to work with them for years."

"Yes. That script. Damn. I read *Monte Cristo* before the festival and your interpretation blew me away."

"You did?" It was like pulling teeth to get my team to read *The Count of Monte Cristo*. I gave up with everyone except my principals.

"Of course. Well, I read about half before. Half after. It's a long book." He grinned in a self-deprecating way. The honesty was more endearing.

"It is."

"My girlfriend read it with me and it only took her a week. She made fun of me the whole time. But it's not my fault. Math major." He ducked his head and laughed like it was perfectly normal for twenty-five-year-old actors with faces like his to study math.

"Seriously?"

"Yeah. She reads fast."

"No, the math major."

"Oh, yeah. That. I don't think my mother will ever forgive me for signing with my agency instead of finishing grad school."

"I'm sorry. You were studying math in grad school? Not just like undergrad?"

He tucked his pen into his script and closed it. "Don't get any wild ideas. I was only a year into my PhD. Barely a grad student."

"I had no idea." I grinned. "And you're playing a doctoral student. I love it."

"Whoa." He waved a hand. "Applied mathematics is nothing like cultural resource management. I can't pronounce half these words."

"Sorry. I'm still going to be impressed."

He flipped his script back open. "I'll let my mother know."

CHAPTER SEVEN

With a reminder from Russ that I was needed on set in twenty minutes, I called my editor. The chances that he would actually pick up were about sixty-forty and not in my favor. It had been three whole days since I talked to him and I was getting antsy.

"I'm not coming up there," was how Phil answered the phone.

"Good evening, Phil. Yes, it is lovely up here. How's the weather in Los Angeles?"

"Don't try to small talk me."

"So you don't want to discuss the Dodgers?" I asked.

"Addy. I'm not coming up there."

"I didn't ask you to come up here." Sure, I was planning on asking him again. But I hadn't yet.

"This is my process. I don't fuck with your process." His point was kind of incorrect. My process involved my editor being nearby so I could go stand over his shoulder and micromanage him. His process involved him never leaving his little backyard studio. When I filmed in LA, our processes meshed. When I filmed not in LA, our processes did not mesh. Of course, most directors simply demanded that their editors did what they wanted. I'd obviously gotten soft in my old age.

"Fine. Rot in your little studio," I said.

"You could have had any other editor on this project. My feelings wouldn't have been hurt."

"I don't want another editor. I want my editor."

"You just want me to be someone I'm not." He sounded like a jilted lover. Clearly, we'd been friends for too long.

"No. It's fine." I sighed. "How are the dailies?"

"Decent. The audio levels are much better now. Especially for the outdoor shots," he said.

I waited but he didn't offer up any more detail. "That's it? That's all you're giving me?"

"You are impossible to work with, you know that?"

"Am I?"

"I sent you notes an hour ago. Detailed notes." He had officially lost the battle with his irritation, and it was bleeding into his voice.

"It's just not the same."

"I am not coming up there," he said very slowly.

"Fine." I pulled up the email he'd sent. "Walk me through your notes."

"You'll stop asking?"

"I'll stop asking."

Satisfied, Phil dove into his notes.

❖

I was so goddamn tired of the woods. I remembered being bored of them back in the first movie. Shooting in the same location for nights on end had that effect. But in a delightful twist of age, I was now apparently allergic to one of the grasses in the meadow between the tree line and the barn. Luckily, I wasn't filming this week because Jay was good, but no talent in the world could make my eyes calm down.

"Cut," I called. "Back to one. Ava, Xavier, a moment?"

Ava and Xavier jogged over. Ava—Emma—was a forgettably beautiful type. Blonde, blue-eyed white girl. She was gorgeous and sexy and ultimately looked like every other starlet. Hair and makeup had been tasked with downplaying her more memorable features. They'd given her blonder hair and a more neutral lip. It helped. Emma had pushed back on her boring wardrobe, but I managed to lie convincingly enough to keep her in slightly ill-fitting clothing without telling her the real reason we wanted her to disappear. I was going to wait as long as possible before telling her she was Black Hat's accomplice. Xavier, ironically enough, would be her first victim.

I was peripherally aware of the production manager telling Hannah we needed to get a move on to the next scene. Hannah politely but firmly redirected her.

"Xavier, I need more from you before you kiss Ava," I said.

He nodded and very sincerely asked, "What does that mean?"

A PA stepped up and handed each of them a bottle of water. Xavier swished and spit his out. He was shirtless tomorrow for half the day and his trainer was restricting water. Doing so seemed a little pointless since the guy had so many muscles, but hey, I wasn't the target audience. Ava took a long, luxurious swallow of her water. Xavier looked at her longingly.

"That. That's the look I need," I said.

Xavier looked at me in question. "What look? When?"

"Before you start kissing. I want you to hold that a couple of beats longer. And look at her like she's water."

Ava laughed and took another sip.

"Laugh now." Xavier shot her a look. "You're the one who has to kiss me when I'm dehydrated."

"It's true. He does taste like a dumpster," Ava said.

Xavier nudged her with a shoulder. Thank God they actually liked each other. Filming scenes with actors who hated each other and were pretending to be in love was exhausting.

I looked around for a PA. "We'll get him a mint."

Ava waved me off and took a step back. "He's fine. As long as I get to watch him parade around shirtless tomorrow, I'll be fine."

"If I'd known we could pay you in pretty boys, your contract negotiations would have been easier," I said.

"Hey, sexual harassment much?" Xavier said.

"You literally told me yesterday that you were tired of being reduced to your intellect and having people ignore your muscles," I said.

"It's true. You did say that," Ava told him.

Xavier's face brightened. "Aww, you two listened to me."

Ava leaned close to me and whispered, "Ignoring his intellect isn't much of a challenge."

I laughed. "Back to one." I pointed back at the tree they were supposed to start at.

Hannah cut in to make sure they were on the correct starting marks.

"Here, Addy. Before we start rolling." Russ appeared at my elbow and held out eye drops.

I glanced at her and immediately looked away. "I don't want eye drops."

"You keep saying that, but you can barely see."

"I can see just fine." I definitely couldn't. I pulled off my glasses and cleaned them on my shirt.

Russ took the glasses out of my hands and cleaned them with a cloth. "Your eyes are puffy and red and these glasses don't have a single smear. Just put in the damn drops. You're like a child."

"And you're channeling my mother."

Russ sighed and left me to squint at my leads making out against a tree.

❖

"We are going to die," Sadie said.

"Calm down," Pippa told her. "We're not going to die."

"That's what people say right before they die."

"Let go of the horror trope. Besides, your boyfriend is the one who sent us out here." Pippa played her phone flashlight over the ground.

"He's not my boyfriend."

Pippa stopped and gave Sadie a very silly look. The moonlight fell perfectly across Pippa's face. She was the most distinctive of the female cast. Her features were too strong, her jawline just a little too sturdy for conventional beauty. Yet, she was stunning.

Sadie was played by Rosie Reeves. She stood out by virtue of the fact that she'd started at Disney as a young child. We'd only cast white women to blur the identity of Black Hat's accomplice. Mick had thrown a fit—not because he actually wanted women of color. No, he just thought there should have been white men in the main cast. He called the casting unbalanced. I called him racist. No one left that meeting happy.

"Pippa, Sadie, you still out here?" Benny called.

"Boyfriend," Pippa mouthed.

"Shut up," Sadie mouthed back. "Over here, Benny," she called.

Benny caught up to them and the trio continued down the forest path. Hannah called cut. She jogged over to me and Claude in video village and hovered behind my shoulder.

"Yeah, that's great," I said.

"We got the shot?" Hannah asked.

"Yep. The shadow was perfect." I backed up the video so she could see it.

"Damn. You're right." Hannah leaned closer. "Gorgeous shot."

"Yeah, yeah," Claude said.

"What was that, Claude?" I asked pointedly.

"I said the shot looks fantastic. Just like you said it would." He rolled his eyes. Which was an odd look on a guy in his sixties with flowing white hair.

Hannah stepped back. "Okay. We're breaking for thirty."

I left her to deal with logistics. Prepping the rig would take a few and the actors were all due for a break. Most of the kids scattered, except for Rosie. She waved me over. I was headed her way when Russ stopped me.

"Rosie wants to discuss the Benny and Sadie scene later," Russ said.

I nodded at Rosie waiting for me at the edge of the meadow. "Wow, thanks, Russ. I couldn't do this without you."

Russ laughed. "Want me to bring over coffee?"

"Please," I said. We emerged from the tree line and the ground became visible.

"Hey, Addy. Are you heading back to your trailer?" Rosie asked.

"Yeah, what's up?" I asked.

"Can I walk with you?"

"Of course," I said. I signaled to Hannah that I was heading back. She gave me a thumbs-up. "Russ is bringing me coffee. You want anything?"

"Green tea, thanks," Rosie said. Russ nodded and veered away from us.

"Russ said you wanted to talk about one of the Benny and Sadie scenes?" I asked.

"Yeah, I know we've got a lot to get through tonight, so I don't know if we're going to get to the conversation by the grave markers," Rosie said.

"I'm hoping we will. It kind of depends on how the next scene goes," I said.

"Yeah, I figured. It's just—I don't know what we're trying to accomplish, you know?"

"You mean in the scene?"

Rosie gave me a long-suffering sigh. "No, boss. In life. What we're trying to accomplish in life."

I laughed. "Sorry. Yes. Okay. We're ramping up the tension between you and Benny of course. But we're also trying to sow some doubt about Sadie's intentions."

"So you want me to hold back? Like I'm not actually into him?"

"Actually no. I want you to press forward a bit. Almost like you're a bit too eager to lock him down."

"Ohh. Okay." Rosie's eyes got big and she nodded a few times. "As if I'm setting him up."

"Yes, exactly." We got to the door of my trailer. "You want to come in and keep discussing?" I asked.

"Yeah, actually. That would be chill." She looked relieved. Once again, I silently cursed Oath for denying us enough time to properly prepare before we started shooting.

"Should we grab Teddy too?" I asked.

"Heck yeah. We talked about it earlier, but we weren't sure where you were going with it."

I spotted a PA and waved them over. "Can you get me a location on Teddy? I'd like for him to join us." They nodded and grabbed their radio.

Rosie and I chatted inside the trailer. She was the youngest of the principal cast, but she'd been in the business a few years longer than the rest of them so she seemed older, more settled. We discussed the set and her performance a bit. She was feeling good about the direction we were going.

The door opened and Teddy came in. "Hey, boss. You called."

"Yeah, Rosie was asking about the graveyard flirting. We thought you should be included," I said.

"Excellent." He sat on the couch opposite Rosie. "So how sexy are we making it?"

"So sexy. The intimacy coordinator is coming in early just to watch," Rosie said.

Teddy looked at me in surprise. "Really? I mean, I didn't know. It's fine. There's just waxing to be done."

"No. Jesus. Don't listen to her," I said.

Rosie started laughing. "There's waxing to be done." She laughed harder. "You have seven chest hairs."

Teddy arched his eyebrow. "That's not where the waxing is needed."

"No one is getting waxed," I said. "Actually, that's not really my purview. Someone might be getting waxed. But not tonight. It's a simple scene. Sadie flirts hard with Benny. No one gets sexy."

The door opened again. It was Russ with tea and coffee. "Hey, Teddy. I didn't know you were here. You want something to drink?" She handed our drinks over.

"Actually, yeah. Some water. The air out at that meadow is killing me," he said.

"Addy too." Russ gave me a pointed look.

"Yeah, yeah. I have allergies. I'm still not using eye drops," I said.

"You want cold or room temp?" Russ asked Teddy as she went to the small refrigerator.

"Cold, please. Who drinks room temp water?" Teddy asked.

"Addy, again. She's very particular." Russ pulled out a cold bottle of water. "You need anything else?"

"We're good. You've mocked me enough. Let me know when the setup is done," I said. She nodded and left.

"So, boss, what's wrong with you?" Teddy asked.

"That's a big question. Care to narrow it down?"

"The water. That's weird," he said.

"In her defense, it's only Americans that tend to drink cold water," Rosie said.

"Thank you." I nodded at her. "But it's actually because my teeth are fake. So my nerve endings are sensitive." I smiled big because that was always the next question.

"No shit?" Teddy asked.

"Hey, so are mine." Rosie smiled too.

"No. I'm sorry, buddy," I said. She shrugged and waved a hand.

"Why do both of you have fake teeth?" Teddy asked.

"Child star. I needed braces. They would have altered my look for too many years. So my agent convinced my mother to have them cosmetically altered," I said.

Teddy cringed. "I'm sorry. That's fucked." He looked at Rosie. "You too?"

"Basically, yeah. In my case it was the network. *Rosie's Rosy World* couldn't have anything less than perfect."

There was another knock at the door. This time it was Claude. "Sorry to interrupt. Addy, you got a sec?"

"Sure."

Claude held the door open and stepped back. Apparently, he wanted me to come outside. I followed him and he closed the door behind me.

"Just wanted to let you know Nelson will be coming up tomorrow," Claude said.

Neat. Because I wasn't stressed enough. Adding another producer to the mix would totally make things better. "Okay."

"I'm sorry. I pushed him off as long as I could."

"It's fine. Just try to keep him under control on set. You know how high strung he can be," I said.

"Yeah. You got it."

"Because when he starts micromanaging, it annoys the shit out of me." I'd nearly pulled a Black Hat on Nelson in the two weeks before we started filming. I had fourteen days to do the work of three months and Nelson's alleged help made everything harder.

"I know. I'll make sure he doesn't mess with wardrobe or lighting or screw with anything else you already approved," Claude said.

"Thank you." Tomorrow we started filming the party sequence. It would take the better part of a week and that was assuming everything went off without a hitch. Nelson was a hitch.

Claude clapped a hand on my shoulder. "Hey, at least it's not Eddie."

"That's immensely helpful. Thanks," I said dryly.

"Perspective." He shrugged.

"You want perspective? At least it's not Sean. That's fucking perspective."

Claude fought a shudder. "I stand, as always, corrected."

CHAPTER EIGHT

Hannah, Scottie, and I crowded around the bank of monitors. Hannah was taking notes and keeping them to herself. Scottie was grumbling into his walkie.

"What the fuck is that?" I asked. Neither of them had an answer. But I was the goddamn director. "Guys. Why is there a blue sheen over my beautifully lit party?"

"I don't know," Scottie said.

"That's not good enough," I said.

Hannah briefly touched my arm. "We're waiting on Drew. He's on it."

Scottie's walkie came to life. He shook his head as he listened. "Drew says there's nothing wrong."

I was inclined to believe him. I could see the lighting. It looked great. Kitschy lanterns were hung throughout the barn and the tables and dance floor that spilled into the meadow. Cool synthetic moonlight bathed the rustic furniture. Fire pits at the edges of the party gave off rich orange tones. It was all perfectly balanced. And yet, it was blue.

"It's got to be the cameras," Hannah murmured to Scottie.

He pouted. "It's not."

"Scottie. Buddy. C'mon," I said. "We've eliminated all the other options."

"What is the problem here?" Nelson asked from behind me.

I spun. Nelson had his hands shoved in his pockets. He was trying to look casual and failing spectacularly. His shoulders were tight. His jaw was set. Splotches of red were visible on his ever-growing forehead.

"We're having a color balance issue," I said.

"Well, fix it. We're losing time and money here."

"We're trying to fix it. There are a lot of moving parts."

Nelson scoffed. "I can see the lights. They're fine. It's a camera issue. Scottie, what's the problem? Where's your team?" He barely asked the question before stalking toward the camera rig thirty feet away. Three people were clustered around it. They were doing their jobs. Nelson was about to make their jobs harder.

"Nelson," I called. "A second?" Where the hell was Claude? Why was I dealing with Nelson's fuckery?

He reluctantly came back. "What? If you're not going to handle it, I will."

I turned to face him and in the process, took a step away from the action unfolding before us. Nelson was forced to keep his back to Hannah and Scottie in order to talk to me. One day, Nelson would realize how often I directed him like one of my actors. Today was not that day.

"Scottie's team is disassembling their equipment to see what the issue is." That was an outright lie. "If we rush them or stress them, we will break something. There are a thousand things that could be causing this. We're working through the list."

"We don't have time for this. We're ready to film." He pointed at the crew standing around. "We're not paying them to stand here doing nothing." As if half of making a movie wasn't paying people to stand around doing nothing.

I looked at my shoes and took a deep, calming breath. It didn't make me calm but it was worth a shot. "Everyone is well aware that we need to get moving," I said. I was wearing a pastel green shirt and leather fucking suspenders. I looked like a Pinterest board for an outdoor wedding. As if I needed Nelson to remind me that we were making a movie.

"How long will this little search take?" Nelson asked.

I didn't know if I should manage expectations and tell him hours or tell him five minutes and make it a problem for myself five minutes from now. Behind Nelson, Hannah waved and gave me a thumbs up.

"Looks like we're already done." I nodded at Hannah.

Nelson turned to scowl at her and her thumbs up. "Good." He marched off. Excellent producing, thanks, Nelson.

"Ready to get rolling?" I asked. As I stepped closer, I could see the monitors. They showed the same light I could see. That was a relief.

Hannah nodded and took off to get everyone back on set before I could ask her what went wrong. Scottie was already back with his crew. He was laughing at something with the camera operator. At least the pall of Nelson wasn't longstanding.

Baird was the only person by the monitors. "Hannah says we've got five minutes," he said in greeting.

"Great. Did she tell you what went wrong?" I asked. Baird pressed his lips together. At first I thought it was in embarrassment or fear, but I quickly realized he was holding back laughter. "Oh, God. What was it?"

"The color balance on the monitors."

"I know, but why was it off?"

"No, literally the monitors. The settings on the TVs were off. Someone changed the preset and it removed the proper color balance."

"Fuck me." I laughed. No wonder Hannah took off. She was probably interrogating everyone who had touched the equipment in the last hour.

"You need anything before we start filming?" Baird asked.

"I'm good. Will you send Jay and Sheila over for a final touch-up?"

"Sure thing." Baird went off in search of hair and makeup.

I wove through the tables in the meadow to get to the open barn doors. The set was hot and I'd already called out someone else for fucking up my continuity so I was extra careful to not make myself my own example.

Wylie was waiting below the hayloft. She was wearing a gauzy short-sleeved summer dress that managed to be both elegant and rustic. It was a hard combination, but Arjun over in wardrobe was quite possibly divine. He'd given her heels that put her two inches above me. God forbid we shoot a scene with two lesbians in a barn without putting one of them in heels. Or Mick forbid.

Jay did a quick brush over my cheeks and forehead before spritzing my face with setting spray. He waited for Sheila to finish with Wy and then they switched. Sheila rubbed a minuscule amount of pomade between two fingers and ran it through the curl above my left eye. She held her breath and the curl stayed.

"Damn, I'm good," Sheila whispered. I laughed. "Well, I am."

"No one is disputing that," I said.

A PA secured the steps so Wy and I could climb to the hayloft. Once we were up, they whisked the metal apparatus away and replaced it with a scene-appropriate wooden ladder. We sat on the edge of the loft on our little pieces of tape.

"Fuck," Wy said.

"What?"

She leaned forward dangerously. There wasn't a pad below us because it would have interfered with the shot. We were not supposed to be leaning forward. The hayloft was a good twenty feet up.

"My shoe," she said.

I looked down and her heel was indeed on the ground. "Smooth, babe."

We watched a PA grab the heel and climb the ladder.

"I told Arjun those heels were a bad idea for the party," Wylie said.

"I'm pretty sure you said heels were a bad idea for running."

The PA handed the shoe to me. I handed it to Wylie. Hannah tried not to roll her eyes.

"You think you can manage to power through?" I asked as condescendingly as possible.

Wy huffed and turned up her nose. "I'm a professional."

I laughed. "Just stop swinging your feet."

"I know Grace better than you do. She would swing her feet." Wy carefully bent to put the shoe back on without falling out of the loft or flashing the crew below us.

"No, she wouldn't."

"She did during their first kiss."

I couldn't actually remember if that was true. "Well, she was a teenager. She's not a teenager anymore."

Wylie rolled her eyes and sighed. She knew I was right.

"Hey, we good?" Hannah asked.

"Yeah. Get the marker," I called down.

The crew fell silent again as the marker dropped. The crane slowly rose, panning up the rough barn walls, then it climbed our legs to our clasped hands on the edge of the loft, to us. Wylie stared out at the empty barn. I stared at Wy.

"We did it," she said.

"You did it."

We were at the start of the third and final act. Grace and Taylor didn't know Xavier and Pippa were already dead. Their bodies would be revealed during the party, prompting the sequence of events leading to the climax. But this, here, was the moment we got to feel their happiness, their hope. It was before the guests arrived, before the carnage began in earnest.

"Not without you. There's no way I could have pulled it off without you." Wy kissed my knuckle. She let out a slip of tongue and grinned at me.

"You're just saying that because I hauled up your ice." I gave the line a teasing lilt.

"There is that." She cupped the back of my neck and pulled me forward into a kiss. "Of course, I know you made Xavier do the heavy lifting."

"Why would we hire your nephew as a farm hand if not for heavy lifting?" I asked.

"You sound like Aunt Jill." Her smile dropped, just a little.

"She'd have been proud of you."

"Or she would have told me to burn this place to the ground."

"No. She loved this place. And you've brought it back to life." I turned to stare out at the barn. We would cut in a shot of the empty tables sprawling into the meadow. Instead, all I could see was the camera directly in front of my face. I fixed my focus on the opposite wall.

"I have, haven't I?" she asked.

"You were right, you know."

Wylie followed my gaze out. "I'm always right." She waited a respectable beat before turning to look at me again. "Wait. Why am I right this time?"

I chuckled. "You said the ranch was where we fell in love. That the love outweighed the horrors. It didn't erase them, but it mattered more. And this, baby, this is love." I infused as much warmth as I could into the brief monologue even though it was only a placeholder.

Lenny would write me something better—something longer. We would play the audio over Black Hat cutting down the first guests to arrive at the party.

"Maybe we should skip the party and make out in the hayloft," Wylie said.

I sighed and stood. "And keep your guests waiting?" I held out my hand to help her up.

She took my hand and got to her feet. "The guests aren't going to arrive for another two, maybe three minutes."

I tugged her close and wrapped my arms around her waist. "Well, if we've got three whole minutes," I whispered before kissing her.

Wy leaned into the kiss. Her body pressed the length of mine. I angled my head so our lips would meet just so. She took my shoulders and pushed until we fell against a wide support beam. I was very aware of the placement of my feet. We had four feet between us and the drop-off. I knew my blocking—I always knew my blocking—but this was a rare moment when missing my mark would result in injury rather than a reshoot.

"Grace? You in here? The lights on the path are out and I can't find Taylor," Benny called.

Wylie pulled back, grinning. We stifled our laughter. "Guess it's been three minutes," she said.

"Up here, Benny," I called. We stepped away from each other, but stayed close enough to touch. "I'm on my way down."

"Hey." Wy tugged me back before I could let go. "Thank you. For seeing me."

I took her chin and kissed her once more. "I'd do anything for you."

"Even return to your nightmare?" She smiled. The pain had been bled from the question and we were just two women in love.

"Even that."

We descended the ladder. I called cut, a PA brought back the safe ladder, we climbed and swapped ladders, and did it all over again. After running the whole scene a couple of times, we reshot the kiss. Again. And again.

One entire take was a close-up of my hands on the back of her dress, gripping her waist, wrinkling the fabric. Another take of Wy running her fingertips under the strap of my suspenders. At least three takes of our lips meeting. The soft descent. My lips cupping her bottom lip. A slip of tongue. We did the fall back into the support beam. Wylie did one take smiling slightly as we fell, then another where she stared deeply into my eyes. One take where she landed hard against me. Her thigh hit and pressed directly between mine. A pulse started. I decided to use it. No one needed to know it was real.

She pressed me back into the beam and kissed me hard. I spread my hands wide across her back and held tight. Benny shouted his line from below. We did a final take where we climbed down the ladder again.

I chugged a bottle of water and sat reviewing the footage while Hannah gave the crew instructions for our next setup. I became aware of someone behind me. Icy water dripped on my shoulder and I looked back.

Wylie wiped at the drop, but it had already bled into my shirt. "Sorry."

"It's fine. Want me to back this up?" I asked.

She shook her head and drank more water. Her bottle continued to drip condensation from the heat of the lamps around us. "God, Drew is amazing. The light through the slats behind us is exquisite." She pointed at the thin pinstripes flashing across the screen.

"I know."

"You're doing much better," she said.

I half smiled. "You can take credit."

"Oh, I fully do."

We watched the rest of the footage, slowing and speeding when Wy asked me to. It felt familiar and it should have been comfortable. But the residual arousal trembling through my chest made relaxing impossible. It wasn't like me to carry emotion beyond a scene. In fact, the last time I had was over a decade before with Wylie in the same damn hayloft.

CHAPTER NINE

I checked my watch to see what my next appointment was. Russ had disconnected my watch from my calendar. She'd done the same with my other ten favorite apps. Sadly, for me, she was right, and it had dramatically improved my focus and productivity. Instead of my calendar, all I had were texts from Russ.

You've got Lenny in 5.

And make sure to ask him about the opening scene. We need to send it to KK's people.

Hannah says her assistant will be here this evening. Camera will be operational for tonight's shoot.

As of three a.m., we'd lost the camera we needed for the next week of shoots. After scrambling—and okay, raging—for an hour, Claude and I decided it was better to lose eighteen hours of shooting rather than try to shift the schedule and film something else. We didn't have the locations, and finding them would take longer than getting a part and fixing the camera. Which was why I was holed up in a conference room, trying to get ahead of twenty other problems. If I couldn't film, there was plenty else to do.

Four minutes later, Lenny let himself into the conference room. "Hey, Addy. Thanks for fitting me in." He dropped a laptop, two notebooks, and his phone a couple of seats down from me.

"Well, Russ has taken an iron grip on my schedule so I'm not remotely aware of it. But you're welcome."

Lenny smiled. "I need to talk to you about the opening scene."

"Oh, good. Kayden's agents need a copy of the script before they come up here," I said. Russ would be so pleased.

"Yeah." He drew the word out. "I'm having some trouble with it."

"What do you mean?"

"I haven't written it," he said.

"What?" I didn't shout, which was big of me. "They'll be here next week."

"I got in my head and now I can't get out. I can write gay." He looked at me pointedly. "Hell, I wrote the iconic gay slasher of the century."

"Okay, calm down. The century has eighty years left." I smirked at him. "And your leads had wild chemistry that sold your arguably heterosexist script."

Lenny laughed. "See? This is why I need help. Everything I write is dreck. And each version gets increasingly offensive."

"That fills me with terror." I was not being facetious. "You're writing a script with at least three queer characters, all played by queer actors."

"Yeah, but I know Grace and Taylor. I don't know how to write a non-binary lesbian. Frankly, I'm not even sure I know what a non-binary lesbian is."

"And you waited until a week before Kayleigh fucking Kayden shows up on set to play said non-binary lesbian before telling me this?" Still not shouting.

"Well, I thought I could pull it off. I googled and that's when things got muddled."

"How so?"

"I realized there was an entire trans cultural history behind the character that I don't have access to." He drew an invisible arc on the table. "And even the most authentic dialogue falls flat because, hey, I'm an old straight guy. And I'm cis, which is a word I only learned two years ago. I didn't even know there were people who used she/they pronouns. Why the hell am I writing this?" he asked.

"Because you're the original screenwriter. And we managed to secure the hottest non-binary pop star who asked if they could die bloody in the opening scene of our movie."

"Okay, and then there's that. I knew it was off, but I didn't know why. And then I started researching, you know, trans culture." He was rambling. Rambling Lenny either meant a weeklong headache for me or he was about to say something brilliant. Or both. "We can't bring on a trans person in a major studio slasher and kill them off in the first ten minutes. That's bad. I'm not fully sure why, but I know it isn't good."

"Shit."

"What?"

"You're absolutely right. Goddammit."

"So what do we do? I've been mulling this for two weeks and I still don't see a solution that results in killing Kaleigh Kayden bloody—as their contract stipulates—and not killing our only trans character."

"It's actually really simple," I said. I felt a little stupid for not having seen it before Lenny pointed it out. "We need to add another character. A trans character who survives."

"Hot dog. You're right."

I laughed at his turn of phrase. It didn't matter how many times I'd heard him say it. "I assume you can shoehorn in another young character?"

"Yes, absolutely. I'm thinking a guy. Or a non-binary person?" He looked at me to see if he'd said it right.

I gave him a small smile. "Yeah, but a masculine non-binary person."

"Exactly. We have too many women to add another feminine character." Lenny started taking notes in one of his notebooks. "Okay, I'll get started on sides so casting has something to work with. I'll keep them gender neutral so we have options."

"Smart. But I'm also okay with it if you explicitly go with a guy."

He tipped his head in acquiescence. "Any other requests for the character?"

"Let's make them a townie who is hired as a ranch hand. But make it seem like they are too eager to be hired so the audience will think they are Black Hat. Which means he'll need to be white."

"Got it. So also tall, dark, and handsome?" He wrote that down too.

"Yep, just like me."

Lenny laughed way too hard. "Sure thing." He closed his notebook and started to stand.

"Hold up. We still need to figure out Kayden's opening scene."

"Damn." He sank back down. "I've got a workable sequence. It's the dialogue that's killing me."

"Okay. How would you feel about bringing in a trans screenwriter to consult?" It was a dicey question. But the relief on Lenny's face suggested it was the right call.

"Yes. Please. That would be great."

"Seriously?" I tried to find my phone to scroll through my contacts. And then I remembered Russ had my phone. "I've got someone who would be a good fit. He's like you. A crotchety old man. Wears a lot of thick cardigans. Grumbles at children. Survives entirely on black coffee and stinky cigars and tall glasses of cold milk. You'll love him," I said.

Lenny scowled at me. "I don't grumble at children." I raised an eyebrow. "Okay, fine. I don't like children. They are very loud. And they always need things."

"See? You and Harold will get along great."

"Why am I just now hearing about this guy?"

"He's only written a handful of screenplays. Mostly shorts." I was skipping the important detail. Lenny was looking at me like he knew I was lying. "And he's twenty-four."

Lenny laughed. "Of course he is." He stood again and gathered his things. "I'll email you about the new character by tonight."

"And I'll see how fast Harold can get up here," I said. When I'd floated the idea of a queer screenwriting consultant initially, Danny had shut me down. This would force the studio to do what we should have done in the first place.

"Sounds like a plan." Lenny doffed an imaginary cap at me because of course that was how he exited a meeting.

I spent the rest of the afternoon on the phone with casting and the producers explaining why we were adding a new character ten days into filming. Mostly it was just me stating the decision and listening to Mick yell. At one point, Russ took my phone with a yelling Mick and set it on the conference table within earshot. After three minutes she handed it back and Mick was still yelling. I eventually kicked it to Claude because it was my job to have creative vision. It was his job to produce the thing.

After that delightful ninety minutes, Harold McCann finally called me back. Just Harold. Not his agent or his manager. Which was probably good because his manager was his ex-girlfriend's brother. The guy was nice enough and decent at shielding Harold, but he didn't know a damn thing about the business. And Harold's agent was not remotely prepared for a contract like the one about to land on his desk. After reassuring Harold that, yes, he was exactly the screenwriter for the job, and, yes, Leonard Pace was excited to meet him, I told him my agent was going to call him.

Paulie responded to my subsequent text with a thumbs up, which meant his assistant was off for the day. I was ready to dive into my email when Russ took my laptop and gave me back my phone.

"You have five hours until we start shooting. You're taking an actual break," she said.

"Arjun needs feedback by tomorrow." I tried to take the laptop back.

Russ folded her arms around the laptop. "Arjun's emails are always a hot mess which is why I read them first and simplify the questions you need to answer."

"Phil is supposed to—"

"Send you notes. They're not here yet."

"Don't do that anticipating my needs bullshit. I could have said anything. I could have said Phil is supposed to send me flowers." Now I was just being ornery.

"Well, the virtual flowers aren't in your inbox either."

"I'm sure there's something else in there that needs my attention," I said.

"There's plenty. But you need a break. A car will be here in seven minutes. You and Wylie are going to Jed's. You'll drink a couple of beers. You'll eat some food. You'll play pool and relax. I will call when you need to head back for tonight's shoot," Russ said.

I opened my mouth to respond, but that honestly sounded amazing. Maybe it was the nostalgia of this place. Or maybe I was just hungry and needed perfect french fries. "You'll call if I'm needed before then, right?"

"I promise. Go," she said.

I walked back to my cabin from the main lodge. It was almost six and the sun was showing no signs of setting. It took me five minutes to grab my shit and get ready. I stripped off my thin sweater. The short-sleeve Henley underneath smelled fine so I just grabbed my bomber jacket and a baseball cap.

Wylie knocked on the door before letting herself in. "Car's here. You ready?" she called up.

I leaned over the railing. "One minute." I grabbed my phone and wallet and went downstairs.

Wy was basically wearing the same thing as me—chinos and a T-shirt. Her shirt was wide and cropped. Something about the cut of her pants, the drape of her shirt was elegant whereas I just looked rumpled.

"Look at you taking a whole night off," Wylie said.

"I'm a new man." I held my arms wide and spun.

She laughed. "Yes, I can see that."

❖

Jed's had changed. The barstools were newer. The broken tube TV had been filled with plastic flowers. Apparently, Jed was still adamant about not having sportsballs playing. The pool tables had been re-felted—they were red now. And the taps now included two California craft beers in addition to Bud and Miller. That was it. The entirety of the change. It still smelled like fried food and spilled beer. The sound system still played a mix of vintage country, seventies rock, and nineties chick alternative. The garage door at the back of the bar was open, letting in sunlight and cigarette smoke from the deck.

"My God. It's good to be back." Wy leaned against my shoulder and gripped my forearm. She was right. This was probably the only public venue in the world where we weren't playing the roles of ourselves—we were just us.

"Pool table." I handed her my jacket and nodded at the table in the corner. "I'll get beer."

"Done."

It was early evening in the middle of the week. Jed's wasn't exactly hopping. There were two bartenders and five patrons. I'd been here on nights where the fire marshal should have been called. They never were though. This place was for locals—including the fire chief.

I approached the bar. Jed was perched on the back counter under glass shelves holding liquor bottles. He had one foot up on a stool so he could use his thigh as a surface for his crossword book. I'd swear he hadn't changed his outfit since I first met him. Loose 501s and a backward San Jose Sharks cap. His black T-shirt was still tight in the shoulders, but it looked like it was getting looser across his belly now. His close-cropped beard had gone from salt-and-pepper to white. He looked up as I got closer. He hopped down and rolled the crossword book to tuck in his back pocket. He stuck the pencil up into his cap so it was pinned against his temple.

"PJ Addison, as I live and breathe." Jed smiled and shook his head at me. "You started filming two weeks ago. What the hell took you so long?"

"Didn't you hear? I'm the director now." I stood on the foot rail so I could lean over the bar and kiss his cheek.

He grabbed a glass pitcher and started filling it. "Well, at least you brought your girl. Otherwise you'd be in trouble." He nodded at Wylie. She tossed my jacket on the table and crossed back to the bar.

"She's not my girl anymore," I said.

"Sure." He winked at me.

"Hey, Jed." Wy stepped up and leaned across the bar. When she kissed Jed's cheek, he turned to grin at her. She used the opportunity to grab a fresh bowl of popcorn from behind the bar.

"Dammit, Wylie. There's perfectly good popcorn on the bar already," he said just like he had every time we'd come in for the last ten years.

"That's finger popcorn." She took a handful from her bowl.

"There's no such thing as finger popcorn." Jed set our pitcher on the bar.

"Fine. Genital popcorn," she said.

Jed paused in his inspection of two fresh glasses. "Good God, woman."

"Can you assure me that all your patrons wash their hands after touching their junk? No, sir, you cannot."

"If I send over some fries, will you stop talking about genitals and my food in the same sentence?" Jed set the glasses on the bar, then put his hands on the counter and leaned forward in an attempt to be menacing.

"Deal." Wylie grinned and carried her popcorn back to our pool table.

I handed my card to Jed to open our tab. "Will you send over some chicken strips too?"

"Yeah, yeah. I'm sure the kitchen is already getting it going." He thumbed behind him toward the kitchen.

"Thanks." I winked and grabbed the pitcher and glasses.

"Glad you're back, kid."

CHAPTER TEN

"You want to break this time?" Wylie carefully lifted the triangle off the racked balls.

I looked up from studying my empty beer glass to boldly meet her stare. "Heck yeah." She hadn't offered for the first three games and I wasn't going to ask.

"Seriously?" she asked.

"I have many talents."

She laughed. "I'll take your word for it." She placed the cue ball in front of me and watched me expectantly.

Playing pool was very much not one of my talents. And I was okay with that. Sure, it was a little embarrassing to try to break and watch the cue ball do fuck all. But it was fun. Plus, most people assumed I was trying to hustle them because I couldn't be that bad when I was, in fact, that bad.

Wylie leaned against the wall and sipped her beer. Maybe I'd miraculously developed a talent in the last couple of years. Or the last couple of games.

I leaned forward and lined up my shot. I could do this. I hit the cue ball and watched it rocket toward the racked balls. It was really flying. Straight at them too. And then it gently tapped them and rolled back an inch. The rest of the balls sort of shifted so they had an impressive quarter inch between most of them.

Wylie howled with laughter. "That was amazing. Truly inspired." She clapped a couple of times.

I bowed. "Why thank you, m'lady."

"Did you get worse?"

"Okay, that's just uncalled for. I'm equally bad. No worse," I said.

"I just call 'em like I see 'em, baby." She circled the table.

"Yeah, well. Let's see if you can do better," I said. She could. We both knew it. But my clumsy shot had put the cue too close to the other balls to do any real damage.

"Didn't you play a gambler a couple of years ago? You played pool in that." She stretched over the table and gave the bar quite the view when her shirt rode up. She hit the cue so it sailed past the balls. For a moment it looked like she missed, but then it bounced off the side and ricocheted back to send them all flying. She looked up at me and grinned. "Well?"

I scowled. "Yeah, they used a double and had someone else take all my shots."

"Movie magic." She waved her hands like a magician and laughed.

I poured the rest of the beer into my glass. I caught Jed's eye and held up the empty pitcher. He nodded. I leaned against the wall. Wy had already sunk three balls and she wasn't slowing. No wonder I was bad. I never actually got to play.

"So are we drunk enough?" I asked.

"What did I do now?" Her shot went wide. She sighed and stepped back.

"Nothing." I leaned over the table and hit the ball. My shot landed, but the ball didn't get anywhere near the pocket.

She arched an eyebrow and waited.

"Jocelyn." I was not drunk enough to ask. There was no drunk enough to ask. But I wasn't sober either.

She sank another ball and plotted the next. "What about her?"

It was my turn to stare and wait.

Wy relinquished the table. "Come on. She's sweet."

"As fuckin' pie." I took a shot and missed spectacularly. "But I don't want to marry pie."

"You don't want to marry anyone," she said.

"As opposed to marrying everyone?"

"Is Jeffrey here? Are you channeling him or something?" Wy looked around dramatically.

"Sorry. I just don't get her. Bubba I understood. Natalie was chill. Jocelyn is—" I stopped talking, not ready to actually commit to an opinion.

"She's what?" There was an edge in her voice. Which was perfectly reasonable considering the idiotic path I'd taken our conversation down.

The waitress—likely the latest in the line of Jed's granddaughter's friends—deposited a full pitcher on our table. "You two need cold glasses?" she asked.

"We're good. Thanks," I said.

She nodded and gathered our empty fry baskets.

"PJ," Wy said.

"Yes?"

"You were about to tell me what my wife is." She crossed her arms and hit me with a stare that was, honestly, hilarious. Now she was just pretending to be mad.

"She's a fan," I said.

"Seriously?"

I gave her a pointed look. "The *Blackbirds* obsession? C'mon."

"I knew it. I knew you were going to bring that up."

"I'm sorry. She's a chaser. I'm not judging her—I mean, I'm trying not to," I said.

"But you're judging me."

"Well, yeah. A little." It was my prerogative. As her ex, her sometimes friend, her costar. I wasn't sure which of those gave me prerogative, but one of them had to.

"She's not with me because she's a fan. She's got a whole life, a whole career that's not about me," she said.

"And that's great. Seriously. Her whole thing is great. I'm just saying she wanted to steal my napkin after I used it."

"Get over yourself."

"Fine." I put my hands up. "I don't see what you see. And that's fine."

"You really don't, do you?" She sounded serious all of a sudden.

"What am I missing?"

"Nothing." She shook her head and surveyed the table. "We're definitely not drunk enough for this conversation."

"Hey, uh, excuse me." A young guy in worn boots and messy carpenter jeans stepped into our sightline. "Sorry. I was just wondering if we could get the next game?"

Wy looked at me and I shrugged. We were barely playing. She handed her stick to the guy. "It's all yours."

"Oh, no. You don't have to cut your game short." He put his hand out to stop her.

"Seriously. We're not playing. And she's the worst pool player probably ever." Wy nodded toward me. "You're doing me a favor."

He laughed and took the stick. "Then you're welcome."

"I'm sure there are some toddlers who are worse players," I said.

"Are you? Are you really sure of that?" Wy grabbed the pitcher and her glass.

"Dick." I grabbed my jacket and beer and followed her outside.

I checked my watch to see if any progress had been made on set. Just one text from Russ. *Stop checking your messages. Relax.* Helpful.

We settled on stools at the railing on the far side of the deck. Below us, the forest dropped away. It was a shallow valley. But it was still deep enough that we were staring at the tops of trees. The foliage was sparser here. I could see flashes of dirt trails between the treetops. There was a faint trickling sound from the stream running through the bottom of the valley. The sun was setting finally, bathing everything in a warm, pink glow.

"I love the way this place smells." Wy took a deep breath and rested her chin on her hand.

"Fry grease?"

"I'm having a moment here. Think you could kill the snark for two minutes?" she asked.

I laughed. "I like it too." When the temperature dropped—like it was now—the scent of warm resin was replaced with cool, damp pine. It smelled fresh and clean. The way only movie sets ever smelled. Or camp, according to Kaleb and Jeffrey.

We sipped our beers and watched the sun set. It filtered through the trees and cast ominous shadows. Wy rubbed her palm against her bare arm. I handed her my jacket and she put it on. Behind us, Jed's started to fill up. Or at least as much as it could on a Wednesday.

"I didn't mean anything by my question earlier," I said.

"Of course you did."

"Okay. But I wasn't trying to like condemn your whole relationship. I guess with the other two, I saw what you saw. Even if I didn't agree with it or whatever. I still understood why you married them. Jocelyn is just—" I searched for the right descriptor and came up with "so vanilla scented."

"Really?" she asked.

"Yes?" I didn't know what I was agreeing to, but her tone suggested I was in dangerous territory.

"No, I mean, you're really going with this line of questioning?"

"What other line of questioning would I go with?" I asked.

"Vanilla scented?" Wy looked incredulous.

"She is."

"You mean she's more femme than Bubba or Nat?"

"I guess. But she's also dripping with sugar. The woman is so damn earnest and sweet. She's crème brûlée in human form."

"I'm sorry. I just want to make sure I'm getting this. Your issue is that she's nice and genuine?"

Well, when she said it that way, I sounded like a jerk. "You've always preferred your partners with a little edge to them."

"And look where that got me. I trusted Bubba when she was fucking her way through LA. And then Nat questioned everything I did—like she thought I was fucking my way through LA. Neither of those edges was particularly enjoyable."

"So you went with a cream puff instead?" I asked.

"Did you make a list of desserts before you started this conversation?"

"I did in fact. I like to keep you guessing." I grinned at her. "That's my edge."

Wy rolled her eyes. "See? That's what I'm avoiding. I know exactly what to expect from Jocelyn. She's reliable. She's honest. She looks good at premieres."

"You mean she's arm candy?"

"There's more to it than that. But, yes, she looks good on my arm," she said. "I don't have to go to events alone and have the press speculate. I don't have to explain every woman I'm photographed at coffee with. I'm not outing every single woman I know."

"I don't follow," I said. She gave me an irritated look. "I get the premiere thing. But how are you outing women?"

"Because when I'm unattached, every woman who is seen with me is presumed to be my girlfriend."

"Oh."

"Yeah."

"That doesn't happen to me," I said.

She snorted. "You never go out. All the paparazzi photos of you are at festivals."

"That's not true." As soon as I said it, I knew it was wrong. "Okay. I don't go out much."

"You never go out. You work. You go home. You see your mother socially twice a year."

"Rude. I see my mother at least five times a year."

"Wow. I stand corrected." She bit back a laugh.

"I just don't like people very much."

"I know. You're a recluse. You would have been a great forties director savant, hiding in a bungalow in the Hollywood hills and emerging every decade to make a great film," she said.

"That sounds ideal, actually."

"See? You don't need companionship. You don't need people."

"People are overrated," I said.

"They are." Wy dragged her finger through the moisture on her glass and drew an evaporating pattern on the wood railing. She leaned sideways to press her shoulder into mine. "Jocelyn is my version of your isolation. Both afford us privacy. That's why I like her. She's exactly what she appears."

"You mean she has her own life that doesn't interfere with yours, but she's available at the drop of a hat."

Wy sighed and straightened so she wasn't touching me anymore. "It sounds crass when you say it like that."

"I'm not trying to demean. She likes being married to the great Wylie Parsons. I get that. I'm a big fan too. But I see you as a real person."

"She sees enough. And she'll never break my heart. She'll never demand something from me I can't give."

"That's fucking depressing." I heard the anger creep into my voice, but I couldn't pull it back. Wy deserved more. Better.

"And it's better to live alone and socialize with your mother five times a year?"

"It's honest at least."

"You don't get lonely."

"Are you asking?" I asked. I did get lonely, but it was better than being disappointed—not that I was going to tell her that.

"No. I know you. You don't get lonely. I'm jealous of that."

"But don't you want some grand romance? Some Hollywood splash? Someone who will see all of you and love every inch?"

Wy turned and stared at me. She shook her head. "Babe, we had that. I fucked it up."

"Oh." I didn't believe her. If she'd loved me that hard, she wouldn't have left. But I wasn't going to tell her that.

"You're just impervious. I mean, I know you're not. But you move through the spotlight and never let it hurt you," she said. I opened my mouth to respond but she cut me off. "Oh, I know you were raised in it and it broke you. But I think you sometimes use that as an excuse. Like you're dodging vulnerability."

I sighed. "Yeah. I get why it seems that way."

She leaned against my shoulder again and took a deep breath. "PJ?"

"Hmm?"

"I love you."

"Yeah. Same." I kissed the top of her head.

CHAPTER ELEVEN

We had about two hours max to rehearse the opening of the party scene. Drew was working double time to make sure we had continuity with the lights. Scottie had promised me a working crane shot, but Hannah was already managing my expectations, which meant the equipment had failed again and they didn't want to tell me until they were sure it was broken. On top of that, Lenny and Harold had finished writing Malone—the new character—but the actor wouldn't arrive for another two days. The current script had Malone skipping the party with very thin reasoning. In the event that Lenny changed said reasoning, we had to shoot a lot of extras milling about and hope Phil could make it look like footage of Malone was from the same time.

Teddy, Emma, and Rosie were off at hair and makeup. Their performances were solid. Wylie, however, was in hell. I was helping her run through the scene with the mayor's teenage daughter who had just watched her parents be killed. The kid was a nightmare. She was thirteen and felt it was her job to single-handedly give all thirteen-year-old girls a bad name.

"Gemma, let's try that again. Since crying isn't working, I think we should revisit the stoicism," I said.

"I can cry on my mark," Gemma said.

I leaned forward but stayed seated. Gemma was height sensitive. Apparently. "I know you want to, but it's not working. So that's why I want to try something else."

"Fine." Gemma sniffed. "What do you want me to do?"

"Quiet stoicism."

She looked at me like I was an asshole. "Stop using words like that. You're trying to make me feel dumb. I'm not dumb."

"Right." I took a careful breath and tried to find smaller words. "I'm thinking if you try to be subtle. Don't overreact. Just be sort of stunned."

"It'll help if you try to hold back your reaction. And lower your voice," Wylie said.

"I know what I'm doing. I don't need your help," Gemma snapped at Wylie. Again.

Wy put up her hands and took a step back. She started to respond, then thought better of it. I could see her jaw clenching.

"Let's take five," I said.

"I'll be at crafty." Wylie immediately took off and left me with the child actor from hell. No loyalty for her director, that one.

"I'll grab Lenny and see if he can offer some character insight," I said.

"Mr. Pace?" Gemma asked. She shook her head. "He's scary." This kid was killing me. Where the hell was her manager?

"What about Harold? The other screenwriter?" I asked.

Gemma was confused. "There's another screenwriter?"

"Yeah. He's cool." In this case, cool just meant under thirty, but that was probably enough for Gemma. "Let's see what he has to say."

"Fine."

I went off in search of Russ or Harold or Lenny. Or anyone who could help me. I spotted a PA I knew. "Simon," I called.

He spun and rushed over. "Yeah? Can I get something for you?"

"I'm looking for the screenwriters."

He frowned. "Mr. Pace is in his trailer. Are there multiple screenwriters?"

I shook my head. "Sort of. Would you go grab Lenny for me? And tell him to bring Harold?"

"You got it." Simon took off.

I looked back. Gemma was where I'd left her. Her manager had materialized and she was yelling at him. That image was enough to send me to crafty. I found Hannah and Wylie drinking coffee and laughing.

"Traitors," I said.

"Sorry, PJ," Wy said with absolutely no remorse. "That's the reason I never want children. I have no patience."

"She wasn't like this at her audition," Hannah said quietly. I appreciated the attempt at discretion.

"She really wasn't." I snagged a cup of coffee and sat next to Hannah. "I sent for Lenny and Harold. See if they can do something."

Wylie set her coffee down. "Harold? That's the screenwriter you brought on to queer the script up?"

"Yeah. He's a good kid. And I think Lenny likes him."

Hannah nodded. "They've been holed up in Lenny's trailer since Harold arrived. So Lenny either likes him or has decided to murder and cannibalize him."

"You think so little of me?" Lenny asked from behind us.

"Maybe it's an absorption of powers thing? If you cannibalize me, you consume my knowledge," Harold said to him.

"Hmm. Worth considering." Lenny sat next to me. Harold sat across from us. They both looked disheveled. Their hair stuck out at odd angles, their glasses were dirty, and their eyes were bloodshot. They were rocking at least three days of unkempt beard growth. Harold's collar was half tucked inside his shirt. One of Lenny's buttons was undone. They both absolutely reeked of cigars and scotch.

"Wow. So you two have been bonding?" I said.

"Why do you say that?" Lenny asked.

"My eyes are watering just sitting at a table with you," Wylie said. She stuck out her hand to Harold. "Wylie Parsons. PJ raves about you."

"Harold McCann." He shook her hand. "Addy is too nice to me."

"Well, now it's time for your comeuppance," I said.

"Okay." Harold frowned. "What does that mean?"

"The kid who's playing the mayor's daughter is making me consider retiring. Like right now. I don't think I should finish this film. I'm going to take up large format black-and-white photography and move to the Canadian wilderness."

Wylie patted my hand. "Sweetie, you hate the cold."

"That's film director PJ. Photographer PJ fucking loves the cold," I said.

"Are you sure? You brought heaters onto the set when it dropped to sixty-eight the other night," Hannah said.

"And?" I asked.

Hannah shook her head. "Nothing. That's perfectly normal."

"So how exactly can I prevent you from freezing to death on an ill-advised jaunt to the Canadian wilds?" Harold asked.

"Coach the kid. Use very small words to explain to her that stoicism is the way to go because—despite what she believes—she can't cry on cue," I said.

"You got it." He nodded with purpose. "One question. Why me?"

"She needs help understanding the character and thinks Lenny is scary," I said. Lenny tried to look offended but couldn't muster the emotion. "I told her you were cool."

"Sure." Harold stood. "I assume she's the preteen who just made that adult man cry?" He nodded toward Gemma and her manager.

"That's the one. Oh, and fix your collar." I pointed at my own.

Harold looked confused until he touched his collar and found it tucked in. "Better?"

"Much better. You look nothing like a young Lenny," I lied.

He saluted us and marched off on a suicide mission.

"Hey, Lenny?" Wylie asked.

"Yeah?"

"Why is your shirt not fully buttoned? And follow-up question, is it related to Harold's collar being messed up?" She propped her chin in her hand and waited for whatever thrilling answer Lenny was going to give.

"Christ, Parsons. Can't a man have his secrets?" He scrubbed at his face.

"Normally, yes. But now I'm intrigued."

"Harold likes to work shirtless. It helps him connect with the work," Lenny said.

"That invites a lot more questions, Leonard," Hannah said.

Lenny scowled at her. "Well, I tried it out. We got a lot done. Maybe it was freeing. Maybe it's superstition. Doesn't matter as long as it works." He was trying for assertive, but it fell flat.

I looked sideways under the table. Lenny was wearing forest green pleated corduroy pants. Looking had been a mistake. Now

I had the imagined image of shirtless Lenny in his oversize corduroys.

"Thanks, Wy," I said.

"For what?"

"I can't unsee it now."

"That went well." Harold rejoined the table.

"It did?" I asked.

"Nope, I was lying. Gemma has locked herself in the bathroom because I accidentally pointed out that she doesn't have a trailer." Harold smiled but it was more of a grimace. "Also, she fired her manager. Her mother is on the way over from the lodge."

"Excellent. Thanks for handling that," I said.

"Happy to help?"

"You two better lose your shirts and head back to your trailer. We're going to need you to rewrite the role," Hannah said. She turned to me. "We can use the screaming kid instead. Give the mayor a ten-year-old son?"

"I'm sorry. Lose our shirts?" Harold asked. "Why would we take off our shirts?" he asked Lenny.

Lenny laughed and stood up. "Come on, kid."

Wylie and Hannah and I stared at their retreating backs. "Did you make that whole thing up?" I called.

"Yeah. We're not goddamn weirdos. Jesus H." Lenny clapped an arthritic hand on Harold's shoulder and leaned in, presumably to relay what he'd convinced us of. Harold started laughing after a minute.

"Will you go track down the ten-year-old and his manager? Make sure he's up for a bigger role?" I asked Hannah.

"On it, boss." She stood and left me and Wylie.

"Incoming," Wylie said. It was all the warning I got before a pair of large hands gripped my shoulders and Diego straddled the bench next to me.

"There's my favorite director," he said.

"Diego," I said.

"I was wondering—" he started.

"No."

"But—"

"The body is already up in the barn. You can take selfies with your bloody corpse after we film it falling out of the rafters," I said for the tenth time.

"Do you know when you're going to shoot that?" he asked.

"Tonight."

He sighed and blinked at me all slow and sad. "But when?"

"Hey, Diego," Wylie said.

"Parsons. You gotta help me."

"You want me to help you convince PJ to let you take photos with the dead Xavier body?" she asked with misleading optimism.

"Yeah. Would you?"

"Not a chance in hell. Sorry." She smiled big.

He frowned. "You're mean."

"You keep pushing and I won't let you take photos at all," I said.

"I'm going to go sit quietly in my trailer. You know, if you need me." He stood. "Can I watch the body fall though?"

"Yes. You can. Hannah will give you plenty of warning before we shoot," I said.

"Okay. Cool. You're the best. Love you." He ran off.

"Did I just become a parent?" I asked Wylie.

"You did." She patted my hand again. "Congratulations. He's real pretty."

❖

The party was in full swing. Grace stood just outside the open barn doors. She was surrounded by people from town congratulating her on the reopening of Durant Ranch. The audience would know by now that the mayor and his wife were missing. Grace hadn't noticed their absence, but she was starting to worry about Xavier. She wouldn't have to wonder much longer. We were getting establishing shots of the party, which meant we were only thirty minutes away from the dramatic body drop.

Hannah called cut and we shuffled the extras and actors around. Diego was hovering behind Hannah per the rule I'd given him. My empty threat had done its job. He was staying out of the way and had stopped asking for updates.

There was only one short piece of dialogue left to get before we sprayed everyone with blood. Benny and I settled into one of the larger tables closest to the barn. Scottie pulled in tight and Hannah called action.

"How long until we can clear out the upper paddocks?" I asked. Benny shook his head. "Patience, Henderson. We're not even done with the east paddock."

"Grace wants horses." I shrugged like it was out of my hands. "I have to get her horses."

"Surveying takes time. I promise we're moving as fast as we can," he said.

Wy approached. She was smiling pleasantly, but there was something strained beneath the surface. "There you two are. Have you seen Xavier?"

We shook our heads. "Last I saw him was up at the main house," I said.

"I can text him," Benny said.

"I already tried," Wy said. "I need him with me for my speech. He's the ranch's successor." She took in a shaky breath. It could have been nerves or fear or irritation.

"Hey, babe. It's fine. I'll run up to the house and find him," I said. "Really?"

"I'll go too." Benny stood. "Give us five minutes."

"Thanks." Wy squeezed my hand.

Benny and I walked off and Hannah called cut. When I circled back to Hannah, Diego was waiting dutifully behind her. We got everyone in place for the body reveal. It would be really nice if we could get it in one go. If not, we'd have to haul the dummy back up, wait for the blood to be cleaned off the set, retouch everyone's makeup. It would be a nightmare.

Hannah called action. Grace thanked everyone for joining her for the reopening of the Durant Ranch. She launched into her speech, her eyes scanning the crowd in search of her nephew. I watched her and pretended I was in love. When she got to the part of the speech where she talked about the physical structures of a farm and how they were like family, she tapped the frame of the open barn doors. Right on cue, the body dropped. It was a grotesque likeness of Diego. It was suspended from its feet so the arms and head swung in a slow back and forth arc. Deep wounds covered his forearms. Fresh blood dripped from them and gently sprayed the ground.

One of the extras screamed. It wasn't the best scream. I already knew we'd have to re-record it. But it didn't matter. The sound launched a flurry of action. I skirted Xavier's corpse and gathered Wylie into my arms. The rest of the scene unfolded perfectly. When Hannah called cut, I caught her eye. She smiled. We'd gotten it.

CHAPTER TWELVE

O h, hi, new favorite person!" Jocelyn kissed my cheek and enfolded me into her arms.

"Hey, Jocelyn." I wrapped one arm around her, grateful for the case of beer I was holding because it occupied my other hand.

"God, look at you." She cupped my face in her hands. "Aren't you supposed to be tired after all those night shoots?" That compliment just landed better every time she used it. Didn't ring increasingly false at all.

"Don't worry. I am. I'm just on a lot of cocaine," I said.

She roared with laughter. It was good I was joking. I knew far too many people who got through arduous shoots with drugs.

"Hey." Wy came down the stairs. Her cabin was the mirror of mine, reversed but otherwise identical. If I remembered correctly, this was her original cabin too. Which meant I was five feet from where I'd first kissed Wylie, twenty feet from the bed where she first seduced me.

"Thanks for being home base," I said. Wy's cabin was way closer to the fire pit. Diego's was next door and Claude was on her other side. But I wasn't going to impose on Diego, and Claude wasn't invited.

"No problem." Wy brushed my shoulder as she went by and it felt more intimate than Jocelyn kissing my cheek.

"This was your plan?" Jocelyn asked. She took the beer from me and laughed when she saw it was Bud Light.

"Nothing bonds a cast like booze and fire," I said.

"Or a rapey director," Wy said.

I pointed at Wylie. "There is that. But I opted to not be a rapey director."

Wy nodded indulgently. "And I support you."

"So we'll drink and play with fire."

"Oh, God. You two are so cheeky. I love it," Jocelyn said.

"You'll have to trust us on this," Wylie said. "If you don't want to be consumed by the shoot, you have to carve out time to be normal." She took the beer from Jocelyn and put it in the fridge.

I followed Wy and leaned against the wall by the fridge. She started handing me cheese. It was an obscene amount of cheese. I piled it all on the counter.

"How is this normal? You never want to use our fire pit." Jocelyn looked at Wy in confusion.

"Yeah, but this one thinks all food should be cooked over open flames." Wy tipped her chin in my direction.

"It tastes better that way." I shrugged.

"Right." Jocelyn nodded but she looked confused. She really needed to learn when we were kidding.

"Plus, she still doesn't know if her stove works," Wy said.

"That's not true." I frowned. "My mother has definitely used the stove in my kitchen." Wy laughed. Jocelyn hesitated before joining her. "And I'm sure Russ has too."

"Your mom cooks at your house but you don't?" Jocelyn asked.

"Gerri does a lot that I don't do. Ski. Drive. Read nonfiction. Talk to people when she's not being paid to," I said.

"You've met her." Wylie touched Jocelyn's arm. "At our wedding. Gorgeous svelte woman. She wore that blue dress you loved."

"Wait. Geraldine is your mother?" Jocelyn turned to me slack-jawed, then delighted.

"Why was my mother at your wedding?" I asked.

"She was invited," Wylie said it like it was the most obvious answer. "You were invited too, but you were at a film festival."

"You invited my mother to your wedding?"

Wy rolled her eyes. There was a knock at the cabin door. Jocelyn looked relieved at having a new task.

"That'll be the kids," I said.

"They're not kids," Wy said.

"Whatever."

"The party has arrived," Molly called from the door. Diego was half a step behind her. "That's right, baby."

"They sound just like we all used to," I said quietly.

"See? I told you they weren't kids," Wy said back.

"I was thinking the opposite. We were kids too."

"Hey, boss." Diego shouldered me out of the way to open the fridge. "Jocelyn said there was beer."

"Grab me one too?" I asked.

"Sure thing." He tore into the case and handed me a can. "You've got to be the coolest director I've ever worked with." He tapped his can against mine. Foam exploded out of the top and he narrowly missed dripping it onto the floor by licking the side of the can.

"I'll take it. Even though providing beer is a very low bar." I cracked open my beer.

"No, no, no, boss. It's that you're destroying the artifice, you know? Like you're not trying to be some mysterious, patriarchal figure." He threw an arm around my shoulders and squeezed. "And you give us beer."

"Spoken like a true artist."

"That I am." He switched the beer can to the hand slung around my shoulders, pulled out his phone and went Live. "Addy is the best director, y'all. She's out here being all stern and directory, but in like a real way. I trust her with my art. I trust her with my life. Do you all know how hard that shit is? To find trust on a movie set?" My face heated with embarrassment. Diego kissed my temple and released me. "Let's check out this party." He wandered off with his phone held aloft to get the best view.

"Oh my God, you're just the dreamiest, bestest, most authentic director I've ever worked with," Wy said in a deep voice.

"Shut up."

"He's right, you know?"

"Yeah, yeah."

"No, I mean it. Can you imagine how much stronger our work would have been if we weren't terrified half the time?"

My face flushed again and my wrists started to itch. "Come on, Wy."

"Fine. I'll stop embarrassing you."

"Addy," Rosie called from outside. "Get out here."

"I'm being summoned." I pushed off the counter and went outside to the courtyard where most of the cast was congregating.

Rosie met me at the door. "There you are. Diego has decided to start the fire, but I don't think he knows how." She pointed at the wide fire pit. Diego had stacked about five pieces of oak in the center. He was holding a lighter to the end of one piece.

"Dammit. Thanks, Rosie." I squeezed her shoulder. "Diego, put the lighter down," I called.

"Addy!" Diego let go of the lighter and the flame went out. "I'm starting the fire!"

"What if I show you how to build it and you can be in charge for the rest of the evening?" I asked as I crossed the courtyard to him.

"Yeah, for sure." Diego dutifully put the lighter in his pocket and waited for me to join him.

I explained the difference between types of wood and why size mattered. He made a dick joke. I showed him how to stack the wood. When we shoved newspaper under the kindling, I made a joke about him not knowing what it was. It landed as well as his dick joke. Once it was built, I let him light the paper.

"I made fire, boss." He grabbed my forearm and squeezed. "Now what do we do?"

"Now I keep an eye on it to make sure it doesn't go out. And you go wash your hands." I pointed at the newsprint handprint he'd left on my arm.

"Oh, shit. Sorry." He held his hands out and studied them. "Yeah, okay. Be right back. Don't add wood without me."

"I wouldn't dare."

He ran back inside Wy's cabin. His was literally one cabin down, but sure. Why not?

My watch lit up with a message from Russ. *En route with Logan. I'll get him checked in and bring him over.* I sent back a thumbs up. Ostensibly, I was using this little party to introduce our newest cast member. But if I was being honest, I planned on doing the party anyway. Logan was an excuse.

"Hey, PJ. There you are. You disappeared." Jocelyn started to throw her arms around me. Again.

I backed away and held up my dirty hands. "Sorry. I wouldn't want to get you dirty."

"Oh, you're so sweet." She leaned up and kissed my cheek instead. This woman could not read body language.

"I'm back," Diego announced. "What now?"

I gave Jocelyn a polite smile and turned to Diego. "Once the kindling catches, we add some slightly bigger pieces. We'll work up to the big pieces of hardwood. A good fire is all about patience."

"Right. Got it." He nodded very seriously.

"Keep an eye on the flames while I go wash?" I held up my hands.

"Heck yeah." He put his hands on his hips and stared intently at the small fire.

I went back inside. On the way, I passed Rosie and Teddy. "Keep an eye on him," I whispered.

They smiled. Rosie nodded subtly. Teddy winked.

Wylie almost ran into me when I walked inside. "Shit, sorry," she said. "I just was going to ask if you wanted me to cut bread."

"No, don't worry about it. Diego has appointed himself my apprentice so I can do kitchen duty." I nodded in his direction.

Wy bit her lip. "Well, if that's not the cutest thing I've ever seen."

"We should bring out beer though."

"Sure." Wy surveyed the courtyard. Rosie and Teddy had moved to seats around the fire pit. Emma and Jocelyn were chatting. Molly looked lost. "Molly, help me carry out drinks?"

Molly turned. "Sure."

Inside, I washed my hands while Wy and Molly unloaded beer and hard seltzer from the fridge. Molly teased Wy about her scene the night before. They asked me when Logan was due to arrive. It was the sort of easy camaraderie I always tried to cultivate on sets.

We carried out cases of booze and unloaded them in the galvanized metal tubs Russ had placed at key points between the padded benches around the fire pit. Wy poured bags of ice on them.

Diego tried to throw the wet plastic in the fire which got him a stern talking to from Emma.

Once Diego had coaxed some decent coals out, I started making campfire grilled cheese. Teddy teased me about it until I handed him the first one. One bite and he acknowledged my cooking prowess. My culinary skills were a limited field, but I excelled at the three things I could make.

Here. Russ texted.

I looked up and saw her walking with Logan. They were still forty yards away from the courtyard around the fire pit. No one had seen them yet. I excused myself and met them on the pathway. Logan towered over Russ. Granted, she was short, but he was easily over six feet. He was wearing rumpled linen drawstring pants and a coordinated cream camp shirt. His face was pure art. All angles and jawline.

"Logan, I'm PJ Addison. It's fantastic to finally meet you in person." I put out my hand.

Logan shook it and smiled. "Same. I'm so excited to be here. It's a dream, honestly."

"Are you ready to meet the rest of the cast? I don't want to overwhelm you."

"Oh, I'm ready. I'm really looking forward to diving in."

"Excellent." I nodded and turned back to the fire pit.

Russ stopped me. "You need anything else?"

"We're good. Just let me know an hour before setup so I can wrap up here and wrangle tonight's cast," I said.

"Sure thing." Russ waved at Logan. "It was nice meeting you."

"You too." He winked at her. "And thanks for the pep talk."

She hid a smile and turned back toward the main lodge. Logan and I returned to the fire pit. The brightness of the flames made the growing dusk seem darker. Laughter carried to us. Molly was telling the group a story that had Diego on the ground howling.

"So what was your pep talk about?" I asked.

Logan chuckled. "I just asked for a vibe check. Since I'm being added after filming started and all that. Ms. Russell assured me I didn't need to worry."

"You don't. And my door is always open. Seriously. I want my set to be a kinder place than I grew up with," I said.

"I appreciate that."

Molly stopped her story as we joined the group. "I'll finish. I promise," she said. Diego regained his seat, still laughing. "But the boss is back."

"Hey, gentlefriends, this is Logan Vernon. He'll be playing Malone," I said. "Logan, this is the cast. Teddy who is playing Benny. Rosie is Sadie. Emma is Ava." They waved from across the pit. "Molly is playing Pippa. You two will be playing non-romantic buddies with unrealized sexual chemistry."

"What up," Molly called.

"Nice to meet you," Logan said.

"You probably know Wylie Parsons. And that's her wife, Jocelyn."

"I'm a huge fan, Ms. Parsons." Logan leaned forward to shake Wy's hand.

"Wylie, please," she said.

"And finally, Diego. He's playing Xavier." I pointed at Diego, who immediately stood.

"Bro, I'm like so stoked to meet you." Diego grasped Logan's shoulder with one hand and shook his hand with the other.

"You are?" Logan asked.

"Yeah. Totally. I've been heckin' curious."

"I mean, same," Logan said.

I settled back into my seat between Wylie and Diego. "How do you two know each other?" I asked.

Logan and Diego looked at each other and grinned.

"We slept with the same chick," Diego said.

"We dated the same woman," Logan said at the same time.

They laughed at each other's description.

"Well, yeah. We just slept together," Logan said. "There were no dates."

"Real boy slayer, that one," Diego said. "Come. Sit." Diego dragged Logan to the cushioned bench next to him.

"So, uhh. Are you going to tell us who?" Molly asked.

"Oh, no," Logan said.

"Frances Stuart," Diego said. The circle roared with laughter. "What? I kiss and tell." He leered at Emma. "Be warned."

Wylie shot me a knowing look. I started praying but I knew it was useless.

"Wait. Like seventy-year-old Oscar winner, old Hollywood dame, Frances Stuart?" Rosie asked.

"She is a very spry late sixties," Logan said. "And aging like fine wine."

"And the woman thoroughly enjoys handsome young men." Diego kissed his own bicep.

"Not just young men," Wylie said. I very carefully watched the fire. "Right, PJ?"

"You mean? Oh, shut the fuck up." Diego grabbed my arm and squeezed. "You too, boss?"

"Goddammit," I said.

"This is not the bonding I imagined, but I'll take it," Logan said.

"Wait. Seriously?" Teddy asked.

"I also don't kiss and tell," I said. "But if I did, I'd say Frances Stuart has a very sexy trio of freckles on her inner thigh."

The circle exploded in laughter and questions.

CHAPTER THIRTEEN

It was entirely my fault. I wished there was someone else to blame. But as I slowly turned another grilled cheese over the fire pit and watched Emma toss her empty seltzer can at Diego, I realized my cast was too drunk to film.

Wy nudged me. "What's up? You look bummed all of a sudden."

I shook my head. "I'm an idiot."

"Why?"

"We're supposed to film two scenes tonight and I got my stars too drunk." I nodded at Rosie and Emma. They weren't sloppy by any means. But they certainly didn't have the control we needed for Ava's breakdown over Xavier's death.

"Uh, yeah. I'm going to have to agree with you there." Wy squeezed my hand. "Sorry."

I sighed. "It's fine. I'll be right back." I handed her the grill basket with the sandwich I was roasting. "Finish this."

Claude was very kind in a very disapproving way when I told him to shut down production for the night. We could have possibly done a different scene, but none of the other actors were on set. And the rest of the principal cast was more drunk than Emma and Rosie. Real bang-up job by the director there.

When I sat back down, Wy turned to me. "All good?"

"Yeah. I think I'm more irritated than Claude was."

"I know just the solution." She nodded sagely. "Teddy, beer for the boss," she called.

Teddy dug into the galvanized bucket of ice next to him and pulled out a beer. "Beer for the boss."

"I thought we were cutting off?" Emma said.

I caught the beer Teddy tossed me. "We were." I sighed again. "But I got you guys too drunk to film."

"Excuse me. We can still film," Rosie said.

"Really?" I tapped the can and opened it. A rush of cold foam spilled onto my fingers. "Do your monologue."

Rosie frowned at me, then stared into the fire and took a deep breath. She turned to Emma. "He didn't believe in the curse. You can't either. Some asshole killed him, yes. But it's just some backwood hick who got a taste of power and…" She hesitated where there was no need for hesitation. Maybe it was an acting choice. Rosie had good instincts. But then she made the mistake of meeting Emma's eyes and they both burst into laughter. "And I don't know the rest of it," Rosie said.

I grinned and saluted her with my beer before drinking half the can. "You're a phenomenal actor in a phenomenal cast. You can't help that your idiot director wanted to drink booze and make campfire grilled cheese."

"Well, in that case, pass me another drink, Teddy," Rosie said.

"I want another Tropical," Emma said. "And I sure wish someone would make me a Gouda and Havarti. Someone who is real good at campfire grilled cheese." She looked directly at me and blinked slowly like I was a cat and she needed to earn my trust.

"Fine." I put together another grilled cheese and wedged it into my grill basket.

"I'm sorry. What is this grilled cheese magic that's happening? Can I have a Gouda and Havarti?" Logan said.

"Sure. We've also got Brie and cheddar and Gruyère and provolone and pepper jack and—"

"That's too much cheese," Logan said.

"There's no such thing," I said.

"Wow. Thanks for holding me accountable, boss. Can I have Gruyère and cheddar?" he asked.

"Sure thing." I put together a second sandwich, spritzed them in olive oil, and sprinkled on kosher salt.

"If fifteen-year-old me could see this, he would fucking die," Logan said.

"Which part?" Wy asked.

"All of it. I'm in a *Dangerous Summer Nights* movie. I'm sitting here with all of you. And PJ Addison is making me what looks like an amazing grilled cheese. I might actually be dead. This is an illusion," he said.

"I know, right? I had such a crush on Addy when I was a teenager," Molly said. She saluted me with her beer.

I rolled my eyes and declined to comment.

"Oh, no. It was Parsons for me," Logan said. "That MTV kiss? Fuck. I was gone."

"Holy shit, yes. It's my root," Molly said.

My face heated and my scalp started to tingle. I glanced at Wy who was studiously looking into the fire.

"Honestly, same," Jocelyn said.

Wy groaned. "Not you too."

"Well, it's not my root. But I watched that clip on repeat. It was sexy as hell." Jocelyn half shrugged. "But you knew that."

I shot a look at Wy and she sighed pointedly. I went back to watching the sandwiches I was holding over coals.

"No, really though. I knew I liked boys and I thought I might like girls, but then you two did that fucking kiss. I mean, the leg. The cheek. The hair." Molly did an aborted movement to push her own hair off her face.

"The leg." Logan nodded vigorously.

"Okay, why have I not seen this kiss?" Diego asked.

"Oh, pull it up," Molly shouted.

Diego was already pulling out his phone. "What do I search?"

Logan leaned over to look at Diego's phone. "MTV Best Kiss. It's the year *DSN* was released." He pointed at the screen. "There. That one."

"Oh, shit." Diego tapped the video. Teddy, Emma, and Molly all crowded next to him and Logan. Rosie leaned politely close, but she wore an apology too. All her first kisses were on YouTube. She understood.

"And the Best Kiss goes to PJ Addison and Wylie Parsons for *Dangerous Summer Nights*." The sound of the crowd roaring was abruptly cut off.

"Can you guys see this?" Diego asked. He was angling the phone screen so Wylie and I could watch.

"Uh, no. We were there," I said.

"Yes, it was, in fact my oh so sexy leg," Wylie said.

"Umm, not disputing the sex appeal of the leg, but it was actually the way PJ grabbed your leg and pulled it up," Molly said condescendingly.

"She has a point," Logan said.

"Play it, Diego. I want to see," Emma said.

Diego tapped play. I didn't need to see. I remembered the night in Technicolor. Wylie had broken up with me three days before. The press, the paparazzi, her dick of an agent had all come to a fever pitch and she snapped. I knew in retrospect that she was grasping for something to control, but that knowledge didn't erase the pain of having lost the first—the only—woman I ever loved. The breakup wasn't public yet. Everyone still thought we were the final, final girls.

We arrived at the MTV Awards together. It was our last public appearance. Jeffrey and Taryn were there pretending to be in love. They knew we'd broken up and tried to draw all the attention so Oath wouldn't come down on me and Wy for being reserved. The irony of the suits suddenly wanting us to look like a couple in public was not lost on us.

Jeffrey and Taryn were up for Best Kiss too. It was a small hope that failed when they called our names. We knew the deal. We would re-create that first hayloft kiss. The one where I pressed Wy against the wall, pulled her thigh up high so she could wrap her leg around me. She'd push my hair off my face—a move that was for the cameras but no one minded because they wanted to see. They wanted all the details. They wanted to imagine what it was like to kiss Wylie Parsons. To have her kiss them back like she loved them. But I knew. And I knew she didn't love me.

But we were professionals, dammit. So we gave our speeches and we thanked the right people and I grabbed Wylie and kissed her like we were the only two girls alive.

"Holy shit. Play it again," Emma said.

"Oh, I'm playing it." Diego tapped the screen and backed up the video.

"Yeah, uh." Teddy made eye contact with me, then Wylie. "Sorry, guys. But that's fucking hot."

"It's iconic, honestly," Logan said.

"It really is. I wore pocket tees for a year after that," Molly said.

"No way! I wore tuxedo pants and graphic tees," Logan said.

Wy started laughing. I kept it together until she caught my eye, then I burst out laughing too. I'd worn the tux pants and a T-shirt with a Vargas girl. Wy wore a pocket tee with a suit. We'd picked out the outfits with our stylists before breaking up and were convinced we looked cool as heck. A decade later, people still asked me to sign pinup girl T-shirts so maybe we did look cool.

Jocelyn raised her hand. "I got the haircut." She winced adorably and smiled at me.

"Yes. The haircut." Molly skirted the fire to fist-bump Jocelyn.

"It was a good haircut," Logan told me.

"I almost fired my agent over that haircut," I said. It was a glorified shag. But it was above my chin and I'd been recently outed which made it all too gay.

"You did? Wait, were they for or against it?" Molly dropped onto the seat next to me.

"Against. I dropped them a year later," I said.

"Over a haircut? Or like your whole vibe?" Teddy asked.

"The vibe. I'd been with them since I was a child. They still treated me like an inanimate object." I pulled the sandwiches out. "These are done." I opened the basket and offered it to Logan. I pointed to his cheddar and Gruyère. "Yours is that one."

"Oh, yes." Logan lifted the sandwich out. "This looks awesome."

"Perfect." Emma reached across Diego and Logan handed her grilled cheese over.

"Is Addy this nice on set?" Logan asked Diego out of the side of his mouth.

"She provides fewer snacks. And more constructive feedback." Diego took a long drink of his beer. "But yeah, basically."

"Plus she's hot," Logan said.

"She's no Frances Stuart, but yeah." Diego attempted another leer.

"I'm sorry, but did you call her by her full name the entire time you were sleeping with her?" Rosie asked.

"Yep," Diego said.

"Absolutely," Logan said.

They all looked at me. "Yes. Obviously," I said. I couldn't very well lie to them.

"She did. Loudly," Wy said sardonically. They all slowly turned to stare at Wy as the meaning of her words sunk in.

Diego was finally brave enough. "Uh, Parsons. Spill."

Wy looked at me. I shook my head. I wasn't helping her. She'd gotten here all on her own. "Frances was kind enough to lend me her winery for my first marriage. Bubba and I sneaked out of our reception and found PJ and Frances in the library," she said.

"Addy was at your wedding? And she was screwing someone else there?" Molly asked.

"She was in the wedding. She was Bubba's best man." Wy made it seem like she was clarifying, but she was just throwing me under the bus.

"I wasn't supposed to be her best man," I said. Which made it much, much worse. As evidenced by the burst of laughter from my cast.

They all started asking questions so I had to tell the story. They howled at the accidental best man. Diego confirmed the exquisite library that Frances Stuart enjoyed fucking—not reading—in. But it was Bubba asking me to slow dance and whispering what she'd just witnessed that made them cry with laughter.

"I'm glad my pain amuses you," I said.

"It's just so, so gay," Logan said.

That made Diego start laughing all over again. "Holy shit. It is."

"That's some next level being friends with your exes shit," Molly said.

"Yeah, yeah."

"I'm kind of sad you didn't come to our wedding," Jocelyn said. "Sounds like you put on quite a show."

"For what it's worth, only Wy and Bubba knew what I'd been up to," I said.

"Which was good considering your mother was at that wedding too," Wy said.

"My God! Stop inviting my mother to your weddings!" I shouted.

Wy gave me a withering look that all but guaranteed she'd invite Gerri to every single future wedding.

❖

We wrapped up the party after three a.m. It felt downright indulgent to be facing a bedtime before sunrise. Teddy, Emma, and Rosie all escorted each other back to their cabins. There was much debate about safety and who could protect whom, which was adorable. Molly and Logan helped Wylie put away the remaining food and booze, which felt very queer. The rest of the cleanup could wait until Russ in the morning.

Diego hovered next to me while I broke up the fire and covered the coals with ashes. He nearly knocked me into the damn pit trying to see exactly how fire safety worked so I told him to move any flammable items away. The only thing nearby was a small pile of remaining wood. Diego thought that was a dumb idea until I told him it was to prevent forest fires. It was a slight exaggeration, but it was better than having him lean drunkenly against me.

I tasked Molly with walking Diego back to his cabin. Logan hung back to tell me how excited he was to be joining my cast. It was kind of a perfect end to a perfect evening. Sure, I'd have preferred to film the scenes, but this was a close second. It was exactly what the best film sets I'd been on as a young child felt like—magical and warm and easy. There was no undercurrent of fear or control. It was like Logan had said—an illusion. And then the illusion crashed. I brought the last of the beer in and put it in Wy's fridge. When I closed the door, Jocelyn was there.

"Shit. Sorry. I was trying to be quiet," I said.

"Oh, it's fine. You know how Wylie sleeps." Jocelyn nodded at the loft. I could hear light, familiar snoring.

"Yeah, there's no waking her once she's out." I washed my hands to get the layer of ash and oil off. "Thanks again for letting me take over your cabin."

"Of course. It was fun to see you all in your element." She walked me to the door, still standing about six inches too close for my comfort. At this point, I was used to it. Jocelyn didn't seem to follow everyone else's rules of propriety.

"I don't know if we were in our element necessarily," I said.

"Oh, you were. Wylie told me you had a gift for putting people at ease. You really do. It's the sort of natural charisma that can't be explained or replicated." She entwined her fingers with mine. "It's really powerful to watch. Thank you for letting me be a part of it."

"Sure." I took a step back and opened the door.

"Good night, PJ." Jocelyn put her arms around my shoulders and hugged me. She pressed a vanilla-sweet soft cheek to mine and kissed, then drew back and kissed my cheek again. And then she kissed the corner of my mouth. I froze. She kissed my lips. I pulled away.

"What are you doing?" I asked.

"I'm saying good night." She smiled like it was perfectly normal.

"I don't think we're at the kissing friends stage. I'm sorry." I took another step back.

She reached for my hand. "I think we both know more is happening here."

I didn't really know what to say to that so I blurted, "It's really not. I'm sorry." I didn't even know what I was apologizing for. Not stopping her lingering hugs before they turned to lingering kisses? "You're married to one of my oldest friends." And I found her saccharine. But that didn't seem kind to say out loud.

"Yes, and you're obviously both more than just friends," Jocelyn said with a useless smile.

"What do you mean?" I wasn't drunk enough to ignore her logic but I wasn't sober enough to follow it either.

"I mean the three of us. We can navigate it however you like. But something is clearly happening here. Wylie can feel it too."

"There's nothing for her to feel." I tried to keep the vehemence from my tone before it bled into panic. I wasn't entirely successful.

"Please. I'm not naive and she's not jealous. She did away with all of those toxic feelings. Wylie wants this too. You, me, her." She leaned up and tried to kiss me again.

I took her shoulders and held her back. "You need to stop."

"Oh, don't be cross with me." She smiled.

I realized in that moment how dangerous Jocelyn was. Not for her insistence on a lie, but for believing it to be the truth. "Jocelyn, whatever you think is happening between me and Wylie or me and you isn't. I don't know what I did to give you that impression, but I'm not remotely interested."

She sighed. "Okay. I understand. I'll tell Wylie," she said like she was doing me a favor.

"Fine. You do that." I left and pulled the door closed behind me.

CHAPTER FOURTEEN

I spent a blissful seventy-two hours filming. We shot our scenes, we slept and ate, we came back and filmed more. There was a lot of Malone we needed to get done, but he was a trooper. He got his lines, he did his takes. It was simple. Lenny and Harold hovered between video village and set, tweaking things. They still reeked like old cigars and the patriarchy, but at least they got along beautifully. It was nice to be right. Even if we were going to have to burn their trailer to the ground when we were done.

I very studiously did not think about Jocelyn and her assertion that something was going on between Wylie and me. I was fully aware that something was always going on between Wylie and me. That tension had been there for over a decade. It didn't mean anything. It was just a fact of life. Like my preference for warm colors or good gin. No. It was the thought that Wylie might want something to come from it. Worse still, that she wanted sweet Jocelyn involved. The Wylie I knew would never entertain the thought. And if—in some *Twilight Zone*—Wylie decided she did want a relationship with me and her wife, she would have the nerve to tell me. She wouldn't pull the coward's move and send Jocelyn to botch the seduction. She knew I couldn't stand the woman.

Unless, of course, I didn't know Wylie at all. I'd been emotionally blindsided by her before. Maybe I really didn't know her. It was too much to consider so I decided not to think about it at all. Except I was. Compulsively. It was the thought that lingered as I fell into exhausted sleep every night and hit me with the alarm every morning. What if I didn't know Wylie? Had never known Wylie?

Which was why I kept my head down and prioritized every scene Wylie wasn't in. I didn't want to see her or talk to her. And I really didn't want to film a scene with her where I had to look at her like she hung the moon. Hannah didn't seem to notice. She thought I was focused on the Malone scenes. Russ did notice but she had the good sense not to point it out. I knew it was a short-term plan but that wasn't a problem if I didn't think about the future.

Claude pulled me aside on the third night after we wrapped. He clearly wasn't handling night shoots any better than I was. His soft gray eyes were underlined by heavy dark bags. He was as energetic as ever though. Once we headed back to the lodge, he would go for a quick two-mile run before going to bed. When he woke up in four hours, he'd go for his morning run. Which was somehow different from the pre-dawn run. It was gross.

"I need you for dinner tomorrow night," Claude said.

"Sure. What's up?" My schedule didn't exactly have gaps, but Claude knew that. If he said he needed me, he did.

"Nelson and Eddie are coming into town. I know Eddie is insufferable, but he holds the purse strings."

"Dammit, Claude." I sighed. We both knew I was going to go.

"I know. But I'll owe you. Eddie likes you."

"Eddie hates me," I said.

"Eddie hates you less than he hates most people." It was a concession but it was correct.

"Fine. But we need to make it an early dinner. We've got four scenes scheduled tomorrow night." I waved Russ over. "What time do I need to be on set tomorrow?"

Russ looked back and forth between me and Claude. "Seven thirty."

He frowned. "It's not even dark until nine."

"Yes, but we need rehearsal time. Everyone else has a call time of eight. I like to build in some time for Addy to relax and prepare." Russ wasn't being entirely truthful. But she was being a damn good assistant. Mentioning my mental state was a sure-fire way to get Claude to agree. No one wanted a high-strung director.

"Right. Fine." Claude nodded decisively. "We'll make it an early dinner and you can leave when Nelson is buzzed enough to relax."

"Perfect. Just let Russ know details."

"Thanks. I appreciate it." His relief was palpable.

I squeezed his shoulder. "I got you."

Russ followed me to the van waiting to transport us back to the lodge. We climbed in and the sway of the van was almost enough for me to nod off. I was tired, but the healthy kind. We were three weeks in and with any luck, would wrap in another two, maybe three weeks. The script was basically done, which meant we had the writers in video village for most scenes. It made everything easier.

In two days, Kayleigh Kayden was due to arrive. They and their team had loved Lenny and Harold's rewrite. We had forty-eight hours to film their scenes. Hannah had us on a tight but doable schedule. The only thing that could derail us at this point was Kayden themself. If they were a handful, it wouldn't work. But everything I'd heard about her suggested they would be a professional.

"I take it you're going out with the producers tomorrow night?" Russ asked.

"Huh?" I replayed what she had just said. "Sorry, yes. Nelson and Eddie are coming into town. Claude wants me to smile pretty and charm Eddie."

"Should I pick up a new personality for you?"

I laughed. "The last three didn't take. I'll just have to muddle through as a curmudgeon."

"Any idea what you'll wear? If you need pressing or dry cleaning, I need time," Russ said.

I did a mental review of what I'd brought. "I guess I'll wear the blue suit."

"Shirt?"

"Surprise me."

"That lavender knit tee?" she asked. "It'll dress down the suit and it's breathable. Plus it will look good with your brown belt and Chelsea boots."

"Perfect. Thanks."

We pulled up at the lodge. It was blissfully quiet. Everyone who didn't need to film was tucked in bed. One advantage of wrapping at dawn. The sky was edging from gray to blue as Russ and I went our separate ways. I climbed the stairs to my bed, stripping as I went. I fell asleep wondering how Wylie had taken Jocelyn's announcement that I wasn't interested.

❖

Claude's assistant had managed to find the only restaurant with white linen tablecloths in a hundred-mile radius. Claude and I were the first to arrive. The restaurant itself was dark. Dark wood, dark curtains hanging on the windows, dark leather seats. The white tablecloths and candles offered bright points of contrast. We were taken outside and seated on the patio. Below us, the cliffs dropped straight to the narrow rocky beach. Near the shoreline, craggy boulders broke the surface. Beyond that, the ocean sprawled. The sunset was unobstructed and blinding. It was lovely and I had no interest in looking at it. I had scenes to shoot. I'd pushed a meeting with Phil for this dinner. Aside from actually liking Phil, I also seriously needed his notes.

"You're not going to pout like that the whole dinner, right?" Claude asked.

I snapped out of my reverie and looked at him. He was teasing. "Sorry. I'm increasingly distracted. I promise to be charming when they get here."

"I know. But before they get here, tell me the truth." He lowered his voice like that would prevent any potential curses that might arise from having asked. "How are you actually feeling about the movie?"

I grinned. Something I didn't need to lie about. "Don't hold me to it, okay?" I asked. He gave me a serious nod. "It's fucking great."

"You think so too?"

"Yeah. Teddy is killing it. And have you been watching the dailies the last couple of days?" I asked. Claude started nodding and grinning. "Logan is perfect."

"He really is. I was on the fence about adding someone so late in the game, but the kid is amazing. Commanding, sexy, charisma for days."

"And he provides a contrast to Teddy's James Dean angst," I said.

"Yes, exactly. Diego is giving us solid comedic relief, but Logan seems to blend the star power of Teddy with the lightness of Diego."

I snapped. "That's exactly it."

"Well, you two look enthusiastic," Eddie said from behind me.

Claude and I stood to greet him and Nelson. We did the requisite handshakes and butch shoulder grips. We shuffled around so they could sit. I counted the place settings and realized there was an empty one right as I heard Wy behind me.

"I don't know why they say Hollywood is a boys' club," she said, laughter in her voice.

"Wylie, darling. This is why I invited you," Nelson said. He leaned forward to kiss her cheek. "Otherwise I'd fall asleep in this sea of drab suits."

We were, in fact, all wearing drab suits. Eddie's pink shirt was more exciting than the other guys'. But even that couldn't overcome the overabundance of sedate. Wylie, however, was exquisite in a white suit. It emphasized the rich sunlight of her hair. She'd foregone a shirt so we got an eyeful of tan cleavage and a triangle of flat stomach. I dragged my eyes back up to find her staring curiously at me. My wrists started to itch.

"I feel like I haven't seen you in a week," she said to me.

This was why avoiding problems was a bad idea. I suddenly had a lot to say to Wylie and no space to say it. But I was an actor and I was a professional. So I smiled like I meant it. She was the only person at the table who would know I was lying.

"I know. Logan has had my attention since he arrived." I squeezed her hand briefly. The producers would read affection in the movement. Wy and I would hash it out later. Without the expensive audience.

"Oh, yes. That's the new guy, right?" Nelson asked.

We all sat and launched into our meeting disguised as dinner. As usual, Eddie made his pinched, sour expression every time we mentioned something that might cost more money. At the moment, that meant any mention of Logan.

"I've been sneaking into video village. Logan is fantastic," Wy surprised me by saying.

"You've been watching the dailies?" Nelson asked. "I thought Addy was too precious to allow that."

"I am." I scowled. This was the first I'd heard about one of my leads watching someone else's performance. There wasn't anything technically wrong with it, which pissed me off more. I couldn't push back without being a jerk.

"Claude is a sucker." Wy nudged Claude. She turned to Eddie. "Believe me, whatever you're paying Logan, you're getting a deal."

"We were just saying that." Claude nodded at me. "He has serious star power."

I half expected Eddie to take a transphobic turn, but he seemed to read the table well enough to hold himself back. That was good. All my energy was currently occupied by not being overtly rude to Wy who kept smiling at me and whispering silly asides. If I had to deal with Eddie being a shit, I'd play my hand with Wylie. Instead, I kept my head down and ate my dinner. I polished off my third glass of wine when Wy stood.

"You'll have to excuse us. Ladies room." She put a hand on my shoulder.

I managed to keep my confusion to myself. It had been a good ten years since Wy invoked ladies' room to get us out of a table. And then it had been so we could make out. I followed her to the bathroom. It was a unisex, single stall. She ushered me in and locked the door behind us.

"What the fuck?" I asked.

"That's what I was going to ask." She crossed her arms and I looked at her tits again. No more wine for me. "You haven't responded to any of my texts for the last three days. Jocelyn said she tried to come on set to say good-bye to you before she went back to LA and you'd banned her from set." Okay, I did do that. "And now you've been weird and cold all evening."

"I've been busy. I don't know if you noticed but I'm directing a picture." I was trying for nonchalance, but I definitely just landed at asshole.

"You've been directing for weeks. That never stopped you from responding to texts," Wy said. She was pissed. Under that she was hurt. Which was pretty fucking bold.

"I'm sorry." Maybe placating her would work. "I really have been swamped. The last couple of days have been constant. But I should have a break soon. We'll catch up then." I tried to nudge her out of the way of the door. She was not nudgeable.

"No. Tell me what's going on. You're acting as though I've wronged you on some Shakespearean level."

"Nothing is going on," I said.

"We had a fantastic night with the cast—which you orchestrated. And then radio silence. I thought I was just being sensitive until tonight. It's damn cold out there, babe." She stared at me and waited, her jaw set.

"It's just Eddie and Nelson." I shrugged. "Not exactly a fun audience."

"Don't do that. Don't tell me I'm imagining it. That's shitty. What changed? What happened?"

"You know damn well what happened," I snapped.

She was surprised at that. "I really really don't."

And suddenly, I felt like an idiot. Because of course she didn't. Either Wylie had acted extremely out of character or Jocelyn had shown me a new, fun part of herself. The answer was obvious.

"Shit," I said.

"What?"

"Fuck."

"You're freaking me out here." She reached for my arm, but I backed away.

"I'm sorry," I said.

"For what?"

"Dammit. We can't do this here." I looked around. The bathroom was beautifully appointed. For a bathroom. But the walls were closing in.

"Hey, stop with the cryptic bullshit," Wy said.

"Jocelyn made a pass at me. She made it sound like you wanted her to. I believed her. I'm sorry." I waited. Wy processed. Someone knocked at the door.

"Fuck," Wylie said.

"I know."

"How are we supposed to go back out there?" Wy's eyes got big and she started to tear up. "I can't go back out there."

"Yes, you fucking can."

"How?"

"One sec." I held up a finger and texted Russ. *Need immediate extraction with Wy.* "Russ will get us out of the rest of dinner."

The knock came again.

"And that?" Wy asked. She suddenly looked around and realized we were in a single bathroom together. "Oh no."

"Hey. I got you." I cupped her cheek and smudged her lipstick with my thumb. Her eyes widened but at least it didn't look like she was going to cry any more. I pulled away and smeared the color across my own lip. "Ready to have an affair?"

Wy laughed. It was shaky but it was better than the alternative. "I'll deny it."

"Hard same. I'm a recluse savant. I don't have illicit affairs." I winked.

"I love you."

"Oh, it's that kind of affair?" I asked.

Wy rolled her eyes and unlocked the door. A fit older guy huffed when Wylie came out. When I followed, he coughed and managed to look scandalized. In his defense, it really was a nice restaurant.

CHAPTER FIFTEEN

"Sorry, boys." Wy slid into her seat. "I had to remind Addy that she's supposed to be charming tonight."

They all laughed. Claude made pointed eye contact with me and wiped his mouth with his napkin. I mirrored the movement with a suggestion of panic.

"I will say, I was nervous," Eddie said. "But I'm feeling much better about the direction of the film after tonight." He grinned at me. It was more avarice than lechery. Capitalist.

"You know Addy. Always the consummate professional. She knows what she's doing and she does it well." Wy took a sip of wine and it was pure lechery. This evening was a disaster. Or a wild success if you were a producer.

Claude's phone rang. "I'm so sorry. It's our AD." He stood. "I'll be back in a moment."

Nelson waved him off. "So how has it been working together again? It's been a few years, right?" he asked us.

I nodded. "I was nervous. I've become so ensconced in directing. I wasn't sure I could wear both hats." In for a penny. "But Wylie really knows how to center me. She's been a wonderful ally on set." I took her hand and kissed her knuckle.

"An ally?" Eddie bit back a smile. "That's fantastic."

"Sorry about that." Claude rejoined us. "That was Hannah. She needs you back earlier than expected," he told me.

I glanced at the time and frowned. "We were always on borrowed time, guys."

"And, I hate to say it, but you're needed as well," he said to Wylie.

"Oh, no. I didn't think I was shooting tonight," she said.

"You weren't. But the first scene fell through so Hannah needs you for a different scene," he said.

Wy sighed like the universe was really depriving her. We said our oh so sad good-byes. Nelson and Eddie offered—threatened?—to drop by while we were filming. I acted like that was a lovely idea. Maybe I could ban them from set too.

I was ready to spend the entire drive back discussing Jocelyn. Wylie obviously wanted to. But our driver existed, which sort of made that a non-starter. As we pulled away from the restaurant, Wy slid her hand into mine. I didn't know what she needed from me, not really. But I could give simple comfort. It didn't make the twenty-seven-minute drive any less tense. I ran endless scenarios in my head, had the conversation fifteen times. Each time, Wy took it differently. Sometimes it was my fault. Sometimes hers. It was always Jocelyn's.

The driver took us back to the set. Russ was waiting. She ushered us, looking very serious, to my trailer. Wylie went inside and I hung back.

"Just FYI," I said to Russ. "In a moment of excellent decision-making, I led the producers to believe Wy and I were having an affair. So uh, that's happening. Or rather, it's not happening, but they think it is." I clapped my hand on her shoulder. "I don't think it'll go anywhere. Just want you to be in the loop."

"Thanks for telling me?" Russ said. Strangely, she didn't actually sound thankful.

"Got to keep you on your toes, pal."

She gave a long-suffering sigh. "I'll knock fifteen minutes before you're needed on set. We're out at Malone's cabin tonight."

"Thanks." The cabin was one of the more far-flung sets. But it was perfectly isolated. Very serial killer in the woods. Or pretty boy lumberjack hipster. Which was the exact balance I'd been aiming for.

Russ took off and I let myself into my trailer. Wylie was standing there looking glassy-eyed, staring at nothing.

"Hey, babe. You want to sit?" I asked.

"Oh." She looked around and saw the small couch. "Yeah."

I left her to that gargantuan task and grabbed a cold water. I handed it to her and sat at the other end of the couch. She drank her water and did some more staring. I waited to see which way the emotional scales would tip.

"Tell me what happened," she finally said.

"You sure?"

"Yes, of course. I need to know."

I owed her the truth. Jocelyn owed her more, but I couldn't control that. "After the fire, Jocelyn kissed me. I told her that wasn't our vibe. She said that you and me were obviously into each other and also somehow into her. I disagreed. Then she tried to kiss me again so I left."

"Wait. What do you mean?" Wy asked.

"Which part?"

"That you were into her? And me?"

"She made it sound like you two had talked about it. And that you wanted her to come on to me," I said.

"Hold up. You're saying my wife told you I wanted to have a threesome with you. And her."

"Yeah. Well, she kind of implied it would be more than that. A romantic relationship."

"I just—" She closed her eyes and shook her head. Incredulous was winning, but anger seemed close behind. "What?"

"Go ahead and process. I've been stewing about it for days."

"Why didn't you tell me?" Cool. There was the anger.

"Because I'm an idiot. I believed her."

"You believed her?" Wy asked. "The fuck?"

"It fucked me up, okay. I was so stuck in my own head I couldn't see clearly."

"What does that mean?"

"I don't know." I could hear my own voice getting high pitched. "She sounded convincing."

"But you know I'm not poly," Wy said.

"People change."

She gave me a dubious look. "That's a big change."

"Right. Yes. That's where I'm an idiot."

"Shit." Wy fell back against the couch and stared at the ceiling. "What am I supposed to do?"

"Talk to your wife."

There wasn't much more to say after that. We knew where we stood. Jocelyn was the wild card. I gently suggested Wy should call her, but that didn't land well. Instead, we just talked. About nothing. About the film, then Gerri, then somehow the fundraiser Wylie had gone to the month before. Talking to her was like listening to a new song but hearing echoes of something old and familiar. Sometime in the middle of recounting a film festival I'd gone to in spring, I remembered how simple it had been to fall in love with Wy. She was easy to be with. She was the only person who didn't require a facade from me. Which was a sad commentary on my life, but one I'd made peace with years before.

Russ knocked when the van arrived to take me out to Malone's cabin. I stood, belatedly realizing I should have changed clothes. Oh, well. Too late now.

Wy stood when I did. "PJ?"

"Yeah?"

"Can I come?"

"Where?"

"To the set. I know it's dumb." Instead of looking away, she caught my eye and held it. Doing so seemed to give her strength. "I just don't want to be alone right now."

"Yeah, of course." I took her hand and kissed her knuckle.

"You sure? I know you like your set clear."

"Babe, it's fine. Come on." I tugged her with me to the door.

Wy stared at me as we rode out to the set. A few times she opened her mouth to say something, then thought better of it. The van slowly filled with warmth and the scent of her shampoo. Gray evening light filtered in making the brightness of her suit luminous. The air felt charged. The comfort of our meaningless conversation had fallen away and been replaced with a sharp tension. It felt like the ache of a battery on your tongue. The kind of childhood dare you somehow regret and never resist in equal measure.

"Thank you," she said when we pulled up.

"Any time."

Logan and Molly were already running lines when we got to the cabin. They didn't initially realize I was behind them so I stayed quiet and listened. They were great together. About two lines from the end of the scene, Logan turned and saw me. He jumped.

"Shit," he said.

I laughed. "Sorry. I was just listening."

Molly started laughing and put her hand on Logan's shoulder. "Careful, Black Hat will get you."

Logan flexed. "I could take him."

Molly nodded appreciatively. "I would watch that."

Wylie came up and stood next to me. "I would too, honestly."

Molly grinned lasciviously. "Yeah, you would."

"Hey, Parsons. Are you filming with us tonight?" Logan asked. "I didn't see you on the call sheet."

"No. PJ and I were having dinner with the producers and tagging along here seemed much more fun." She leaned into my shoulder.

"That explains why you're all hot and fancy," Molly said.

"There you are." Hannah emerged from around the side of Malone's cabin.

I turned to include her in our circle. "Just sneaking up on Logan for fun."

"Sounds like a blast." Hannah consulted her watch. "Drew says we've got about ten to rehearse the scene before lighting is done."

"Cool. Let's work on blocking." I waved Malone and Pippa ahead of me. "I liked what you two were doing just now. Malone, remember to be more bro-like. You're the one white guy in the cast so you're representing casual misogyny."

"Similar to what we did yesterday in the bar scene?" Malone asked.

"Yes, exactly. I've haven't seen any of Phil's edits yet, but everyone agrees that your dailies are solid."

"What about me?" Pippa asked. "I know Pippa isn't into him. So how do you want me to react to him hitting on me?"

"I'm envisioning you two as buddies. Pippa is hot and she knows it. So she's dismissive. Being hit on is just like a Tuesday," I said.

"Okay. But she's not offended, right? Because he doesn't really mean it."

"She's not offended. But he definitely does mean it. If she gave him any indication that she was down, he'd sleep with her in a heartbeat. But he'd also forget about sleeping with her the second they were done."

Malone and Pippa stopped on the path between the house and the woodshed. We did some basic blocking, then I had them run the dialogue with movement. I tweaked a couple of things and asked them to run it again. Something was wrong but it wasn't Logan's or Molly's acting.

"Hannah?" I called out.

She was at my side in a moment. "What's up?"

"Malone looks wrong, but I don't know why." I watched Malone shuffle his feet and stare at the ground. He glanced up and locked eyes with me. When he realized we were studying him, he frowned.

"Okay. Can we unpack that a bit?" Hannah asked.

"I don't know. Malone, will you spin for us?" I called. He did. "Do it again, but slower."

"It's the sweater," Wylie said.

"What?" I asked.

"He's a townie. He's a ranch hand. And you've got him in a designer cashmere sweater."

"She's right. I'll get Arjun," Hannah said.

Five minutes later, Malone was wearing a thick navy and saffron overshirt. It was still designer but it was ranch hand designer. He looked perfect. Wylie looked smug but she deserved to. Arjun had Logan wear a white undershirt. I didn't know if it was actually one of Black Hat's or if it just looked similar. He unbuttoned Malone's overshirt low enough to give us flashes of the white underneath. It was the exact red herring we needed to make the audience think Malone could be Black Hat.

Throughout filming the scene, and then during the next scene—a beast of angles and ominous shadows—I stayed focused. But I was always aware of Wy. To anyone else on set, it looked like she was just observing. Maybe even participating a little. I'd ask her opinion on a line and she'd answer. But she was barely aware of the movement around her. Instead, she was thinking. As the night waned, she moved in and out of my orbit, coming ever closer.

I watched the last shot of the night come to a close. Hannah called cut. She looked to me for confirmation that we were done and I nodded. I turned to Wy, standing five feet away. She came closer and I slid my arm around her waist. I felt a measure of possession. It wasn't romantic or even sexual. Or maybe it was both. Wy was mine—had always been mine—and now she was hurt. It was my job to absorb that pain so she wouldn't carry it alone.

CHAPTER SIXTEEN

My world was dictated by the sun. I had Kayleigh Kayden for two days. They needed to sleep. The crew needed to sleep. I did not need to sleep. I needed more sunshine.

The cast was banned from set since Black Hat was having a big moment and none of them could meet Rob. Their absence made the set feel barren. Maybe that was only because I didn't really know the actors I was working with for the day. Hannah did most of Rob's direction so I wouldn't interact with him. We also had two day actors who would disappear almost immediately. Their corpses would have more screen time than they would. I sort of knew Kayleigh but only from the incidental Hollywood party. We'd toasted each other with overpriced champagne but never had a substantial conversation.

The real reason I felt alone was none of that. Directing could be a lonely gig. I usually enjoyed my isolation. But all I could think about was Wylie. It had only been a matter of hours since I'd seen her. Had she spoken with Jocelyn? Did time give her space to get mad at me? Was she hurting?

After spending the first half hour on set checking my phone and my watch, I gave them both to Russ. If anything pressing came through, she'd tell me. If it wasn't pressing, she wouldn't.

We spent the first day on exposition. Kayleigh was one of the local kids hired to prep the ranch for Grace and Taylor's arrival. The other two locals had gone off to swim at the river and an ominous loneliness settled around Kayleigh. The sun climbed higher, burning out the shadows and creating a false safety. It was *Texas Chainsaw* but stripped of any bad men or power tools. Just an empty, hollow ranch and a kid with an overactive imagination.

With the sun at its peak, we discovered the body of one of the locals. Kayleigh stood in the open barn door, sweat drawing streaks in the dirt on their neck. And then something dripped. Kayleigh wiped their cheek absentmindedly only to recoil when they realized it was blood.

That shot took half my goddamn day. Nikolai had a glycerin compound he swore by for simulating sweat. I'd used it. It had a lovely eucalyptus scent. Except, of course, Kayleigh smelled the bottle and announced they were allergic to eucalyptus. Claude helpfully agreed that Kayleigh's manager had provided a list of their extensive allergies—including eucalyptus. Apparently, no one had thought to give the FX makeup guy the list of her allergies. I had a small, quiet tantrum.

Hannah instructed Nikolai to mix more of the sweat bottle without eucalyptus. He didn't have any more glycerin and getting more would take at least an hour. I had a slightly larger tantrum.

We tried water. It was a classic for a reason. But the water didn't stick and run the way I wanted it to. I wanted to try lube, but the only lube Nikolai had was banana scented. Kayleigh was also allergic to banana. I didn't ask Nikolai why he only had banana-scented lube.

Calls were made and PAs were sent to buy unscented lube, which proved to be more difficult than it should have been. Arjun and Drew finally stepped in and managed to save the shot. Drew rigged up heaters to increase the temperature on set. Arjun put Kayleigh in a thermal undershirt with the sleeves cut off so it wouldn't be visible. And Kayleigh sweated for real.

We got the shot. Kayleigh ignored the first blood drop and wiped away the second. They nailed the reaction. An immediate horror followed by confusion and a sort of denial. Then they stepped back into the darkness of the barn and looked up. There was a slender arm hanging from the hayloft, blood gathering and slowly dripping from a chipped fingernail. Even then, Kayleigh didn't believe it. They started to climb the ladder. Halfway up, we would reveal the full body. The corpse was painted in ribbons of blood. Were they wounds or blood spatter? It didn't matter. She was very, very dead. Kayleigh bravely climbed the rest of the way and checked her friend's pulse. When they knelt, they found the second body. We didn't see his face because the girl's body was piled on top, but the realization that there were four legs and three visible hands was garish and jarring. It was too much. Too many body parts, too much blood, too much death.

By now, my sunlight was waning. We were shooting through the open roof of the barn so we only had a short time to get the shot. If we didn't, Phil would fix it in post, but it would add hours. Kayleigh cried over their friend's body. We watched their face as the shadows behind them materialized into movement. Black Hat was in the hayloft too.

We cut and took a short break. Hannah ran through rehearsal with Rob. FX makeup prepped Kayleigh to get stabbed. They swapped the undershirt for a rig with a blood pack and a tube.

"You doing okay?" I asked Kayleigh.

They looked up from the plastic being taped to their torso and grinned at me. "Yeah, totally. How am I doing?"

"Great. You're a natural," I said.

Kayleigh frowned. "Do you say that to all the frivolous pop musicians the producers force you to work with?"

I laughed. "How many pop stars do you think I've worked with?"

"Didn't you spend a year just making art house music videos?"

"Fair enough." It was only six months, but they weren't wrong. "I assure you that you're doing excellent. Your reaction to the body was awesome. Everything I was hoping for."

"Fuck yeah, it was." She did a little dance and the woman taping their ribs cleared her throat. "Sorry. Sorry. I'll keep still."

"You're doing fine, sweetie," Nikolai's assistant said. "We're almost done."

"For this next piece, I want you to keep with the theme of confusion," I said. "When he stabs you, your initial reaction should be kind of baffled. And then almost immediately a mix of physical pain and fear."

Kayleigh nodded. "Yeah, okay. I got it."

"Cool." I glanced around for Russ. We still had a few minutes before we'd start rolling again.

"Addy?" Kayleigh asked.

I turned back to them. "Yeah?"

"Thanks. You've been super chill."

"Of course. You really are killing it. Keep it up," I said.

Russ approached to pull me aside. "Hannah says you've got ten."

She led me away from the wild energy of the set. I asked her for my phone and she made me eat a salad before she'd give it to me. That gave me all of two minutes to read the complete lack of messages from Wylie.

"You let me think I had a message," I said.

"You do. Your mom wrote you." Russ pointed at the misleading icon.

"You know damn well that's not what I'm looking for."

Russ shrugged and half-smiled. "Gerri sent you a fascinating article on sharks in South Africa. Maybe you should read it before judging."

I glared and handed the phone back.

We got excellent footage of Kayleigh being stabbed. I'd opted for a more challenging shot where we saw the long knife burst forth from between Kayleigh's ribs. It would be easier to show the knife going in than out, but it was a hell of a lot more compelling to watch the damage it wrought. The tube taped to Kayleigh's torso leaked a steady stream of dark blood. With every subtle movement, it would shift and dribble.

For the last shot of the day, Kayleigh shoved Black Hat off the hayloft. I would have preferred to film the whole sequence, especially because we were paying stunt men to stand around. Instead we opted to shut down for the night.

My phone was still distractingly silent so I settled in to watch every piece of footage from the day. I told Scottie and Hannah I didn't need them so they immediately pulled their chairs closer. Video village was not the most comfortable place to review dailies, but I ignored my initial discomfort and after five minutes was lost enough to not notice.

The initial shots with morning sun were solid. Hot young people doing hard labor was always a good way to build interest. I took notes for Phil so he'd know which takes I preferred.

Claude barged in and tried to ask me a bunch of distracting questions so Hannah led him away. Russ handed me a sandwich and stood too close until I started eating it. I had no sense of time other than the fact that it was dark. I promised Russ I'd drink water and get some sleep. I might have been lying. But I was a decent enough liar that she agreed to leave for the night.

"I knew you'd be here," Wylie said.

I spun around. Scottie fumbled to stop the footage. Wylie was standing, looking out of place in the sea of empty chairs that made up video village. She was wearing baggy jeans with the knees torn out and a cropped T-shirt that was so threadbare it was see-through. Her eyes were puffy.

"Yeah, I want to see if there's anything we need to reshoot while Kayleigh is here," I said.

"I figured." Wy nodded a couple of times and glanced at Scottie. "Could I maybe watch too?"

"Yeah, totally." I stood to make room for her.

Scottie stood too. "Actually, you can have my spot. I watched all this as it came in." He backed away. "You good?" he asked me.

"Yeah. Thanks. You made some serious magic today."

"Anything for you." He gripped my arm briefly. "See you bright and early."

Wylie sat in Scottie's abandoned seat. "Are you sure this is okay?"

"Do you promise to be real terrified when you film with Black Hat?" I asked. I wasn't actually concerned about humanizing Rob, but I wasn't not concerned either.

"I mean crashing your work time." She folded her arms and gripped hard enough to leave pale dimples in her skin.

"I knew what you meant."

Wy nodded. "Okay."

"Do you want to talk?"

"Maybe in a bit," she said.

I hit play and we watched two takes of the swimming hole discussion. After that was a lot of B-roll of Kayleigh working around the barn. They piled junk and waved away clouds of dust. Dirt settled in their cropped hair turning the burnished gold flat and pale.

Wylie shifted in her chair for the second time. "I talked to Jocelyn."

I stopped the video. "How did that go?"

"Bad." She studied the image on the screen for a long time. I waited. Finally, she looked at me. "She didn't deny any of it. But she basically said it was my fault."

"That's shitty."

"Yeah, it really is." She took a deep breath and dropped her gaze.

"How did she figure it was your fault?" I asked. I really was curious.

She shrugged. "She said she felt like she was losing me. And that was her attempt to keep me?"

"That doesn't really make sense."

"Apparently, she felt like she never really had me. She isn't wrong. There was always some element of a business transaction in our marriage. But that didn't mean it wasn't also a marriage, you know?"

I took Wylie's hand. "Sure." I was lying. But what did I know? It wasn't like I'd ever been married.

"According to Jocelyn, I never fully committed to her. She said I wasn't capable of it." She lifted our joined hands, then dropped them. She drew her thumb back and forth across my knuckles.

"That's fucked up. She's wrong. You're totally capable of love."

"No, no. You misunderstand. She said I wasn't capable of loving her." Anger hit her voice hard. "And that I'd never loved Bubba or Natalie."

"That's bold."

Wy's eyes snapped back to mine. "She said I wasn't able to really love anyone else because I was still in love with you."

I stared at her in shock. My first thought was denial. That thought was correct so I moved on to secondary anger on Wy's behalf. That was a terrible thing to say to someone you claimed to love. It was a terrible accusation. I took a breath to fervently support Wylie, but she hit me with the second punch before I could.

"I think she might be right."

CHAPTER SEVENTEEN

I'd planned to spend most of my night watching dailies. Instead, I accomplished fuck all. No dailies, no notes, no sleep. Dawn took forever and somehow still came too soon. The sunlight was making my headache worse. But feeling shitty was a luxury. So I buried my anger at Wylie, chugged some coffee, and swallowed whatever pills Russ handed me.

The stunt team was already set up for Kayleigh's jump from the hayloft. She was supposed to kick out the rotted boards over the hay door, then leap into the pile of old hay below. Kayleigh insisted on doing the kick stunt, which was fine. They did a couple of rounds of practice before Josh, the stunt coordinator, declared them ready. Thankfully, Kayleigh wasn't interested in doing the jump. I wouldn't have let her for a multitude of reasons and I really wasn't up for explaining those reasons.

The kick was excellent. I didn't bother telling Kayleigh that we would end up filming it six more times to have plenty of footage. There simply wasn't time for them to film it again and again. We had the footage with their face, and that was all we needed. Kayleigh's stuntman nailed the jump on the first attempt. We reset and had him do it again. Then we moved the mats and got footage of Kayleigh jumping a nice sedate three feet.

Mid-morning, we broke to set up the next shot. I mainlined more coffee while rewatching the Kayleigh jump on my monitor. Russ pulled me aside.

"Trade you phone for screen?" she asked.

"Why?"

"She keeps sending messages," Russ said.

"Then turn it off. I'm filming. I don't want to talk to her."

"You wanted to talk to her all day yesterday."

"I wasn't mad at her yesterday. Today, I'm mad," I said.

"Sure." Russ pocketed the phone. "No phone. Phones are bad."

"I'm working."

"Obviously."

"Pretty sure you're mocking me," I said.

Russ pursed her lips and shook her head. "Nope. You're clearly having a day. When you have days, it's best to agree and ride it out."

My scalp started to tingle and my skin got hot. "I don't like when you placate me."

"Well, you're an asshole when you're not placated."

Dammit. She was right. "I know."

"Addy, we're ready for you," Hannah said.

"Stay focused here. The rest will keep." Russ took a step back.

"Thanks."

Kayleigh did their run from the pile of hay to a split-rail fence with Black Hat chasing them. They climbed the fence and fell over the top. The stuntman stepped in for the fall. I wasn't about to let Kayleigh do that either.

Then we set up the shot that would establish the tone of the entire film. Kayleigh started on the ground where they'd fallen. They stood and looked back, but Black Hat wasn't there. Scottie framed the shot looking over Kayleigh's shoulder at the barn. The setting sun saturated everything in heat and light. The barn was dull, peeling red. The pines were a heavy green velvet. Dry, overgrown grass swayed in the gentle breeze. Bent stalks with smears of blood showed Kayleigh's path. It was the swath of a dying animal.

Kayleigh turned and found their hero. A tall bareheaded cowboy silhouetted by the sunset standing in waist-high grass. At first glance, it looked like the other local kid.

"Help! Please! He's going to kill me." Kayleigh limped forward. Their dark golden hair was plastered with drying blood. She kept a hand pressed to the deep wound in their left side. Dark blood seeped through their fingers with every step toward salvation.

And then the cowboy moved his hands out of the tall grass. He settled the black Stetson on his head and angled the brim down. Then he reached back slowly and pulled the knife from his belt.

Kayleigh screamed as they realized it was him.

The sequence was simple from there. Black Hat came toward them. She turned and tried to climb the fence again. He pulled them back and the camera hovered overhead as he stabbed them repeatedly. Blood painted the tall grass. The camera slowly spun. Black Hat looked up at the sky and Phil would cut to title sequence right before Rob's face was visible.

My intent was to invoke the original *Dangerous Summer Nights* ending sequence. Except we were reversing key elements. The daylight, the beginning rather than the ending. And Black Hat triumphing, of course. Whereas in the original, queerness was the final girl, here I wanted to have the patriarchy left standing. It would make his destruction more meaningful in the end.

Sean never gave a shit about the meaning behind what he was doing. His intent was never to make a statement. Sure, he thought he was doing subversive interesting shit. But he only signed off on Lenny's idea of two final girls because he wanted to watch us make out. Which we knew because he announced it during filming. Often.

Plenty of politics and money had gone into my decision to direct this picture, but ultimately, I wanted to reclaim this. It was part of my legacy and I was tired of it being tied to Sean Murray. I'd been plenty famous before *DSN,* but it was central to my brand in a way my other work just wasn't. Sean had spent ten years taking credit for acting choices I'd made, a script Lenny had crafted, a legion of fans who gave the movie life and meaning. But not this one. This one was mine.

❖

Half the cast insisted on getting to meet Kayleigh since I'd banned the actors from set. So we'd rented out the top floor of some restaurant in Thackerton, and in twenty minutes, I was supposed to be there being welcoming and shit. My whole body hurt from lack of sleep and—let's face it—being old. Russ had given me ten minutes to shower and change. The shower would cure me. I was sure of it.

I sent Russ back to my cabin to grab an outfit for me. I couldn't very well wear the dusty chinos and Chelsea boots I'd been in since dawn. I'd been under the hot water all of three minutes before I heard the door to my trailer open. I rushed through my already truncated shower. I towel dried my hair and stuck my head out of the miniature bathroom.

"I'm almost done. You have my clothes?" I said. Russ didn't respond. "Russ? Where are my clothes?"

"I was wondering who you could be talking to, but Russ makes sense, I guess," Wylie said.

"Jesus fucking Christ. What are you doing in my trailer? Get out." I ducked back into the tiny bathroom.

"No, we need to talk."

"Now is not the time to talk," I said. I slicked my hair back with product. As it dried the curl would come out. Given my choice, I'd blow dry. Or better yet, go over to hair and have Sheila style me. As it was, I had zero minutes to get across town. I'd have to settle for curls instead of fluffy curls.

"We can talk while you get ready," Wy called.

"We are not talking right now," I yelled. I pulled on the terrycloth robe hanging on the back of the door. I couldn't yell if I was naked. It was a rule. "We have to go play nice with the cast tonight. And I don't have clothes. And I'm mad at you." I walked into the central room of the trailer so I could glare at her as I told her I was mad.

"PJ." Wy sounded real put upon.

Russ opened the door and walked in with my outfit for the evening. "Fuck." She drew it out. "I thought I locked the door."

"Clothes, please." I put my hand out. "And make Wy leave."

"I'm not leaving. I can't sit through another polite, icy dinner with you. We need to talk this through," Wylie said.

Russ looked back and forth between us before sighing and shrugging. She wasn't going to remove Wy. "The green short sleeve you wanted isn't here. I don't think we brought it from LA. So I grabbed the blue striped one instead."

"The one with wooden buttons?"

"Yes."

"Fine." I took the bag of clothes Russ was holding out to me and brought it into the bedroom at the back of the trailer. "What's my timeline?"

"You need to leave in six minutes. Your driver is waiting," Russ said.

I kicked the door shut. As I got dressed, I could hear them talking. There was a pressure shift as the trailer door opened. One set of footsteps walked down the steps. I had a feeling Russ had left and Wy was waiting for me.

I walked out barefoot in my jeans and loose cotton tank. Wy was sitting on the couch. I studiously ignored her as I sat to pull on my worn loafers and cuff my jeans to mid-calf.

"I wasn't trying to say I was in love with you, you know?" Wy said.

My silence couldn't hold up to my temper. "What the hell else could you have possibly meant?"

"Just that I'll never love someone the way I loved you. Love you."

"Past or present tense? You're really pissing me off here." I looked around for my watch and wallet. The watch was on the counter. Russ probably had my wallet.

"Both. It was romantic love when we were kids. You were my first love, asshole." Wy leaned forward as she spoke, but she showed no intention of leaving. "And of course I still love you."

"Then why the hell did you pass off the blame for your failed marriages on me? It's barely funny as a joke. It's fucking devastating when you say it and mean it."

"I'm sorry. I phrased it poorly. But you didn't give me a chance to explain. You just left," she said.

"Of course I left." I heard the volume increase in my voice and worked to lower it. "This movie is killing me. I'm exhausted. All I wanted last night was to review footage and instead I have you showing up all vulnerable with the weight of your fragile marriage. That's not fair."

Wy scowled. "Well, sorry I'm not always perfectly articulate. I would also rather not be dealing with my marriage falling apart right now."

"I know you didn't plan this, okay?" I stopped rushing around. There was nothing else to do to get ready. And this conversation was clearly happening whether I wanted it to or not. I crossed my arms and glared at Wy. "I'm not asking you to handle this perfectly. That's not possible. I get that. But don't come to me and ask me to help you process. It's a shit position to put me in."

"You're right. I'm sorry. For what it's worth, I don't blame you. Not for any of it."

I took a deep breath. It was time to tell the truth. "I know. I blame me a little. So I don't love it when you agree."

"What? How?"

"I don't know." I shrugged. "I kind of wanted you and Bubba to fail because I was still mad and hurt."

Wylie started to grin but had the good sense to hold it back. "And you never really clicked with Nat."

I nodded. "And I can't stand Jocelyn."

"So, just to be clear, you feel guilty for not adoring the women I marry?" Wy lost the battle with the smile.

"Okay, well I don't like when you say it that way."

She started laughing.

"Shut up. Can we go to dinner now?" I asked.

She finally stood. "Yeah. Thanks for talking to me."

I pulled on the blue shirt but left it unbuttoned. "You didn't give me much choice." I looked down at my outfit. "Do I look okay?"

"Yeah, yeah. You look hot." She slid her hands in her pockets and mirrored my pose. "How am I?"

I checked her out. Another shapeless designer T-shirt. She had the sleeves rolled to display the faint lines of muscle in her arms. She was wearing high-top Vans and short shorts. All of it should have looked slovenly and yet. "Fuckin' hot."

"Let's go before Russ has a heart attack." She grabbed my hand and dragged me out the door.

CHAPTER EIGHTEEN

The building was Victorian. Tall narrow windows lined the far wall. A narrow pseudo-balcony ran the length of the facade on the third floor. I pushed one of the windows out. The ancient wood creaked and released a faint shower of dust and leaded paint into the plants hanging from the rail. Below me, the proper balcony was set for dining. There was no way it was legal to have the windows open, but I wasn't going to ask for permission. The restaurant was on the taller west side of Thackerton's main boulevard. The black night and shower of stars were naked enough to feel obscene. The treetops beyond were more of a rumor than reality. I knew they were there, but I couldn't see them.

"I'm fairly certain someone will take issue with you sitting in that window." Wylie handed me a drink.

I leaned back against the window casement and took a deep breath. The cool air tasted sharp like gin. My drink smelled warm like pine. "Naw. I'm a movie star."

"Well, in that case." Wy pushed open the next window over. She straddled the windowsill and propped one foot on the rail of the balcony. Half her face was blocked by the window frame between us. She smiled and saluted me with her drink.

"The headlines are going to be gorgeous," I said.

"What headlines?" she asked.

"Final girls' final fall."

Wy laughed. "It'll sell the fuck out of the movie."

"Oh, then let's wait to die until after we wrap."

"Deal." She held out her glass and I tapped mine against it.

"There they are!" Diego shouted. He spilled into the room. His usual MO was to fill space with noise. Instead, he stopped suddenly enough that Teddy ran into him. "What the fuck are you guys doing? Get out of the windows." Diego waved us toward him.

"It's fine," I said.

"It is absolutely not fine. You're going to fall and die and I'll be sad and probably carry a lifetime of guilt for not having prevented it." He reached back and braced himself against the doorframe.

"Bro. It's fine." Teddy slid past him and crossed the room to hug Wy and shake my hand.

"Theodore, back away from the window," Diego said. It really wasn't clear if he was kidding.

"My name isn't Theodore," Teddy said.

I looked up at him in question. "Really?"

"Edmund," he said.

"Oh, shit. Yeah, Teddy is the right call," I said.

"What about you? What's PJ short for?"

Wy laughed. "It's not. Her legal name is PJ. Her mom thought it was quirky."

"No way." Teddy braced his arm against the wall and leaned out over my head to look at the stars beyond. "Shit, that's pretty."

"Guys. Seriously. Can you please come inside?" Diego had backed up so his shoulders were pressed to the wall.

"Wait. Are you serious?" Wy asked.

Diego nodded. He was breathing hard.

"You're afraid of heights?" she asked.

He swallowed and nodded. "It's bad. And I know it's dumb. But I really want to make fun of Teddy for being named Edmund, but I can't even think, you know?"

Wy shot me a look. "Fine," I said. I stood. Wy swung around and climbed out.

"Good. Now can you close those?" Diego asked.

Wylie gave him an indulgent look and closed the windows. "How do you ever film anything with heights?"

"Thanks." He took a deep breath and stepped into the room. It was a long, open space. Much too big for our small party. "I, uh, don't."

"You don't film anything with heights?" Wy asked.

He shook his head. "It's in my contract. I can film by windows or on balconies, but I have to take Xanax and meditate. It's like a whole process. I just wasn't expecting it here."

"Holy shit." I snapped and pointed. "Lenny rewrote your death scene because of this."

Diego nodded. He was looking more calm now that we were safely inside and the danger had passed. A waiter led Rosie in and dropped off Teddy's and Diego's drinks. Diego asked for water as well.

"Why do you all look so tense? Can we sit?" Rosie pointed at the long table in the center of the room.

"We don't all look tense. Just sweet lil' baby Diego." Teddy squeezed Diego's shoulder as they sat next to each other.

"Fuck off. Edmund." Diego shrugged Teddy's hand off.

Teddy laughed. "It was my grandfather's name."

"You know Edmund is nothing like Teddy, right?" Wy asked. "Like you see that?"

"Oh, I know. I'm not the one who came up with it. But, for the record, Teddy is a common nickname for people named like Edward or Edgar."

"Common? Or it was common a hundred years ago and now your parents are just assholes?" I asked.

"Fair enough. My grandfather went by Ted. So I became Teddy," he said.

"How exactly did we get to the origins of Teddy's name?" Rosie asked.

Teddy launched into an explanation that included a dramatic re-creation of Diego's panic. He was on the floor, gasping for air when Logan walked in followed by Kayleigh and Molly holding hands. Luckily for Diego, that shifted conversation to an entirely different type of teasing.

"What. Is. Happening?" Diego asked.

"What do you mean?" Molly asked.

Diego pointed. "This. What?"

Logan gripped Diego's shoulder as he sat next to him. "KK and Mol? That's been happening for months."

"No, it hasn't. We would know about it," Teddy said.

"Months," Molly said.

"Umm, hi." Kayleigh waved with their free hand.

Diego got up so he could shake their hand. "Hey. Hi, Kayleigh. Diego. Have you been dating Molly for months?"

"So nice to meet you, Diego. And, yes, it's been about eight months," Kayleigh said.

Diego turned to stare at me and Wylie. "What. Is. Happening?"

"You didn't know about it?" I asked. I was fucking with him. This was definitely the first I was hearing about Kayleigh dating one of my cast members.

"You knew too?" Teddy asked.

"Is this because we're straight cis guys? Are you discriminating against us?" Diego asked.

"Yes. Absolutely," Molly said. She and Kayleigh sat across from Diego.

"It's literally all over the lesbian internet," Logan said.

"But you're not a lesbian," Diego said.

Logan shrugged. "I was one once."

"Parsons, did you know about this?" Diego asked.

"No. Neither did PJ. She's messing with you," Wylie said.

Diego's jaw dropped and he gave me the most over-the-top awestruck look. "You're a real asshole, you know that?"

"I've been called worse."

"Are you all being serious? You really didn't know?" Molly asked.

"No. How would we know?" Diego shouted.

Teddy sighed. "I didn't know either."

"They hard launched on Insta months ago," Logan said.

"Oh, well, if they hard launched I guess I should have known," Diego said.

Emma chose that moment to arrive. She looked around the room before landing on me. "What's wrong with Diego?"

"He just found out Molly and Kayleigh are dating," I said.

Emma sat in the last seat. "He just found out? They've been dating for months."

Diego stared at Emma, finally rendered silent. Teddy put his arm around Diego's shoulders and squeezed. "It's okay, buddy," Teddy said.

Diego looked around the table. "No one else is secretly dating, right?"

"It wasn't a secret," Molly said.

"Whatever. An open secret." He zeroed in on me. "You're not actually sleeping with Parsons, are you?"

"Jesus. No. She's married," I said. Maybe too vehemently. But he'd hit a little too close to Jocelyn's accusations for comfort.

"Actually, I'm divorcing my wife," Wylie said.

Everyone except Diego turned to stare at Wylie. Diego just started laughing. I was right there with them. Especially Diego with his maniacal laughter.

"Shit. You almost had me," Diego said.

"I'm serious. My lawyer is drawing up paperwork. And my manager is already coordinating with the studio to decide when to announce in conjunction with the film's release," Wy said. "Welcome to Hollywood, kids. Even your divorces are marketed."

I said nothing. I was wavering between annoyance that she'd neglected to tell me during our discussion thirty minutes earlier and annoyance that she chose to announce to the whole cast—and apparently the studio—rather than tell me. Then again, it wasn't really my business. Wylie could get married and divorced with impunity.

"Oh, wow. You're serious. I'm sorry, babe," Rosie said.

Wy shrugged. "It is what it is."

Diego turned to me. "What did you do?"

"Me? I didn't do anything," I said. I tamped down my sudden rush of anger.

"Come on. I may be out of the lesbian internet loop, but even I know you two are endgame," Diego said. There was a thump under the table and Diego jumped. "Ow. Dick." He glared at Molly.

"They're real people. Don't apply fictional standards to them," Molly said.

Diego rubbed his leg. "I was just fucking around."

"I didn't even know she was getting a divorce," I said. If Wy could drop bombs, so could I.

"You didn't even tell the love of your life that you're getting a divorce?" Diego sounded a little too incredulous. Molly kicked him again. "Ow!"

"Mol, he's filming a nude scene in two days. Don't bruise him," I said.

"I'm defending your honor, boss," she said.

"And my honor appreciates it."

"Leave him alone, honey. He's having a rough night," Kayleigh said to Molly.

"I am?" Diego considered then agreed. "I am."

"He just found out he's being discriminated against as a cis het man. Which is absolutely a thing," Kayleigh said, her voice full of sympathy.

Diego leaned over to Logan. "They're picking on me."

"I don't want to say you invited it, but you kind of invited it," Logan said.

"I'm sorry," Rosie cut in. "I know Diego likes to be the center of attention, but I want to know more about the divorce. What happened? Are you okay?" she asked Wy.

Wy shrugged and carefully avoided my eye. "We had different ideas about what our marriage was."

"So it wasn't your wife trying to eye-fuck Addy?" Molly asked. Diego kicked Molly this time. "Ow. Dick," she said.

Wylie looked confused. "When was this?"

"Any time they were in a room together," Molly said. Kayleigh was watching Molly's face. The rest of the cast were looking intently at the ceiling or table or their nails. "What? They're getting divorced. We can talk about it now."

"I'm sorry. You all saw this?" Wy asked. The confidence with which she'd announced her impending divorce had drained away. Now she just sounded sick.

"Come on, Parsons. You knew, right? It was kind of disturbingly obvious," Logan said.

"No. I didn't."

"Oh."

Silence descended. It was painful. Socially awkward, sure. But the hurt etched on Wy's face outweighed my irritation.

"I'm sorry. I don't think I'm up for dinner." Wy stood. "Is that okay?" She directed the question at me.

"Yeah. Yeah. Totally," I said.

She left. I drank my gin and tonic and ignored the faces of my cast slowly turning to stare at me.

"Are you serious?" Diego asked.

"What?"

"You're really not going after her?"

"You guys really need to let go of this idea of me and Wy. We're just friends," I said.

"Uh. Yeah. That's the point," Rosie said. "A friend wouldn't let her be alone right now." She was right. Damn it.

"Shit." I stood. "Kayleigh, working with you was fantastic. Let me know if you want to make more movies, okay?"

"Yeah?" they asked. "Thanks. It was way better than I expected."

"Good. I'm glad. I have to go now." I pointedly looked at Diego, then everyone else. "Be nice to Kayleigh. Have a good time tonight."

They called out their good-byes as I jogged down the stairs. I emerged onto the busy street. No sign of Wylie. The cars from the studio were down the block waiting for us. I couldn't be sure, but I didn't think any of them were missing. After another scan of the street, I turned left and started walking. At the end of the main stretch, I turned again and walked along the river. The road curved back toward the strip of old Craftsman and Victorian houses that sat above the main street. I went down a narrow gravel driveway that opened up into Jed's parking lot.

Wylie was inside sitting at the bar. She already had a beer in front of her. Only two inches were gone. Jed saw me approaching and started pouring a beer for me. He set it next to her. She looked up at him in confusion. He nodded toward me. She turned and slumped when she saw me.

"I'm sorry. I just couldn't do it. I know it's unprofessional to leave halfway through a cast dinner," she said.

"Are you serious?" I sat and propped my forearms on the bar.

"About what?"

"You're allowed to have feelings. Like, yeah, probably not the best way to announce your divorce, but I'm thinking you didn't intend to do it that way," I said.

"No. No, I wasn't planning it. It just kind of came out."

"Is it okay if I sit here with you for a bit?" I asked.

"Yeah. I guess that would be all right." She leaned sideways against my shoulder.

I drank some of my beer. Wy breathed deep and wrapped her hands around my arm. I kissed the top of her head. My irritation suddenly felt petty. I was so involved in my movie and my performance and my self-imposed role that I'd completely ignored Wy's obvious distress. Sure, in two days we were filming a scene that would require us to be naked and making out for hours on end. And I definitely had about thirty-seven meetings tomorrow. And, yes, all of that made my life complicated in the short term. But Wylie was staring at the rest of her life and taking account. I wouldn't speculate on her feelings even though I could make some guesses. What I did know was that Rosie was right. Wy needed a friend.

CHAPTER NINETEEN

"Come in," I called at the knock.

Emma stuck her head in. "Hey, boss. I'm early. Is that okay?"

"Yeah." I waved her into my trailer. "Grab a seat. Russ said you like Topo Chico." I held up the glass bottle of mineral water.

"Heck yeah. Wait. Do you want something from me? Is this a subtle way to get me to agree to something I don't want to do?" She sat at the table across from where my open notebook and script were.

I laughed. "No. I just think it's good form to make people comfortable. Especially when we're talking about filming sex scenes."

She turned faintly pink. "I was half kidding."

"Don't make it a thing, kid. Directors are assholes to young actors. You're right to ask." I grabbed my own water. "You want a glass or do you like the bottle?" Russ had already told me she preferred the bottle, but I asked for good measure.

"Bottle. All the way."

"You got it." I set our drinks and sat across from her. "Okay, I'm going to say this until you get sick of it. I want you to be comfortable. If you're not comfortable, tell me. Even if it's not rational or it feels silly."

Emma smiled. "Got it. I trust you."

That was a solid start. I asked some questions about what sort of touching she was and wasn't comfortable with. We reviewed the nudity in her contract. Then I outlined the basics of the sex scene we would be filming. We both took notes, though probably very different ones. She asked a couple of questions about blocking. When we got to her character's motivation, I stopped her.

"So this is one of the reasons I wanted to meet privately. I mean, delicate material and all that, but I'll still want to meet with you and Diego together before filming," I said.

"Sure." She drew it out. "What did I just miss?"

"Nothing yet. I'm going to tell you something, but it cannot leave this room."

Emma nodded, looking very serious. And then she stopped nodding and started smiling. "Shut up. Is it me?"

I grinned back. "You're the killer."

"No way! How? I mean, I can't be Black Hat." She leaned closer with every sentence.

"He's your brother. In the final showdown, he's going to be killed pretty quickly, but then you'll put on his hat and take his knife and slaughter a few more people."

Emma's face lit up and she started to bounce. "This is so fucking cool."

"You're going to be great."

"Oh, I am. I'm going to nail this."

"I know you are," I said. Lenny had given me two choices and this was absolutely the right one. "We're going to schedule you with Arjun later this week. He's altered a couple of black hats so we can make sure they will look right on you. We want it to be a little big, but we don't want you to swim in it. It's a delicate balance."

"Yeah, totally." She was still grinning. "Okay, so Arjun knows. Anyone else? I don't want to blow it."

"Hannah, Claude, Scottie, Russ. It's a small group and they've known for weeks so if it leaks, we'll know it's you."

Emma suddenly was very serious. "It won't. I won't tell anyone."

"Perfect." I grinned. "This is where it gets fun. During your scene with Xavier, you're going to look over and lock eyes with Black Hat."

"Oh, creepy incest killers." She chuckled at herself.

"Basically, yeah. Y'all aren't fucking, but you have an unconventional relationship."

"Well, we're killing together so that's pretty unconventional."

"Exactly," I said.

"But Diego can't know."

"No, he can't. I'll call it emotional distance while we're rehearsing and filming."

"Will Black Hat be on set?" she asked.

"No, we'll splice him in during edits. But we'll have a marker in place for you."

"Got it. When in the scene will this happen?" She turned back to her script and flipped back and forth between a couple of pages.

"Here." I leaned over and showed her my blocking notes.

"Oh, that makes sense." She read through and copied part of my notes onto her script. "And how long will the eye contact last?"

"I'm actually not sure. We'll shoot enough for Phil to work with. He and I will make that determination later."

"Sounds good."

"Okay. Do you want to like jump around or dance to get your excitement out? Because once you leave…"

"Once I leave, I'll be feeling great because this conversation about getting topless and sexy on screen is the easiest one I've ever had with a director." She gave me a shy smile. "Besides, Rosie is the only one who will notice my mood. And she'll accept that explanation."

"Great. Cool." I stood. "I'm meeting with Diego later today. Natasha will be here tomorrow morning."

"She's the intimacy coordinator?"

"Yes. You'll dig her."

"Okay, so we all will meet tomorrow morning and then we film in the afternoon?" Emma asked.

"You got it."

At the door, Emma turned back. "Could I get a hug? This has been a lot."

"Yeah, of course." I hugged her.

She squeezed and sighed before letting go. "Thanks, boss."

❖

The swimming hole we were shooting in was two hours south of Thackerton. It boasted an enviable lack of water movement. The river running through Thackerton was fast, cold, and rocky. Basically dangerous in every way it could be. This little slice of river moved at a nice sedate pace and the shoreline invited lazing about. Of course, it was still freezing cold because—like every other river in Northern California—it was made of snow runoff. Diego and Emma were wrapped in thick robes so they didn't have to hang out on set in very tiny bathing suits but also so they wouldn't be shivering when it came time to film.

"I got to tell you I'm worried, boss," Diego said.

I gave him my full attention. This was the moment I'd been prepping for. I was ready to do anything possible to make sure he and Emma were perfectly comfortable. "Oh, okay. What's going on?"

"That water is cold. Shrinkage could be a real issue," he said very seriously.

"Huh?"

"My penis, boss. I'm worried about my penis." He held his serious expression for all of ten seconds before bursting into laughter.

"Wow. I sure do love discussing penises. Especially yours," I said.

"Hannah said you're trying to do a reversal with objectification. I just don't want you to be disappointed." He paused and made sure I was looking at him before continuing. "By my penis."

"Don't worry. Arjun has a backup swimsuit with padding in case your penis is disappointing on film." Turnabout was fair play. If he wanted to make me discuss his genitals, I'd take it seriously.

Diego started laughing again. "Damn."

Hannah thankfully interrupted. "We ready?"

"You ready?" I asked Diego.

"Let's do this." He took off the robe.

We had a bare-bones crew. Filming a nude scene was awkward enough without fifteen unnecessary PAs watching. As such, most of the crew had left their assistants behind. It felt intimate, which was probably good. Natasha was hovering close enough to intervene, but separate. She was the best intimacy coordinator I'd ever worked with. Which was why I insisted the studio hire her. She was about twenty years older than me and had a very no-nonsense grandmother energy. But like a hot grandmother. It was confusing.

I was damn glad we'd gotten her if for no other reason than to have her dictate my own sex scene. Every time I'd tried to block it, I just panicked and gave up. Turns out that blocking a sex scene that you're in is basically just daydreaming about fucking your costar. And in my case, that costar had been worked up about her wife for the last week, which made sexy daydreaming about her awkward if not downright inappropriate. Hannah had some thoughts for the scene, thankfully. Natasha was my ace though. She'd tell us what to do and where to put our hands and tongues.

Normally, I was good at this. Sex scenes were just like any other action scene. You were telling a story with bodies and movement instead of dialogue. That was my jam. Granted, I was struggling with framing Xavier's genitals but that was only because I didn't really understand why his genitals were attractive. How would I know what to highlight? It was good Hannah was attracted to men. She could objectify Xavier—respectfully—all day.

We spent a good forty-five minutes filming Xavier standing up out of the water. Ava was stretched out on a towel in the background. The frame started on Ava, then the focus rapidly shifted as Xavier stood in the foreground. The shot ended with his swim trunks to the center right, filling half the screen. The short, loose material of the swimsuit clung to his dick. Water dripped from the bulge and ran down his legs. In the background, Ava was gorgeous and sexy and yet entirely overshadowed by Xavier.

"Is it exactly as you imagined?" I asked Hannah. We were leaning close to the screen in the center of video village.

"It really is. It's so beautiful." She gave me a dreamy smile. If I didn't know that we were looking at glorified dick pics, I'd think she was watching baby ducklings befriend a cat or something.

"And that's why I put you in charge here."

"Is this the most you've ever stared at a guy's dick?" Hannah asked.

I nodded. "And it's not even close."

"Okay, I'm going to review blocking with Diego and Natasha. You take Emma," she said.

"Sounds like a plan."

We split. Hannah went to show Diego which rocks were soft pads painted to look like rocks so he wouldn't injure Emma or himself. I took Emma to the side, far enough away that Diego couldn't hear or see us.

"Look over my right shoulder. There's a small cluster of leaves painted purple. You see them?" I asked.

Emma nodded. "Yep. That's where Black Hat will be?"

"You got it."

"Okay. So Diego will lift me up so I'm sitting on that rock and then you're doing a slow pan up to my face?"

"Yeah, he'll be going down on you so the camera will trace up his back. His head will cover your crotch. Then we get boobs, then face."

"I'm thinking I'll start with looking down at him, then very obviously turn and stare at brother dearest," Emma said.

"Yes, that sounds perfect."

"Can I play with Xavier's hair? Like I'm directing him?" she asked.

"I think so. Let's ask. Make sure Diego is okay with it."

Natasha saw us approaching and waved us closer. "Good timing. We need to talk hand placement for the lift."

"I can do ass or hips," Diego said. "What's your preference?"

Emma shrugged. "I don't have strong feelings. What will look better?"

"Let's try it and see," I said.

They took off the robes again. Diego grabbed Emma's hips, lifted, and set her on the rock. Then he helped her down and tried it again but lifting her butt this time.

"What do you think?" I asked Hannah.

"Actually, I think I like hips. Butt seems obvious. And his arms look better with the hip lift."

"Agreed. Plus setting her down is more seamless."

Emma leaned on Diego's wide, bare shoulder and called to us. "What do you think?"

"Did one feel better to you?" I asked.

"Not really."

"Cool. We liked hips," I said.

"I gotchu." Diego lifted Emma back down. It was unnecessary, but they had an easy intimacy already. They strolled back to where Hannah and Natasha and I were watching from.

"I wanted to ask if I could play with your hair while you're going down on me?" Emma asked Diego.

He grinned and nodded. "Yeah, that'll be good. Wait. Are you thinking like soft sexy playing?"

"No, more like I'm directing you, I think," she said.

"Good. Perfect. Xavier needs direction."

"He really does. He's a very silly boy." Emma ruffled his hair.

We shot a ton of footage of the initial kiss. Xavier started by pulling Ava to her feet. He continued the motion so she was flush against him. They kissed and kissed. We got footage that made it look like he was untying her bathing suit top. In reality, Xavier couldn't get the thing untied to save his life. He dropped the top on the ground. They did the lift and landed hard against the rocks. She arched against him.

The pan up Xavier's back to Ava's stomach to her breasts to her face was exquisite. She turned and looked directly at her marker. And then she smiled subtly. Just a quirk at the side of her lips. Then she opened her mouth a little and arched again. It was everything I wanted and more.

Ultimately, I had nothing to complain about. The whole shoot had gone off without a hitch. My actors were happy. The film was great. But the closer we got to finishing the scene, the closer we got to filming the next sex scene. Natasha was only here for a day. It was a tight turnaround. We'd shoot a pretty intense make out with Benny and Sadie later tonight. But the bulk of the evening was dedicated to Grace and Taylor getting sexy. Sure, Lenny had rewritten it so it wasn't soft core porn, but it was still a sex scene. With my costar ex. Who was giving me whiplash between pissing me off and making me feel bad for her.

CHAPTER TWENTY

It was just after ten p.m. and Hannah, Natasha, Wylie, and I were sitting on set at the Durant ranch kitchen table. We could see the entryway, the hallway, and the living room where the scene was set. Drew and his team were rigging lights in the living room and ignoring our conversation. Hannah's notes had gotten us through the front door and to the hallway. Apparently, she assumed her director would take over from there. Which was quite presumptuous of her. They were all being exceedingly tolerant of having to block and rehearse thirty minutes before filming.

"The couch is an obstacle. Do you want to go around it to the left? Or you can vault over it?" Hannah pointed with her pen so we could see the trajectory she was imagining.

"We could fall over it," Wy said. "Like if one of us pushed the other backward onto the cushions?"

"Oh. Ohh." Hannah grabbed my forearm. "Can you lift her?"

I looked at Wylie and shrugged. "I don't know. I could when we were younger. But I'm old now."

"Let's try it," Natasha said. "If you can, Hannah will walk us through what she's thinking."

"You up for it?" I asked Wy.

"Yeah." She stood and looked around. "Where do you want us?"

"Start against that wall." Hannah pointed. "You're making out, then Taylor lifts Grace. Then you walk with her over to the couch and set her down on the back."

"Got it," I said.

Wy leaned back against the wall. I pressed close as if we were kissing. She smelled like lemons and mint.

"Okay, now reach down and grab her thighs," Hannah said.

I crouched a little and slid my hands around her thighs. Wy gripped my shoulders to steady herself as I lifted.

"Good. Grace, put your arms around her neck."

Wylie wrapped her arms behind my head. "You okay?" she asked.

"I'm good."

"Back up from the wall. See if you can walk comfortably with her," Hannah said.

I took a step back. Wy tightened her legs around my waist. As she clenched her muscles, she rose up a little so I had a face full of boobs. My glasses got knocked askew and Wylie laughed.

"Sorry." She leaned back and adjusted my glasses so they were back on my nose.

"All good." I grinned at her. This suddenly felt silly.

"That's perfect. Now set her on the couch," Hannah said.

When I set Wy down, she dropped her hands onto my back. The warmth of her palms soaked into my shoulder blades. "What do you think?" I asked Wy.

"It felt good. I think we can make that work," she said. "You? Was it comfortable?"

"Yeah. It didn't feel like a struggle at all." I backed up and offered her my hand so she could jump down.

"That was great. Natural. Hot." Hannah waved us back to the table. She set her phone face up. It had a photo of me lifting Wy. Hannah swiped to a second photo where Wy had her legs wrapped around me. I didn't know she'd been taking pictures, but I appreciated it. It gave me a visual. "Here's my thought," Hannah said. "The original *DSN* had that iconic leg grab. So we're playing on that image, but expanding it."

"Shit. That's fantastic," I said. It wouldn't be a true redux without the leg grab. Fans of the franchise would eat it up. Plus it was a nice evolution of Grace and Taylor's relationship.

"You'll have to be intentional with your hand placement." Hannah swiped back to another picture where she was zoomed in on Wylie's thigh as I grabbed it. I could easily see the parallel she was aiming for. "Because we want it to be obvious to anyone who's looking for it."

"That shouldn't be difficult for you," Wy said. "This is great, Hannah."

From there it was a matter of deciding when and how clothing would be removed. Hannah sold me on keeping Taylor's boots and pants on. She had a vision of Grace shoving her hand down the front of Taylor's jeans.

I had a decent idea of what Hannah was thinking, but more importantly, I loved where her head was at. She was taking charge, which was good from a mentorship standpoint, and even better from an on-the-edge-of-disassociating standpoint. And I really was. I kept having flashes of hayloft make outs—two weeks ago, ten years ago. Our first on-screen sex scene. Three days later when we'd actually slept together for the first time. Last week when Wy told me she'd never love anyone the way she'd loved me. Two nights ago when she told me she felt more stupid for thinking her marriage could last than sad that it was over. The lines between Wylie and Grace, me and Taylor had always been permeable. The flow of time from the past to the present had never felt emotionally linear. So I sat paralyzed on the cusp of a very technically manageable scene, thinking about what the inside of Wylie's mouth tasted like and pretending that I was indifferent.

We broke so Hannah could finalize the set and Wy and I could change clothing and get hair and makeup. Natasha went to crafty for another cup of tea. On the way back to set, I met up with Wylie.

"How you holding up today?" I asked. It was the first time we'd been alone since Jed's.

"Much better actually. I needed to reframe my anger and my sadness, you know?"

"Sure."

She smiled. "You're just agreeing with me, aren't you?"

"Yep. I have no idea what that means."

She laughed. "The whole thing just kind of blindsided me. So I needed to understand what I was upset about, who I was upset with. Does that make sense?"

"Yes, that I can follow," I said.

"I had a good session with my therapist yesterday." She shot me an odd look. "And then I talked to your mom last night."

I didn't react with either mockery or irritation, which I thought showed growth. "And that helped?"

"I know you think Gerri is a lot, but she's pretty wonderful."

"Yeah, I get it. But she's easier when she's not your mom. Her expectations shift," I said.

"You don't need to convince me. I remember what it was like when you were twenty-six and she still insisted on driving you places because you didn't have a license."

"And she could never seem to find the documentation I needed when I made a DMV appointment."

Wylie put on an affected Geraldine accent. "But she certainly wasn't trying to prevent you from getting your license."

I laughed at the too-accurate impression. "She would never."

"But she did keep you from becoming a child star statistic," Wy said carefully.

"She's the one who made me a child star!"

"She's a complicated woman."

I sighed. This was an old conversation for me. I'd had it with countless friends, girlfriends, costars. When Gerri was good, she was wonderful. When she was bad, she was fair to middling. "But she helped you?"

"Yeah, she helped me."

"Good."

Hannah and Natasha were waiting on set for us. "There they are." Hannah stood. "You two ready?"

Wylie took my hand and started swinging them back and forth. "Yeah, let's go guarantee an R rating."

"It's a horror movie. If the violence doesn't get us an R rating, I'm not sure we deserve it," I said.

"Will you shut up and fuck me?"

Wy was only teasing, but I still got wet. So that was cool. Not at all uncomfortable.

"Okay, we're starting with the lift because that's the most physically taxing." Hannah pointed to the markers taped on the floor.

"Wow. So you don't think I'll be able to do it when I'm tired? That hurts," I said.

"There's no speculation here. I know you won't be able to do it when you get tired," she said with a straight face.

"Don't get mad at Hannah for telling the truth." Wy found her marker and dragged me by my shirt so I was standing directly in front of her.

Hannah stepped close and studied our clothing. "You two are fully engaged in the make out at this point. Let's have Grace's shirt unbuttoned."

"Sure. Why not?" Wy started unbuttoning her shirt.

Hannah nodded until she got a look at the bra Wylie was wearing. "Did you approve that bra, Addy?"

I looked at Wylie's tits. For my job. She was wearing a navy cotton bra with cream lace detailing on the underside of the cup. It was not the bra I'd approved. "No."

"Dammit." Hannah grabbed her walkie and stomped off.

Wylie leaned back against the wall and casually tugged her shirt closed. It didn't really do much for coverage. Not that I was looking.

Hannah marched back. She was not happy. "What underwear are you wearing?" she asked me.

I tugged my waistband down but the jeans and belt didn't have much give. "The black boyshorts."

Hannah leaned close and looked down my pants. She stared at my underwear with a critical eye. "Bra?"

"None. Isn't that what we decided?"

"Yeah. That's good."

Arjun's assistant sprinted across the lot, and within five minutes, Wy was in the proper bra. This one was also navy cotton but without the lace. Her tits spilled ever so slightly out of the cups whenever she moved.

"Okay, let's give this another go." The marker snapped and Hannah called action.

Wylie played her fingers over my neck, the pressure at once firm and delicate. She kissed me slowly. Then she opened her mouth just a little. I pressed deeper. She moaned and the vibration lit through me. I slid my hands down to her thighs and lifted. She wrapped her legs around me. As I crossed the room to set her on the back of the couch, she tugged at the back of my shirt. When I set her down, she pulled away just long enough to strip my T-shirt off.

I kissed up her neck and pushed her shirt off her shoulders. The movement pressed my chest against hers. It would look hot on camera, but it would also keep my nudity solidly in the side-boob arena.

Wylie clutched at my shoulders while I unbuttoned her jeans. When I started to tug her pants off, we tipped back over the couch. Wylie laughed quietly as we went over.

"Cut," Hannah said.

I turned and caught the T-shirt Hannah had tossed to me. "How'd we do?" I asked as I pulled the shirt on.

"Fucking great." She waved us over to the monitor. "On the next take we're going to focus on the T-shirt removal. Grace, take your time pulling it up."

"Do you want me to just go slow? Or am I doing anything extra with it?" Wy asked.

"Both. If you could pull it tight like you're doing here." Hannah paused the video and pointed. "I like the lines you're creating in the shirt. It directs the eye up to your hand."

"Got it."

We ran through the lift a few more times. Between the making out and the sensation of Wy's chest pressed against mine, I was getting uncomfortably wet. Usually, that would only be PJ knowledge. But one of the next shots was Wylie sticking her hand down my underwear.

Scottie's team repositioned the cameras to get our fall onto the couch. The first three times we did it, Wylie and I screwed up the fall so the camera caught way too much nudity. The fourth time, Wylie kept her hand firmly around my waist and was able to keep our torsos pressed together. We reset and managed to fall correctly again.

Generally, sex scenes were decidedly unsexy. Too much careful positioning. Too many people watching on even the most closed sets. This scene, however, was fucking with my head. Maybe it was hard to maintain my professionalism while making out with someone I'd slept with. Of course, Wylie and I had filmed a fair amount of these scenes in the last ten years and it hadn't gotten to me before. Not like this.

When we got to the point where I was supposed to strip off Wy's pants, then kiss her stomach, I suddenly found that I wasn't alone. I could smell how turned on she was. Which made me feel better about objectifying her and much, much worse about finishing the scene. It made me question each movement and moan. Was she performing or was she feeling what I was feeling?

Natasha did her job to the letter, of course. But she was operating with only half the information. She couldn't very well compensate for us being wildly turned on since she didn't know about it. By the time we wrapped for the evening, I was dehydrated and aroused and exhausted. Hannah tried to discuss the next day's call sheet, but I just stared at her bleary-eyed.

Wylie put her hand on my shoulder. "Hannah, we're dead on our feet. Can't you review this in the morning?"

"Yeah. Sorry." Hannah dropped the clipboard she was showing me. "Go get some sleep."

"Come on, let's head back." Wylie took my hand and tugged me out the door. We walked to the waiting car, but she didn't let go of my hand.

The ten-minute drive from set to our cabins was excruciating. Whatever exhaustion I'd been feeling leeched away with the sensation of Wy's fingers entwined with mine. Each passing moment heightened the feeling until all I was aware of was the gentle heat of her hand and her breathing in the quiet car.

The driver dropped us at the mouth of the path leading to the private cabins. The sky was just starting to turn navy from black. The treetops to the east were becoming faint silhouettes. We walked down the path, winding between towering pines that littered the walkway with brittle, dry needles.

Wylie stopped. She looked up at the dark canopy and inhaled the cool biting pine air. Then she pushed me off the path until my back was pressed to the wide trunk and kissed me. It was sweet and soft considering the heavy making out we'd been doing for the last few hours. There was something simple and genuine in it. She held the kiss for a moment. Long enough to remove any doubt about the nature of her intentions.

She pulled back. "I thought you should know."

"Know what?"

"You're not the only one who feels it." She smiled and walked away.

CHAPTER TWENTY-ONE

A ddy? Addy, wake up." Someone was shaking my shoulder. I had a flash of Wylie kissing me the night before, and warmth spread through my body.

I reluctantly opened my eyes. Russ was leaning over me. "What?" I realized Russ wouldn't come into my cabin and wake me unless something dire happened. The warmth left. I sat up. "Shit. What's wrong?"

"Everyone's fine. Paulie asked me to wake you."

"Why?"

Russ shook her head. "Here." She handed me my phone. "I'm going to make coffee."

I stared at the phone in my hand. Paulie was on the line. This couldn't be good. "Hello?"

"Addy. Sorry for waking you. And waking Chloe."

"It's fine. What's going on?" I checked the time. Just after five a.m. I'd been asleep for an hour.

"They dropped all charges against Sean," Paulie said.

"What?"

"They suddenly decided they didn't have a case. All charges have been dropped."

"Fuck. Shit. God fucking dammit." I got out of bed and tried to find pants.

"The announcement dropped fifteen minutes ago. It's all over the news, but when the West Coast wakes up, it's going to explode."

"No fucking shit."

"The studio hasn't released a statement, but I honestly don't know how they are going to react."

"They wouldn't be stupid enough to continue working with him," I said. Paulie didn't respond. "Right, Paulie? Tell me they wouldn't bring him back."

"They can. Contractually."

I stopped trying to wrestle pants on one-handed. "What do you mean?"

"He's still an EP. I didn't push to remove him because he was facing a wall of serious charges. I didn't think he was a threat. I'm sorry." He stopped and I could hear his breathing. "Christ, I'm so sorry. We were negotiating to get your whole team in place and I just dropped the ball."

I was livid, but I knew I wasn't mad at Paulie. "It didn't occur to me either."

"Well, I'm still sorry."

"You know how you can make it up to me?"

"Anything."

"Find out Oath's plan. Like now. Drive to Danny's house and wake his ass up. Buy Mick and Nelson breakfast. I don't care what you do. But get me information."

"You got it," Paulie said.

"Has Cary talked to Taryn yet?"

"He's on his way to her house right now."

"She's in LA?" I asked.

"Yeah. We're hiring additional security to keep the paparazzi away. And make sure she feels safe, of course."

"Okay. Good. That's good. Keep me updated."

"Will do."

I hung up and sat on the end of my bed. Today was going to be hell. The rest of this goddamn shoot was going to be hell. This was a mess. And no matter how fucked up I was about it, Taryn was going to be worse. I looked at my phone and made a decision. I tapped Gerri's name. It rang for a while before she answered.

"Hello? Sweet P, are you okay?"

"Hey, Ma. I'm okay."

"What's going on? It's early," she said.

"I know. I'm sorry for waking you up. I kinda thought I'd get your voice mail."

"No. Your calls always come through." Of course they did. She wasn't tech savvy, but she wouldn't risk missing me calling. "What's going on?" she asked.

"They dropped the charges against Sean Murray."

She gasped. "Why? Oh, no. I'm so sorry."

"Yeah. I'm sorry too. It's bullshit."

"Oh, God. How's everyone else? Is Taryn okay? Does Wylie know?"

"That's actually why I'm calling. Wy and I are on set together. But I'm worried about Taryn," I said.

"You want me to fly to LA?" she immediately asked.

"Would you?"

"Yes, of course."

I finally breathed a bit easier. "Thanks, Ma. You're the best."

"The poor thing must be devastated."

"Probably. This is a fucking mess."

"Don't worry about Taryn. You just finish that film. Then we'll go somewhere beautiful and isolated and you can lounge on a beach. How does that sound?"

"Honestly, great," I said. Russ came back upstairs with a mug of coffee. She set it on the bedside table and sat in the chair in the corner of the loft. "Okay, I have to go. But Russ will book you a flight for this morning. She'll email you details."

Russ pulled out her phone. She didn't even know who I was talking to or where they were flying, but she was ready to go.

"Sounds good. I love you."

"Love you too, Ma. Bye."

"Bye."

"Your mom coming here?" Russ asked.

"LA. I'm sending her to Taryn."

"Of course. What's the plan for you today?"

"Fuck." I didn't have a plan. "I guess I need to check in with Claude. And probably warn Wy." I rubbed my eyes. They felt sticky and gritty. "I'm at the mercy of the studio. Paulie is tracking down the execs to get some answers." I was at a loss of what to do. All I had was unfocused anger.

"Okay. Go jump in the shower." Russ nodded at the bathroom. "I'll get your mom booked while you do that. Then we can wake Claude and Wylie."

"Great. Sounds good. Thanks."

"I got you." She went downstairs.

I chugged my coffee. Russ had added my traditional four ice cubes to make it perfectly drinkable. By the time I was showered and dressed, Russ was already on the phone with someone.

"He's right. That doesn't bode well." She turned and saw me coming downstairs. "She's here. I'll update her. Keep me in the loop. Thanks." She hung up. "Paulie's office," she told me.

"What's the latest?" I asked.

"Paulie can't get any of them on the phone or in person. They're shutting him out. He thinks they're already meeting with Sean's people."

"Fucking assholes."

"Yep." She handed me my watch and a key. "That's Wylie's key. I'm going to wake up Claude's assistant. Well, he's probably already awake. But I'm going to get you a breakfast meeting."

"Perfect. Thanks."

"Yeah. No problem, boss."

Outside my cabin, Russ and I split. She headed to the main lodge. Most of the assistants were staying there with the rest of the crew. I walked to Wylie's cabin. Claude's cabin was next door. His lights were off. So he was asleep still.

I let myself in. "Wylie," I called up. It was too much to hope for that she would actually wake up at that. "Wylie, wake up." I went upstairs.

She was sprawled diagonally and passed out. This was the real reason her marriages never lasted. The woman did not share bed space well.

I touched her shoulder. "Wy. Babe. Wake up."

She rolled over and smiled. When I didn't smile back, she studied me. "What's going on?"

"Sorry to wake you."

"It's cool." She sat up. "But why? What's up?" She looked at the clock and sighed.

"Sean. They dropped all charges."

"The fuck?"

"And we don't know what the studio is doing, but Paulie thinks they might let him back in."

Wylie stared at me for a minute. "Nope." She lay back down and pulled the covers over her head.

"That's fair." I stood. "Just thought you'd want to know."

"Dammit." She sat back up and tossed the covers off. "Will you go make coffee?"

"I'm on it." In the time it took me to make coffee, I got three separate texts.

Paulie said, *You've got a video conference at eight with execs.*

Russ texted almost the same thing. *Studio call at 8 in conference room.*

Taryn had texted a screenshot of a message from my mom saying she'd be in LA that afternoon. Taryn had drawn baby blue hearts on the message.

"What are you grinning at?" Wylie asked as she came downstairs.

"Taryn."

"Oh, God. How is she?"

"Better now, I think. Gerri is on her way to LA," I said.

"See? Your mom is the best."

"I'm not arguing that today." I poured two mugs of coffee and set one in front of Wylie.

"So what's the deal? How is Oath responding to the Sean news?"

"I don't know yet. Apparently, I have a meeting in two hours."

"You can't let him on set," Wy said.

"I know." I had a sick feeling that in two hours, that decision would be out of my hands.

❖

Claude was already waiting in the conference room. The video screen was up on the wall, but no one had joined yet. He stood when I entered.

"I don't like this," he said.

"You don't?" I might have sounded a bit more incredulous than I should have.

"Jeez, give me a little credit."

"Sorry. Everything just feels off. I don't really know what to expect right now," I said.

"Yeah. I'm right there with you." He glanced at the time. "Sean's a slippery bastard. And Danny's so far up his ass—"

The screen flickered as Danny started the meeting. It only took a moment for Mick, Nelson, and Eddie to appear as well. I couldn't read anything from their expressions.

"Hey, everyone." Danny smiled and my stomach dropped. He looked fucking thrilled. "I assume everyone's heard the good news?"

Mick and Eddie nodded. Nelson gave a reserved smile.

"I'm not sure I'd call it good news," Claude said. I vowed to buy Claude the most extravagant gift I could find.

"Don't fuck around. This is the reputation we built our studio on, man," Danny said. He sounded jovial. Like he was arguing with Claude about cupcake flavors. Cupcake flavors he was passionate about, but cupcakes nonetheless.

"That's a bit extreme," Claude said. "Sean is one man, not an entire brand or an entire studio. And he's a prick."

"I don't care if he's a prick. The man makes damn good movies. He knows what he's doing," Mick said.

"Or he's a well-connected white man who surrounds himself with just enough talent to cover his egregious missteps," I mumbled.

"What was that, Addy?" Danny had an edge suddenly. Apparently, Claude could critique, but I couldn't.

"I said he's a talentless hack," I said loudly. "And being a prick is the least of his flaws. He's also a controlling asshole who overcompensates for his inability to direct by abusing his cast and crew. And he's a fucking rapist."

Danny leaned in close to his computer. "What are you on? He was cleared. This morning! That's why we're having this meeting!"

"No, they dropped the charges against him. That doesn't make him any less a rapist," I said.

"We'd rather not brand the man a felon without just cause." Eddie sounded very reasonable as he said unreasonable shit. "Innocent until proven guilty and all that."

"Well, since I'm the only one who's actually had to film with him, I'm going to take my experience over the monolith of the justice system," I said.

Claude put a patronizing hand on my arm. "Let's not get worked up here. We don't know that Sean is a rapist." I opened my mouth to yell at him too, but he squeezed my arm and gave me a look. I decided to trust his lead. For the moment. "But Addy makes a good point. Sean is an absolute terror on set," Claude said. He made it sound like he was oh so reluctant to point that out.

"Be that as it may, he gets results," Mick said.

"A lot of people get results. And they do it without verbally and emotionally abusing everyone around them," Claude said.

"If you ask me, this cast could use a little tough love," Eddie said.

"Excuse me? This cast is fucking killing it." I'd never actually had the desire to hit someone until right then. And it was a four-way tie.

"The dailies are solid. You're right," Nelson cut in. "But we'd really like to see production sped up a little. The budget is just tight, especially with adding a new cast member. You understand that, right?"

It was pretty obvious what they were angling for. And it was exactly what I had been afraid they would do. But I'd managed to convince myself they wouldn't be that depraved. Or that stupid. I suddenly felt very calm. "What exactly are you guys proposing?" I asked.

"Now that he's cleared to travel outside New York, we're going to send Sean up there. He's chomping at the bit to get back to work," Danny said.

"No," I said.

"What?"

"Sean Murray isn't allowed on my set," I said.

"He's an executive producer. You can't ban a producer from set," Mick said.

"I just did. This meeting is over." I stood.

"If you won't accept studio help with this, frankly, flagging movie, we'll be forced to replace you," Danny said.

I stopped walking toward the door. "We're three-quarters of the way done. You can't replace me."

Mick shrugged and tried to look casual. "I'm sure Sean could step in and finish it. He understands your work pretty well."

Heat flooded my hands and scalp. It was a scalding, invasive itch that spread over my body. I knew it was anxiety, but that didn't help me control the reaction at all.

"Are you guys serious? You can't seriously be threatening to replace PJ Addison with Sean Murray," Claude said. He was pissed. Which was nice.

"We're not threatening anything." Danny smiled insincerely. "This is hypothetical. If the director wouldn't allow the producer on set, we'd have to examine her work with a close lens. And if we found any issues, then it might be better for the studio, for the cast, if we found someone who could step in."

"The optics alone—" Claude started shouting.

"Fine." I gave Claude a look to shut him up. Arguing with Danny wasn't worth it. "That's fine. When can we expect our recently exonerated EP to arrive?" I asked.

"Tuesday," Mick said.

"Great. Good meeting, guys." I reached over and left the call.

"What the fuck just happened?" Claude asked.

I couldn't respond. I just stared at the empty screen.

"Addy, are you okay?" He touched my arm.

"No."

CHAPTER TWENTY-TWO

There you are," Wylie said from behind me. She closed the cabin door. "Russ has been looking for you."

I was sitting in my solitary chair, staring out at the sun-drenched treetops. "I'm glad you're here."

"Yeah? You want to tell me about your meeting?" She crossed the room and stood in front of me.

I looked through her. The view didn't matter anyway. "No. I want another beer."

She hesitated. "How many have you had?"

"One. The others were too far away." I pointed vaguely in the direction of the kitchen.

"Okay?" She went to the fridge and pulled out a beer. "You know it's eleven a.m. right?"

"Is it?" I took the bottle and drank a third of it.

"Now will you tell me how the meeting went?"

"Nope," I said. Wylie grabbed the beer out of my hand as I raised it to my lips. Beer spilled on my chest. "Hey!" I finally looked at her.

"Sorry. You can drink yourself into a stupor once I get some answers." She held the bottle up out of my reach.

"Fine." I brushed away the beer, but it had already soaked into my shirt. "Sean's going to be here Tuesday. Can I have my beer back?"

"What? No."

"No, I can't have my beer or no, Sean's not coming here?"

"Both."

"Well, I tried that tack with Danny and Mick and the producers, but you know how they react when someone tells Sean no." I reached for the bottle. Wy lifted it higher. I stopped trying.

"What do you mean?" she asked. She really wasn't giving up here. Which was a bummer.

"I mean I told them Sean Murray wasn't allowed on my set. They explained that I couldn't ban a producer from set."

"And that's it? He's just allowed on set?"

"No. No, sweet Wylie." I laughed. "They were good enough to point out that they would have to replace me as director if they didn't like what I was creating. And wouldn't you know it? Sean is familiar with my work and he would have no problem stepping in to finish the film."

"That's bullshit. You can fight that."

"I mean, yeah. I could," I said. "I'm not gonna."

"Why the fuck not?"

"Because it'll just drag out this shit forever, and ultimately, Sean Murray gets to disrupt my life. Again. He gets credit for my work. Again." I was too tired to fight. That was what it came down to. But I felt pathetic saying that part out loud. "Plus, no matter what happens with the movie, it'll forever entwine my name and my work as a director with his."

Wy stared at me for a moment, then drank half my remaining beer. She handed me the bottle and I drank the last few inches. She stomped toward the kitchen, then turned and stomped back the other way. After a few minutes of pacing, she stopped and stared at me. I ignored her. I was tired in my soul, but I was also just fucking sleepy.

Wy put her hands on the armrest and leaned into my space. "What are you going to do about it?"

"I don't know." I sighed. "Finish the movie. Do damage control. You know, try to keep him from assaulting anyone on set."

"Let's be a bit more proactive." She started pacing again. But this was different pacing. This was productive pacing. It was somehow even more exhausting. She wanted me to do things.

"Like how?"

"How many more scenes do we have involving nudity or highlighting sexuality?"

"I don't know."

She stopped pacing so she could yell at me. "Come on, PJ. I need you right now. Sit up and have a fucking conversation. When we're done you can drink and wallow if you still want to."

"Fine." I pushed myself up into a less reclined position. I was still going to slouch though. Dammit. "What?"

"Think about scenes Sean will use to take advantage of people. Costume fittings he will force his way into. Physically intensive scenes where he can get handsy."

"Hand me my script." I pointed across the room.

It started with glancing through the script. When it became clear that there were only ten or so dicey scenes left to film, I suddenly became serious. I could film ten scenes in three days. Wylie watched me. She didn't prompt or ask questions. She just waited.

"Where's my phone?" I asked.

She shrugged and went to check the kitchen. I glanced at the handful of surfaces downstairs. "Here." She held up the phone.

"Thanks." I grabbed it and called Russ.

"PJ, where are you? Did Wylie find you?"

"Yeah. We're at my cabin. Listen, I need you to get me Claude and Hannah in the production office," I said.

"Sure. When do you need them?" she asked.

"Now."

There was a slight pause. "Anything else?"

"No, but tell Hannah we're completely redoing the schedule for the next three days."

"You got it."

Wylie was watching me when I hung up. "You want another beer?

"No. Asshole." I grabbed my script and my notebook. "I'm going to go mitigate this shitshow. You want to come? Earn that EP credit?"

"Fuck yeah." She smiled and it was a little too smug for my taste. If only smug wasn't sexy on her.

❖

Claude was already in the production office when we arrived. Hannah followed us in a minute later and dumped a pile of index cards and Sharpies on the conference table.

"Any chance you were joking about the schedule?" Hannah asked.

"Nope. Sit," I said. They all sat and gave me the floor. "On Tuesday Sean Murray is going to arrive and presumably torment everyone until the end of the shoot."

"What the fuck are you talking about?" Hannah asked.

"Sorry. They already know." I waved at Wy and Claude. "This morning, the DA dropped all charges against Sean. A couple of hours later, Danny gleefully informed me Sean would be here ASAP."

"So what's the plan?" Claude asked. He seemed quite relieved that my moody silence had passed.

"We're going to figure out which scenes we don't want Sean on set for and we're going to film them all in the next three days," I said.

Hannah's eyes went a little wild as the implications of that approach hit her. She took about ninety seconds and then reached for her script.

"The scene with Grace and Taylor in their underwear in the kitchen," Claude said.

Hannah stood and waved me out of her way. She dragged over the freestanding whiteboard and wrote *Grace/Taylor kitchen pep talk*. Then she added *Malone shower* and *Ava/Xavier intro*.

"The bar dancing scene," Wylie said. Hannah added it.

"The costume fitting for Pippa's meadow outfit," I said.

Hannah shuddered at that suggestion. But then she added three other fittings—two that I hadn't considered. After twenty minutes, we'd created a relatively definitive list and ranked them by importance. I was prepared to wrangle them into some semblance of a shooting schedule, but Hannah very much did not want my help.

She tilted the whiteboard so I couldn't easily write on it. "I'm sorry. You're just going to fuck with my process."

"Fair enough." I didn't laugh at her sudden possession of the board, which I thought was big of me. "I need to tell the principal cast what's going on anyway."

"You want help with that?" Claude asked.

"Yes, I don't trust that everyone on set will side with us over the studio so we have to be discreet."

"Agreed. Hundred percent."

"I want to help too," Wylie said.

"I kind of assumed," I said.

Claude pulled up his calendar. "I've already got an afternoon meeting scheduled with Scottie. I'll loop him in."

"I've got a fitting with Arjun," Wylie said. "It's not until four though so I've got time before."

"I'm rehearsing with Teddy and Rosie at six. I think." Why didn't I invite Russ to this meeting? I didn't keep track of my own schedule.

"No go," Hannah said. She pointed at the board. We couldn't read it, but she was real insistent that those scribbles mattered. "We're going to have to start shooting at four thirty this afternoon. That's firm."

"You got it, sir." I saluted.

"I don't have time for banter." Hannah didn't even look up from furiously writing on an index card. She was mocking up a color-coded board on the conference table. "You go find Emma, Rosie, and Molly right now. The girls are priority as far as Sean is concerned so that's on you. Parsons, you've got Teddy, Diego, and Logan. They've started lifting together at noon on days they aren't shooting."

Wy stood then hesitated at the door. "Where do they lift?"

"The gym at the lodge." Hannah still didn't look up. "Make sure no one else is in there before you start talking."

Wylie nodded and left. Claude was watching Hannah attentively. You'd think the producer would be calling the shots, but Hannah was on a roll and neither of us was going to derail her.

"Claude. Your job is a bit more ambiguous. Arjun and Scottie are definite priorities. Lenny and Harold too." She switched a pink and a yellow card, frowned, then switched them back. "From there you need to be more circumspect. Test the waters with all the department heads. If you can get hair and makeup on board, that's great. They will be able to intervene and keep Sean from being alone with anyone in the cast."

"Sounds good," I said.

Hannah looked up, furious. "What are you still doing here?"

"Leaving." I hightailed it for the door. On the way to my trailer, I called Russ. She immediately answered. "Where are you?" I asked.

"Your trailer. What do you need?"

"Cool. I'm headed to you. And I need a location on Emma, Rosie, and Molly. Then I need you to head over to the production office and get a handle on my schedule for the rest of the day."

"Got it. See you in a minute."

"Thanks."

Russ was on the phone when I let myself into my trailer. She finished her conversation, then wrote some notes in her cheap notebook. "Rosie and Emma are in Rosie's trailer running lines for the scene they thought they were shooting today."

"Do they know anything that's going on?"

Russ started shaking her head before I even finished talking. "I need to go track down Molly, but I'll tell you when I find her. If you need me after that, I'll be in the production office with Hannah." She waited long enough for my brief nod, then took off.

Rosie's trailer was a few down from mine. I knocked on the door. There was a burst of laughter from inside before Rosie called, "Come in."

I opened the door and found Emma and Rosie laughing wildly. "Sorry to interrupt."

"You're not." Rosie waved me in. "Emma is trying to convince me that I missed out by not attending a traditional American high school."

"You did!" Emma laughed some more.

"Well, I'm with Rosie. If it wasn't in an aughts rom-com, then it's outside my wheelhouse," I said.

"See?" Rosie gestured at me. "*Easy A* is a far better way to get the high school experience. Right?" She looked back at me and her smiled dropped a bit. "You look real serious."

I gave a wry smile. "I am. Sorry." They both sobered and straightened up.

"What's going on?" Emma asked.

"You guys have heard about Sean Murray?" I asked. They nodded. "The charges against him were dropped this morning."

"Yeah, I saw that," Rosie said. "Is it bumming you out? I've heard his sets were hell."

I almost laughed. Her question was perfectly appropriate in a just world. This was not a just world. "I wish it was only bumming me out. Oath is sending Sean to set. He's still an EP and they think he can help speed up production."

That set off a round of expletives and questions. I tried to answer, but finding answers that made sense was difficult. I was trying to avoid explicitly telling them about Danny's threat when Molly showed up.

"Hey, Addy, your assistant said you were looking for me," Molly said.

"Yeah, come in." My watch lit up with a call from Russ. "Sorry. Can you two catch her up?" Rosie nodded so I answered the phone. "Hey. Molly just got here."

"Good. Baird is running over the call sheets for today. You've got thirty minutes to fill Emma in before she needs to head over to makeup," Russ said.

"Baird? Is he in the loop?"

"Yeah, Claude brought him in. Baird's his nephew."

"That tracks." I realized all three of my cast members were watching me intently. "I got to go. But thanks, Russ." I hung up. "So we're all caught up on Sean Murray fuckery?"

"Well, I know the facts, but I'm still real confused on the reasoning," Molly said.

"It's the patriarchy."

Molly nodded very seriously. "Oh. That explains it. Thanks."

"Basically, I'm here to warn you and put in place some safeguards. You three are the most at risk. Claude and Hannah and I are working to make sure you won't be put in any bad situations."

"Hold the fuck up. You're putting in place safeguards to make sure the producer can't rape us?" Rosie asked.

"Yep."

"That's untenable."

"Agreed. If I were you, I'd be calling my agent and my manager and my lawyer and my mother. Actually, I already spoke with all of those people today—including my mother and I'm thirty-six years old. Now, I'm not telling you to do it just because I did. I'm just saying that's my approach."

"Noted?" Rosie very obviously wrote on a napkin *call agent + mom + lawyer.*

"Of course, we're all going to end up in various forms of contract negotiations and litigation and bullshit. I can't control any of that. What I can do is film the nine scenes where you and the other cast members will be the most vulnerable before Sean shows up on Tuesday."

"As in vulnerable to sexual assault? Seriously?" Molly asked.

"Yes and no. I don't think anyone is currently at risk of being sexually assaulted by him. He's far too scrutinized at the moment. But he can still say skeevy shit or touch people inappropriately—you know, those lesser assaults that we're all supposed to brush off."

"Right." Molly frowned and nodded.

"The culture on set is going to shift. I'd like to keep it in the realm of on edge rather than outright fear," I said.

"Yeah, I've been on both types of sets. Edgy is definitely better than fearful." Rosie nodded sagely. "But, for what it's worth, I much prefer the work hard, play hard vibe you've currently got."

"You and me both, sister," I said.

There was a knock at the door. "It's Baird, I'm looking for Addy." I opened the door. "Hey, you've got call sheets?"

Baird handed me a thin stack of paper. "You need anything else?"

"Not at the moment. Thanks for this." I handed call sheets over to Emma, Rosie, and Molly. "This is today's new call sheet. It's not too packed, but we're also going to be squeezing in fittings and such."

"Not too packed? This is five scenes." Molly held up her sheet.

"Yeah, but we're front loading. This way, if we need to reshoot or reschedule, we'll have time tomorrow or Monday," I said.

"How is Murray going to react when he finds out you shifted the schedule like this?" Emma asked.

I shrugged. "He'll be pissed. But if I don't shift the schedule, he'll be pissed about something else."

"What's the plan for once he arrives?" Rosie asked.

"Claude and Hannah are working on it. For now, let's plan on drinks and pool at Jed's Tuesday evening. We can review logistics privately there."

"Jed's?" Rosie asked.

"Yeah, what's Jed's?" Emma asked.

"Shut your damn mouth," Molly said. "I knew it was real."

Rosie and Emma looked at her in question.

I grinned. "Yeah. It's real."

"There's a restaurant or a bar or something—this Jed's. It's somewhere in Thackerton or near Thackerton. No one really knows. The original *DSN* cast spent all their time there. But it's only very obliquely referenced on like behind-the-scenes videos."

I laughed at her fairly accurate description. "We made a pact with the OG cast. None of us ever revealed it."

Molly interrupted. "Even when asked point-blank ten days into shooting."

"Well, I'm telling you now. If you walk north on the main street in town, right where the road curves back and shifts up to those big houses overlooking the town, there's a gravel road. You follow that and you'll find Jed's."

"This is fucking sick," Molly said. "I can't believe you actually told us."

"Why did you tell us?" Emma asked.

"The reason for the original pact was to create a haven away from Murray and his hellish set. Now it seems like you all need that. Sorry."

"That's kind of a bummer," Rosie said.

"Yes, I agree. Patriarchal bullshit is a bummer."

CHAPTER TWENTY-THREE

I walked into Jed's four days later tired, hungry, and twenty minutes late. The pool tables were silent. The bar was empty aside from one well-aged person of indeterminate gender wearing an impressive fringed vest.

Jed saw me come in and smiled. "There you are."

"Where is everyone?"

He nodded toward the patio. "Out back. Here. Take these with you." He set two tall icy glasses on the bar.

I inspected the drinks. "What are they?"

"Vodka sodas. Two of the kids asked for them."

"I didn't know you served vodka sodas," I said.

Jed shook his head and pulled his crossword book out. "This is a bar, you know."

"I heard that rumor." I grabbed the glasses.

"So that dickhead is back," he said without looking up.

"At least your bar sales will improve."

Jed gave me a hard stare. "Don't need the bar sales."

"That much is obvious." I pointedly looked at the dated decor.

He held back a grin. "Food will be out in a couple." He returned to his crossword.

I carried out the drinks and found everyone. They had pushed a couple of tables against the railing so they could look at the view. Wylie was on the far left next to an empty stool. She was leaning forward and laughing at something Logan was saying. Her blond waves fell into her face and she casually brushed them back. I hadn't really been alone with her since we found out Sean was coming back. For the last four days, I'd been ignoring a slowly growing realization—I couldn't be with her. I couldn't make myself vulnerable to Wylie again. Wy was a force. My life wasn't constructed to withstand her. Sean was an asshole for a multitude of reasons, but right then I was pretty okay with putting everything on the back burner to cater to his fuckery. Because I was not prepared to unpack those feelings.

"Addy!" Molly shouted when she saw me. The group turned as a unit. If nothing else, the Sean Murray crash course in cast bonding was still functional. Of course, they all liked each other before so maybe we could have skipped the Sean part.

"Hey." I set the glasses down and sat on the last stool. "Jed sent these out."

Wylie handed the glasses to Rosie who handed them to Molly and down the line until Teddy and Emma had their drinks.

"How's it going, boss?" Diego asked.

"It's a nightmare, Diego, thank you for asking."

"Here. This will help." Diego grabbed the last empty glass on the table and poured beer from one of the pitchers. Then he stood and carried it around the table to present it to me with a flourish.

"You're a genius," I said.

"Could I get you to say that on Live?"

"No."

He shrugged and went back to his seat.

"So how was everyone's first day with Sean on set?" I asked. They all looked at each other like they were waiting to see who would go first.

"Do we need to call on you?" Wy asked. They laughed but none of them talked. "Okay, Rosie, you go first."

Rosie was surprised. "Me? Sure. Uh. It was strange. I was sort of comforted by the fact that I knew exactly who was dangerous and who wasn't. And I wasn't alone all day so your system worked." She looked to Molly who nodded.

"Same," Molly said. "I barely interacted with Sean. The only time I spoke with him, Jay immediately started touching me up. He was very cool about it—Jay, I mean."

"That's good." I nodded. Jay had enthusiastically been on board with the plan, but he was also pretty chill in general so that tracked. "Anyone else? Teddy?"

"Right." Teddy took a sip of his vodka soda. "This morning I was feeling okay. Very secret agent. I had my mission. I knew what to do. And then I saw him talking to Emma and I went over to intervene, you know?"

Emma nodded along. "Sean said some stuff that seemed perfectly appropriate but was just off. I got that stomach thing. Like something is wrong and you need to get the heck out? You know what I'm saying?" Rosie and Molly and Wy agreed.

"I know exactly what you're talking about," Teddy said a little loudly. "But I've never felt that way before. It was gross. Like all my hair stood on end and I knew he was a bad, bad man." He realized the girls were all looking at him with varying degrees of sympathy. "Oh, God. And now I'm interrupting you to explain a feeling you already know."

"Mansplainer," Diego said.

"Dickwad," Teddy said.

A waiter brought out enough bar food to sustain a drunk army. Diego asked for another couple of pitchers of beer. Molly asked for a pitcher of water. We shuffled around paper-lined baskets.

Wy leaned over while they were distracted. "How you holding up?"

"I don't even know. I'm too tired to think," I said.

"Poor baby." She squeezed my thigh, then left her hand on my leg. I was miraculously very awake. Amazing how I could spend four days deciding I was better off without Wy and lose all reasoning the moment she touched me and whispered in my ear.

"Doing okay, boss?" Logan asked.

"Hmm?" I looked across the table at him. "Yeah, I'm all right."

"'Cause your eyes just got all big and you seem like you're kinda hyperventilating," he said.

"Just trying to stay awake," I said.

He nodded along, but it didn't look like he believed me. Wylie glanced back and forth between us like she was simply paying attention to conversation. Under the table she slid her fingertips up the seam of my pants. It did not help me regain my chill.

"So, Teddy, how did Sean react when you went over to interrupt?" I asked pointedly.

Wylie chuckled low and soft and moved her hand to my knee. The movement didn't uncomplicate my feelings.

Emma started laughing. Teddy frowned at her. "I blew it," Teddy said.

"You didn't at all." Emma continued laughing. "He asked me if we were still on for pickleball later."

"I panicked." Teddy looked miserable.

"Well, we're starting a pickleball league now," Emma said.

"Wait. Is pickleball a metaphor?" Logan asked. "Are we pickling your ball right now?"

"Logan, baby, you're always pickling my ball," Emma said.

He grinned and winked at her.

"How did they make that sound sexy?" Molly asked.

"They didn't," Teddy said. "Like objectively."

They started bickering about what made something objectively sexy so Wylie interrupted them. "Anyone else have a Sean interaction?"

"We did," Diego said. "Me and Logan." He and Logan frowned at each other.

"Well, out with it," I said.

"We were taking a nap together between filming," Logan said.

"And Sean woke us up with some vaguely homophobic bullshit," Diego said.

"When you were engaging in the classic heterosexual pastime of two men cuddling? I'm shocked," I said.

"See? That's the sort of homophobic bullshit Sean said." Diego sounded big mad.

"Pointing out that something is gay isn't homophobic," I said. "I'm a big fan of gay things. Sean probably had a negative connotation. Mine was a celebratory connotation with just a little bit of mockery."

"She has a point," Logan said to Diego.

"I'm seeing that," Diego said to him.

"It was a non-sexual nap," Logan said to the group.

"A bro nap," Diego said.

"Sure." I nodded.

"The point is, Sean made it into something else," Diego said.

Logan frowned. "He definitely has a fundamental misunderstanding of which of us is queer and in what way we're queer."

"I think he thinks we're both cis guys, but I'm gay?" Diego checked in with Logan who nodded.

"So what did you say?" Molly asked. She looked very interested in how her cis het costar would react to such an accusation. I was also very curious, but I at least kept it to myself.

Diego shrugged. "Nothing. But when Logan walked away I sure as fuck made sure Sean saw me watching his ass."

"I do have a fine ass," Logan said.

"Totally, bro." Diego reached over the table to fist bump Logan.

"Do you all think we can keep this up for another thirteen days?" I asked. Everyone nodded.

"But let's cram the schedule. See if we can get it down to like ten or eleven," Rosie said. "I'd rather lose sleep to a rigorous shooting schedule than lose it to stress over Sean Murray." Her costars all loudly agreed.

"Fair point. Plus then the studio will be happy," I said.

"Is this what the first set was like?" Molly asked.

Wy turned toward me. "Sort of. It became this." Her eyes searched my face as if I could explain how the original set had slowly devolved.

"But we didn't know at the beginning. Keep in mind this was over ten years ago. Sean's behavior was common. It wasn't until he assaulted our friend that we realized," I said.

"I'm sorry, but how? That guy is clearly a fucking creeper," Teddy said.

"Yeah, but we were femme presenting women in Hollywood," Wylie said. Teddy looked at her in confusion so she explained more. "So we spent a lot of time learning to ignore violent language because it was all violent language. If we listened to our fight-or-flight all the time, we wouldn't have been in the business," Wylie said.

"Or, you know, the world," I said.

"So you just gave up?" Teddy asked.

"Not exactly." I shrugged. "We fought back with the tools available to us."

"He would have destroyed Taryn's career. And he still wouldn't have faced any real consequences. So we asked what she wanted," Wylie said.

"And she wanted you to leave it alone?" Rosie asked quietly.

"Actually, no," I said. "She wanted us to quietly destroy his reputation. So we launched a whisper campaign. Taryn went on to have a wildly successful career. He's been dogged by vicious rumors for his."

"You all are still friends, right?" Molly asked. We nodded. "How is she doing now that he was released?"

"Yeah, have you talked to Gerri?" Wylie asked me.

"Yep. They're having a grand old time." I rolled my eyes. "Spa days and massages and falling asleep by the pool."

"I'm sorry. Gerri?" Molly asked.

"My mother," I said.

"Your mother?" Molly repeated.

"My mother."

"You're here filming with Rapey McGee and your mother is having spa days with Taryn Masson?" Molly asked.

Wylie started laughing. "Mock now, but on the worst day of your life, PJ will send her mother to your doorstep. And Gerri will give you a reason to continue living."

"Wait. You weren't kidding when you said you called your mother?" Rosie asked.

"I rarely kid about calling my mother."

"Does that mean we should have actually called our agents and mothers?" Emma asked.

"And managers and lawyers." I thought I'd been pretty clear about that.

"Yeah, and if any of those people—particularly mothers—want to visit set, now's the time," Wylie said.

"So like, is this the plan? Just keep watching each other to make sure no one is alone with Sean?" Emma asked.

"Yes?" I said. "He's less likely to be a low-key creep if there's an audience."

"I'm not brimming with confidence here," Rosie said.

"Fair enough. Actual logistics. Tomorrow, Wylie will be working with Emma and Molly. You're all shooting together in the evening so you'll be running lines in the morning. I'll pop in on rehearsals," I said.

"What about me?" Rosie asked.

"You're doing the same with Teddy," I said. He looked up and nodded very seriously. "You've got a late afternoon scene. Avoid set until afternoon, then rehearse together in one of your trailers."

"What about you?" Teddy asked.

"I'll have Russ with me all day. But she will also be keeping tabs on all of you. If you're going to have a gap in coverage, she'll send Baird over with a pressing issue."

"He's the twelve-year-old PA who's anxious all the time, right?" Rosie asked.

"That's the one."

"This is awkward, but what about me?" Logan asked. "What if Sean realizes I'm trans and doesn't handle it well?"

"Fair question. Diego, how do you feel about falling in unrequited love with Logan?"

Diego nodded enthusiastically. "I feel great about it. Except the unrequited part." He turned to Logan. "Have you ever tried being gay?"

"Yeah, buddy. We've been over this." Logan spoke slowly and patiently. "I used to identify as a lesbian."

"Unrequited it is." Diego shrugged.

"Hey, Diego?" Molly asked. "Have you ever tried being gay?"

"Hmm. Well, no." Diego turned and looked at Logan. "But come on. If you're gonna give it a go, you can't do much better than this guy. He's real hot."

Molly leaned back and pressed her lips together. "Hard to argue that logic."

"So should I just follow him around?" Diego asked me.

"I mean, try to have a little chill. But yeah. You two are now officially best friends. And you're going to watch him a little more than a straight best friend should," I said.

"Got it." He turned to Logan. "Share locations?"

"Oh, heck yeah. Best buds." Logan pulled out his phone.

My watch lit up with a call. Sean. "Fuck." I nudged Wylie. "Sean is calling me."

"You don't have to answer it," Teddy said.

"Yeah, I do," I said. They all started to protest. "Hey, cool it. I can't ignore a call from my producer even if he is a terrible person." I stood and moved away from the table as I answered the call. "Hello?"

"PJ, Sean here."

"Hey, Sean." I pressed my lips together and waited.

"Listen, I've been watching these dailies and I've got some concerns. Can you come into the production office this evening?" he asked. Sure, it was eight o'clock at night. Why not?

"Tonight?"

"Yeah, you're still around, right?" His tone suggested that I wasn't allowed to leave set.

"Actually, I'm in town having dinner with Wylie." I glanced over and found the cast watching me with bated breath. Diego, Emma, and Logan were all tightly holding hands.

"I bet you are." Sean laughed. "Eddie said you two are getting, uh, close again."

I sighed. "Sure, Sean. I can cut my dinner short."

"Great. I'll see you shortly." He hung up.

"I've got to head back to the production office," I said.

"The fuck you do," Teddy said.

"Yeah, that's not happening," Diego said.

"Guys, I appreciate the masc thing, but I do have to go." I drained my beer and stood.

"Then I'm going with you." Diego got to his feet.

"Nope," I said. He hesitated at the firmness of my tone.

Rosie touched Diego's arm. "We've got to trust Addy here. Besides, it would be weird if you showed up to her meeting with her."

Diego scowled. "I just don't think anyone should be alone with him in a production office. Especially late at night."

"It'll be fine. I'm well versed in dodging Sean's bullshit."

Diego frowned and it was real cute. But he also sat back down.

"I'll walk you out." Wylie got up.

"Sure."

We headed out through the bar. When we got to the gravel path, she threaded her arm through mine. The trees closed in overhead like a delicate shield. The smell, the sound of gravel and wind in the pines was all comforting and warm. But it was a false comfort.

"We haven't really had a chance to talk since you got the call about Sean," Wylie said.

I nodded. I wanted to tell her the truth. I wanted to lie. I said nothing.

"How are you doing?" She asked it real slow like she was waiting for me to talk and let her off the hook.

"I don't know."

"You don't know?"

"I mean, I don't think I can do this," I said. She stiffened and her breath hitched. So I pulled that punch. "I mean, I can't focus at all right now. My head's not on right."

She relaxed infinitesimally. "Right. Of course."

"I just need to finish this picture. You know, before I can do anything." It was a coward's move. But I was a coward. "Sorry."

She shook her head. "It's fine. I probably need to do the same. I haven't even filed my divorce paperwork yet and I'm already—well, I should probably take some time."

"Yeah."

Wylie stopped walking and half turned back to the bar. "Okay. Be careful with Sean."

"Yeah, I'll be fine." I walked away and pretended I couldn't feel her watching my back as I disappeared behind the trees.

Chapter Twenty-four

Sean was staring at the shooting schedule when I walked into the production office. His sandy brown hair was charmingly mussed. He was perched on the conference table with his sneakers on a chair. He was—as always—trying to project a cool he didn't have. He'd landed in the director's, then the producer's chair by an accident of birth and circumstance and lived in fear of someone realizing he wasn't actually anointed by God.

"Addy." He straightened, then kicked out the chair he'd been resting his feet on. "Have a seat."

I stared at his dusty footprints on the fabric for a moment before sitting on the conference table. "What's up?"

"Been reviewing the dailies. Solid work." He clicked a few things on the open laptop next to him. Doing so allowed him to avoid eye contact. It was a tactic he'd long used to seem busy and important. "You've really come a long way as a director."

"Thanks."

He waited for me to say more. I didn't so he continued. "I'll get right to it then. We're going to need to reshoot a few scenes."

"Really?" I generally wasn't one to pontificate as it was. But there was something particularly wonderful about watching Sean wait for me to explode with anger and just not reacting.

"Yes." He turned the screen toward me. It was paused on a shot from Ava and Xavier's sex scene. Because of course those were the dailies he was reviewing. "Xavier doesn't have any chest hair."

"Okay?" To be fair, Diego didn't have any body hair. Wax was his friend.

"It doesn't really work for the character. I mean, he's a guy," Sean said.

I waited for him to expand on the connection between guy and chest hair, but apparently that was the whole connection. "And?"

"He's a laborer. Salt of the earth guy. He needs chest hair."

"I'm not following."

Sean looked at me like I was very dense. "Men have chest hair. Especially farmhand type men."

"They also have back hair. But Xavier's a smooth sort of fellow. We knew that when we cast him."

"Well, it'll need to be reshot," he said.

"Just that scene? Or the four other scenes where he's shirtless?" I asked. I was intentionally being obnoxious because I figured he'd back off once he realized the extent of what he was asking. No such luck.

"All of them, of course. Are there any others in the script that we haven't shot yet?" He definitely should have already known the answer to that. He was the goddamn producer after all.

"Possibly." I did my best to pretend this was a legitimate meeting rather than an excuse for Sean to throw his weight around. "We're still fine-tuning his death scene. I was planning on having him shirtless for that."

"Okay. That's easy enough. I'll let wardrobe know he needs a shirt for the death," Sean said. So kind of him.

"What about his corpse?"

That made Sean look up. "His corpse?"

"When his body drops in the barn. The corpse is shirtless."

He screwed up his nose into his overdone thinking face. Sean's father had steered him away from acting with good reason. "I think the corpse is bloody enough to obscure his chest. Editing will take care of it."

"I'm sorry. You really want to reshoot five scenes so Xavier can have chest hair?" I couldn't believe we were having this conversation. "Diego has so many muscles. Chest hair is superfluous. He's very butch."

Sean scoffed. "That's the issue."

"Him being butch?"

"No." He managed a blend of being patient and condescending. "You calling him butch. You don't have a concept of heterosexuality and what makes it sell. Or not sell."

"So I'm too gay to properly film a hot guy?" I asked.

"It's just a culture issue. You forget that we're selling this to straight people. It's not a knock against you," he said very reasonably.

"Okay, well, there are plenty of straight people on set. Hannah and Claude are well aware of straight culture. I'm not worried."

"I am." Sean spun the laptop back around so he could pull something else up. "See, the Xavier thing stood out to me, but I didn't really see the whole issue until this." He turned the screen toward me. This time it was paused on me and Wylie, topless. It was one of the shots that would never make it to the final cut because you could see both our nipples. I swallowed my disgust that Sean had been sitting alone in the production studio at night watching video of me and Wylie get sexy.

"What's the problem here?" I asked.

"Wylie has armpit hair."

"Yeah?"

"You just can't do this. Like it or not, the movie has to appeal to young, heterosexual men. This." He pointed and shook his head. "It doesn't. I'm sorry. It's gross."

"It's gross?" I heard my voice go up and did my best to rein it in. He was trying to bait me. "It's two topless conventionally attractive women kissing. Are you sure you understand what appeals to young, heterosexual men?"

"Conventionally attractive women?"

"Yeah."

He grinned. "I love your confidence, kid. Always did. But also, no. Taylor's haircut is too unconventional for that to apply. Not to mention the whole vibe." He waved his hand at my general outfit. "We can't have pseudo butch on one woman and armpit hair on the other. It's just too much." There were some shades of early Oath discussions about me and Wylie in his tone. It was familiar, but no less insulting.

"Here's the thing," I said. "You can barely see her armpit hair. The audience who is into that sort of thing will see it. The audience who isn't won't even notice it."

"That's not the point," he said.

"Then what is?" I asked.

He launched into full lecture mode. "This is a mainstream movie, PJ. It's not one of your quirky little indie movies."

"And hot chicks only have armpit hair in quirky indie movies?"

"Yes." He was relieved that I finally made a connection. "So we'll have her shave, obviously, and get this reshot. I'll have to talk with makeup about getting body hair for Xavier before we reshoot his shirtless scenes. Either way, I think we can slot you and Wylie in on Friday." He pointed to the packed shooting schedule.

"It'll take longer than that to get Natasha back up here. She's pretty booked," I said.

"Who?"

"The intimacy coordinator."

Sean laughed. "Okay. Well, I think we'll manage without her."

"No."

"Come on. Don't get all squirrelly on me. You and Wylie have shot dozens of scenes like this. And a bunch of them were even for movies." He grinned at his funny joke. "You can handle—"

The door to the production office loudly opened and Teddy walked in grinning. "Oh, shit, you are in here." He walked right past me with his hand outstretched. "I didn't get to say anything earlier, but I'm a big fan, Mr. Murray."

"Thanks. It's Teddy, right?" Sean shook Teddy's hand vigorously.

"Yeah. Yes. Wow. This is so cool. I mean, no offense to Addy, but I'm just so stoked to work with you. I've seen a ton of your movies." Teddy angled away from me. It was a subtle move that seemed to suggest he wasn't even acknowledging my presence.

"That's really nice to hear," Sean said.

"Can I get a photo with you, Mr. Murray? My brother is going to lose his shit." Teddy was already pulling out his phone. He was laying it on thick. I was pretty sure he was an only child.

"Only if you call me Sean. Cut out this Mr. Murray shit." Sean put his arm around Teddy's shoulders.

"You got it." Teddy smiled like Christmas morning and took a couple of selfies. "Sorry. I wasn't trying to interrupt your meeting or whatever." He stepped back.

"It's fine, Teddy." I slid off the conference table. "I'll have Hannah add those scenes into the schedule," I told Sean.

"Perfect. I'm glad you're not pushing back on this," he said.

"Hey, you're the producer." I put my hands up. "If you think it's necessary, we'll get it done."

"It really is." Sure. The sex scenes were real necessary to reshoot.

"Okay. Well, I'm beat. I've only had about four consecutive hours of sleep this week. I'll catch you tomorrow," I said.

"Yeah, I noticed you completely rearranged the schedule for the three days before I got up here," Sean said.

I shrugged. "You know how it is. Constantly shuffling people and equipment and all that." I kept walking toward the door as I spoke. "Anyway. Good meeting. I'll let you two chat." I let myself out and booked it out of there.

I'd made it all of three steps out the door of the production office before I heard Diego shouting.

"Addy, are you around here somewhere? Hello? Addy?" He was fifteen feet away and facing the opposite direction. He clearly knew exactly where I was.

"What are you doing?" I asked at a perfectly reasonable volume.

He turned very dramatically. "Oh, there you are," he said loudly. "Russ said you were on set somewhere. I've been running lines and I sure do need some help."

"You're a very bad actor," I said.

"That's why I need help with my lines, Ms. Addison."

"You're like a bad caricature of a schoolboy."

"Did someone ask for a schoolboy?" Logan rounded the corner with a flourish.

"Wow. What an entrance! You're very handsome and with such presence, sir," Diego said.

"How drunk are you two?" I asked.

They each took one of my arms and led me to Diego's trailer. "We're not drunk," Logan said.

"Unless you count drunk on life," Diego said.

"This is the exact opposite of the chill I asked for," I said.

Diego opened the door to his trailer and Logan lightly pushed me inside. They followed me in. Diego stood in front of the door and crossed his arms. "Have a seat." He pointed at the couch.

I sighed and sat. Arguing seemed useless. Plus I was admittedly curious.

"Would you care for a room temperature water?" Logan held out a bottle toward me.

"Can you two just tell me what this is?" I asked. Logan shook the water in my direction so I took the bottle. "Thank you for the water. Now, what's going on?"

"We discussed it and decided you're old and bad at making choices," Logan said.

"I love where this is going," I said.

Logan sat next to me. "We also realized you're correct. Sean probably won't face any consequences. Or if he does, we won't be able to help that process along."

Diego sat dramatically on my other side. "We can, however, make sure he knows that we know and that we won't allow for that sort of assaulty behavior."

"Or general chicanery," Logan said.

Diego nodded. "Yes, we are the only ones allowed general chicanery on this movie set, thank you very much."

"So you sent Teddy in to what? Threaten Sean?" This was why I tried to take a firm hand. They were only going to make things worse. For themselves if not me.

"Hold up there, boss," Logan said.

"Threatening would make it obvious and would open any and all of us to Sean's underhanded tactics. We're not complete idiots," Diego said.

"We're just going to be annoyingly, constantly present." Logan put a large, warm hand on my shoulder and squeezed.

Diego gripped my other shoulder. They must have rehearsed this. "One of us will always be with Sean. Teddy is playing the fanboy angle right now. He'll be the primary."

"The primary?" I asked even though I knew I shouldn't.

"The primary."

"Yes, primary."

"I'm just not clear on the point. We're already covering to make sure he's not alone with anyone," I said.

"Yeah, and that's great. But we want to be there to shame him whenever he says something gross. Use our masculine privilege for good." Diego put his hand over my head and Logan fist-bumped him.

"And Wylie signed off on this?" I asked.

They laughed. "God, no," Diego said.

"The girls are having this conversation with her right now," Logan said.

"She left after you did and we discussed it and decided you two are wrong." Diego nodded at his own assessment.

"We're not judging you guys. Honest. It's just, ten years ago, putting up passive-aggressive roadblocks was a solid way to approach a creep with power. But it's a new decade, baby." Logan was far too pleased with his own description. "Now, the way to deal with dudes like Sean is to call them out."

"Not in a challenging way," Diego said.

"Yeah, just in like a bro way." Logan pulled up a list on his notes app. It was titled *Operation Sean Sucks Ass* and consisted of my name and Wylie's name. "So we would like a list of everyone in on your sucky plan so we can make them aware of our awesome plan."

I opened my mouth to tell them their idea had merit. Sharing this burden sounded fucking great, honestly.

Diego cut me off before I could say anything. "And don't argue. Our minds are made up."

"Let it happen. We voted."

"It was unanimous," Diego said.

"Claude," I said.

"Huh?"

"Claude. He's on board."

"Oh, fuck. That worked? Okay." Logan added Claude's name.

"Just give me that." I held out my hand for his phone. He handed it over. I started above the line and went all the way down to Baird and Simon. It was a comfortingly long list. "Can I go get some sleep now?"

The boys nodded. "Which side of the bed do you prefer?" Logan asked. I gave him a look. He started laughing. "Kidding. Jeez."

CHAPTER TWENTY-FIVE

I was standing in the long grass, surveying the edge of the forest where Xavier would be dying as soon as it was dark. Scottie's crew was up in the trees making sure our camera angles wouldn't be impeded by any ill-placed branches.

Russ pulled me aside and handed me a phone. "Eddie," she said. I turned away from the people on ladders. Hannah was hovering behind Russ. They both looked somewhat giddy. At least someone was enjoying this gambit.

"Eddie, hey. How's it going?" I asked.

"Fine. What's this I'm hearing about adding another location? We're a week away from wrapping." He sounded annoyed.

"New location?" I knew exactly what he was talking about. "Oh, right. The river. Yeah, the location we used before has a tree down or something. We can't get the equipment down to where we shot before."

"What river? When did we use a river location?" he asked. I could hear his assistant speaking in the background. "From the opening sequence? The swimming hole? I thought that was finished."

"The swimming hole? No. I mean, yes, same location. But we also filmed the Ava and Xavier sex scene there. Now that we're reshooting it, we need the location again." I could hear him trying to cut in so I continued. The key was to sound distracted and urgent but factual. "Like I said, it's inaccessible so we've been scrambling to find a suitable replacement."

"What do you mean reshooting?"

"All the scenes where Xavier is shirtless. The whole chest hair thing?" I asked as if I had also just found out about this.

"What chest hair thing?"

"Sean feels that Xavier's character needs chest hair. So we're reshooting all his shirtless scenes. It's only four…" I trailed off like I was reading my notes. "No, sorry. Five. Only five scenes. The fifth is why we need the intimacy coordinator back on set." Okay, I was laying it on thick. Then again, I was just being a team player. Sean said it was necessary so it was clearly necessary. Who was I to argue?

"Hold on. We're reshooting perfectly good footage on a production that's behind schedule because Xavier needs chest hair?" By the end of his question, he was shouting. For once, I welcomed the shouting.

"Yes?"

"And other than chest hair, the scenes are fine?"

"Yes."

"Yeah, that's not happening. Not a chance in fucking hell," he said.

I did a little dance. Hannah and Russ saw my reaction and danced in response. "Sean seemed to think it was necessary."

"He's wrong."

"What about the other sex scene?" I asked. I was perfectly innocent here. Just clarifying.

"What about it?"

"Grace has armpit hair. It's visible in a few of the cuts. Sean thought that ought to be reshot as well." I closed my eyes and hoped.

"How visible?"

"I don't know. I didn't notice until he pointed it out," I said.

"Weren't you in the scene with her?" Eddie asked.

"Yeah, of course."

"And you didn't notice?"

"No."

"Good Lord. Yeah. We're not reshooting that either. Please tell me there aren't any more," he said.

"Let me check." I counted to ten. "No. It looks like that's it."

"Okay. Good. Don't reshoot anything. I'll talk to Sean, tell him that's off the table."

"Sounds good."

"Everything else going okay?"

"Yep. Barreling toward the end." It was the only answer he wanted to hear.

"Great. Okay. Talk soon." He hung up.

"It worked?" Hannah asked.

"Like a goddamn charm." I gripped Russ's shoulder. "I will never doubt your network of assistant buddies."

"I'm glad we got it done," she said.

"Seriously. That was wildly impressive."

"Okay, calm down. Let's not make it into a bigger deal than it is." Russ pressed her lips together and stared at me.

"Why did you just get weird? Hannah, did she just get weird?" I asked.

"I didn't get weird." Russ shook her head at me. "I just don't want you to think there's some secret network of assistants I can tap into."

"Well, you clearly know Eddie's assistant."

"I do know her, yes." Russ nodded slowly.

"Addy's right. You just got super weird," Hannah said. Russ started to scowl. "Is it super embarrassing? Did you meet her at a lightsaber competition?"

Russ sighed. "No."

"Sex party?"

"No." Russ started to walk away.

"Holy shit. Did you sleep with Eddie's assistant?" Hannah asked.

"No," Russ said. "All right. Yes. Once. We didn't date or anything."

"Hold up." I hustled to walk with her. "You called a one-night stand to get a favor for me?"

"Yes." Russ sighed again.

"That's like real dedication. That's a chit you don't call in lightly."

"I know."

"Did I know you also slept with women?" I asked. Behind us, Hannah laughed.

"Yes."

"Cool. Good talk."

"I'll take it as a win that you don't think about who I'm sleeping with," Russ said.

"We have an odd dynamic. Should I be paying you more?"

"Probably."

❖

"Stop touching that." Nikolai gently smacked Xavier's hand away from his chest.

"I'm sorry. It just feels so cool. Like it looks like my skin but I can't feel it at all." Xavier's fingertips inched up his chest. "Addy, touch this."

"No, thanks. I don't want to feel your naked chest," I said.

"But it's not my chest. It's latex."

I stopped looking down at the artistically strewn leaves that Xavier was about to be dragged through so I could give him a stern look. "It took hours to prep you for this scene. If you screw up your makeup, I'm putting you in a T-shirt and everyone will be deprived of another shirtless scene of you. Do you want to wear a shirt when you die?"

He shoved his hands in his pockets. "No, ma'am."

Nikolai covered a laugh. "You're all set." He gathered his toolkit and left us to our final review.

Xavier and Black Hat squared off for the climax of their fight. I called action and Xavier lumbered forward. He was reminiscent of a boxer in the ninth round, still determined to finish and clearly incapable of doing so. He wiped away the blood from his mouth and swung at Black Hat again. Black Hat stepped back and let Xavier's momentum throw him off balance. In the ensuing stumble, Black Hat pulled out the knife.

I called cut. "Xavier, can you watch your feet this time? I want the audience to see the knife for a full beat before you do."

Xavier gave me a thumbs up. Nikolai was wiping away the blood from his chin and setting the next round to drip, which meant Xavier couldn't speak or move his face.

We ran the sequence until I was satisfied. The actual stabbing went well, but then we spent far too long on Black Hat pulling the knife out of Xavier's chest. I wanted blood spatter flying off the blade. Instead the blood stubbornly clung to the knife. Nikolai tweaked the blood until it had a better consistency.

Xavier died beautifully. We had just finished dragging his body away for the last time when Sean came striding onto set. He waited impatiently for us to call cut before he pulled me aside.

"I thought we'd decided to shoot Xavier's death with a shirt," he said.

"Xavier's naked chest is kind of a feature of the character. I wanted to showcase it in his final scene." I was careful to keep my tone even. If I slipped into gloating, Sean would never let this go.

"But the chest hair." Sean was doing nothing to hide his agitation.

"We need to move on to the next shot. Can we put a pin in this so I can tell Hannah we're done here?" I asked.

"No. We're not done here. We need to completely reshoot this." Sean pointed at Xavier who was taking selfies displaying his bloody chest.

"Didn't you talk to Eddie today?" I asked.

"No. He called about twenty times." Sean laughed. "Did you talk to Daddy and ask him to back you?"

I tried to take a calming breath, but it didn't calm me at all. Suddenly, I couldn't think of a single reason to keep my temper. Eddie had tried to call Sean. Sean blew him off. And now I was faced with a producer with his head willingly up his own ass. "You are such a fucking dick, you know that, right?"

"At least I can fight my own battles." He grandly crossed his arms. The movement made me wonder if he'd practiced this in his trailer before coming to belittle me.

"Get over yourself. Eddie called me. He was all up in arms about the location for reshooting the Xavier/Ava sex scene. I stupidly assumed you had already talked to him about why you wanted to do reshoots, but it was the first he was hearing about it."

"Addy, I'm sorry to interrupt." Hannah touched my arm. "But I need to know if we're breaking."

"Yes, we are," I said.

"No, you're not," Sean said.

"Can you grab Russ for me?" I asked Hannah.

She nodded and darted off.

Sean scoffed. "You think your assistant is going to resolve this? Christ. No wonder this production is behind schedule."

"Okay, you need to stop being an asshole. I'm asking for Russ because she's got my phone. If you won't take Eddie's calls, I'll put him on speaker so he can tell you to get out of my way."

"I need to get out of your way?" Sean shouted. "You're fucking yourself sideways. I'm trying to help, though God knows why."

"I was doing just fine for the first six weeks of filming," I said.

"You were not fine. You were dangerously behind schedule. Your dailies are filled with red flags." He was trying to piss me off. It was working. "There's a reason Danny called me as soon as I was available," he said.

It took every ounce of my willpower to not pointedly ask him why exactly he wasn't available before last week. Doing so would feel good for all of thirty seconds before he started crowing about there being no case against him and pissed me off ten times worse than I already was.

"Take the help being offered." Sean put his hand on my shoulder. He was trying for paternalistic, but his touch made my skin crawl.

"Sure. Fine. We're a team, right?" I asked.

"Exactly."

"Hey, here's a thought. Why don't you start your team building by taking Eddie's goddamn calls?"

He bristled. "Eddie is five hundred miles away. I'm the producer on the ground. My opinion is worth a little more at the moment. You'd do well to take advantage of my experience."

Claude finally interrupted. "Everything okay here?"

"I'm great. I've got to review my next shot." I started to push past Claude, but I spun back when I saw Russ approaching. "Sean needs help operating a telephone. The other producers would like to tell him we're not reshooting anything, but he's not taking their calls."

Claude quickly hid his surprise at my tone. "Right. We'll get this sorted out."

Russ fell into step with me as I walked back to my trailer. She didn't say anything as we walked. I let the door slam behind us. Russ silently watched me pace the small space. I felt surprisingly good. It helped that I knew I'd followed the right channels. It made the telling off more righteous.

There was a knock on the door. Russ glanced out the window. "It's Hannah," she said.

"Come in," I called.

Hannah opened the door. "What the hell was that?"

"Sean's been ignoring Eddie's calls all day. He had no idea the reshoots were vetoed," I said.

Hannah laughed. "Of course he didn't."

"Is Claude still talking to him?" I asked.

"Nope. They were passing a phone back and forth—talking to Eddie, I'm guessing. And then Sean left set. He was so mad." She continued laughing.

"He's gone?"

"Not permanently. But for the night at least."

My next breath felt remarkably easier. "I'll take a night of peace."

CHAPTER TWENTY-SIX

Maybe it was a desperate attempt for control or normalcy. Or maybe I was just tired of secret, quiet conversations. The reasoning didn't matter. I was going to do a table read for the movie's finale. Dammit.

Russ set up the biggest conference room with pointless little name placards and bottles of water and scripts hot off Lenny and Harold's printer. Per my youthful cast member's plan, all the kids showed up early to rearrange the seating. Logan and Diego forcibly moved Claude and Hannah and the writers' seats so they were behind the girls. I made the mistake of asking where Teddy was and was told the Primary was making the Target late in order to force him to sit where they wanted him.

It was very annoying. It was also a decent execution of a decent plan.

Of course all of this made it so Rosie read her script first because the boys were fucking around. She turned to Molly who was marking up the set directions for her and Diego to read. Their characters were dead, but they weren't going to miss an opportunity to annoy the hell out of Sean. I appreciated their commitment to the cause. Molly and Rosie whispered about killer Ava. Across the room, Emma watched them realize that she'd already known. She smiled and texted them. It was a delight to watch.

When Sean and Teddy arrived, Sean gave an insincere apology for making us wait. They sat in the two available chairs. I skipped introductions since everyone knew each other and instead announced that Molly and Diego would be reading set directions. Sean cut into my speech.

"Sorry. I know you all have been working together for a minute, but I haven't officially introduced myself. I'm Sean Murray, former *DSN* director, current executive producer," he said grandly.

The cast looked at him, then each other, then me. Then they collectively looked right back at their scripts. It was painfully awkward. I loved it.

"Great. So. As I was saying, Molly's and Diego's characters are dead so they will be narrating. Take it away," I said.

Molly launched into the description of the previous scene. The party, the scattering guests. I did my best to keep my eyes down. I listened to the cadence of dialogue and took notes. The first shot was Benny finding Sadie dying in the woods. She tried to tell him things. He shushed her and told her someone would come to help.

Diego cut us over to Grace and Taylor fleeing through the woods and Ava innocently finding them. We spent some time on basic exposition before Diego chimed in with footsteps to drive us toward the cabin. Molly cut back to Benny sobbing over Sadie's body.

"You're okay. It's okay," Benny said.

"Benny attempts to keep pressure on the wound in Sadie's stomach." Molly kept her voice moderated, emphasizing the subtlety of Benny's careful movements. "She's unconscious. He realizes with gruesome confusion that he's pushing out her intestines whenever he touches her."

"Exterior. Malone's cabin. Grace, Taylor, and Ava run toward Malone standing on his porch," Diego said.

"Get inside. He's here," I called, frantic.

"He's in the woods. Inside. Now," Wylie yelled.

"Who? What are you talking about?" Malone asked.

We continued shouting at Malone. He greeted our panic with deceptive repose. I made a note that I wanted him to play up the confusion rather than pure creepy calm.

From there, the final showdown was action heavy. My table read idea was a bit silly in retrospect. Molly and Diego fell over themselves describing the action.

"Black Hat appears behind Malone!" Molly shouted.

Wylie screamed.

"Black Hat stabs Malone in the back! Once, twice! Malone drops to his knees!" Diego shouted.

"Grace runs forward! Ava and Taylor hold her back!" Molly shouted.

Diego dropped his voice to a low rumble. "Black Hat steps past Malone. He's Michael Myersing that shit. Stalking them. Slowly walking toward the stairs. The women begin to back away. The forest at their backs is so close, but they're never going to make it."

"No. No, no, no," I said.

"Malone shoves himself to his feet and grabs Black Hat. In a single, beautiful movement, he snaps that motherfucker's neck. Black Hat's black hat falls off his head. We see his blank eyes for the first time as the body drops," Molly said.

I glanced at Lenny and Harold. They were rapt.

"Malone slumps against the railing. He's alive but barely," Molly said.

"Ava moves forward. She's tentative. Like she's approaching a deadly animal—and she is," Diego said. "She checks Black Hat's pulse. Then she takes up his knife. With the weapon secured and the threat neutralized, Grace and Taylor approach the house. As they mount the steps, Ava picks up Black Hat's black hat and settles it on her head. She stands and her face is cast in shadow. She has become him."

"My brother never did have the stones to do what was necessary," Ava said.

"Ava stabs Malone again. She twists the knife and shoves him to the floor. She resumes Black Hat's methodical stalking, descending the stairs toward Grace and Taylor," Diego said.

Wylie screamed again.

"No. It's not—You can't be—" I stumbled over the words, a plea in my tone.

"Run!" Wylie shouted.

Diego cut away from us to Benny stumbling through the woods. "Ava appears. Her silhouette is clearly half Black Hat, half young, hot woman. Benny doesn't notice the hat. He approaches her, his bloodied hands out in placation." We had another patch of action where Ava seemingly killed Benny. I took fast notes about how I wanted the shots framed. "The Final Girls sprint through the forest. Ava chases them. She's given up on stalking—now she just wants the kill," Diego said.

"They emerge into the clearing around Malone's cabin. The bodies on the porch haven't moved. We see Black Hat's unblinking eyes. His bare head makes him grotesque. They carefully step over Black Hat, then Malone. Malone coughs. He's still alive!" Molly shouted.

"Oh, shit. Malone," I said.

"She's here," Wylie said. She made no effort to lower her voice. It was simply an announcement. It was perfect.

"Come on, Grace. I just want to talk." Ava's voice was sweet, singsong. "You owe me, bitch."

"Don't listen to her," I said.

"You want to talk? Let's talk," Wylie said.

"Grace vaults down the stairs and faces off with her nephew's killer. The two women dance around each other."

"Come on. Tell me how I've wronged you," Wylie said. She was on the edge of shouting, but not quite there. Anger made her voice hard. "Tell me what my family did to make you want to kill people. Tell me how it's my fault."

"You killed my father." Ava spat the words.

"Taylor slowly approaches the stairs. Grace sees the movement but keeps her focus locked on Ava. They're hot as hell and pissed off. This is a reinvention of the angry lesbian and it's a damn revelation," Molly said. Harold had clearly influenced Lenny's writing, but I was undecided on whether that was a good thing.

"Then he probably deserved it," Wylie said.

"You bitch."

Lenny had given us an ending worthy of the series. I was filming Taylor's death in the hopes that Oath would let the franchise die with her. I was also filming her survival to avoid reshoots when they inevitably decided I couldn't kill her.

"And cut," I said. "That's a wrap on our climax. Thanks for doing this, everyone."

Diego and Molly led a round of applause. They directed it toward me, but I pointed at Lenny and Harold. Both guys nodded their thanks and grinned.

"Okay. Let's break for thirty, then meet back here. I'd like to review my notes with you all as a group rather than individually. I'll still be meeting with some of you, but for efficiency's sake, I'd like to get the bulk of my notes out in this forum. Sound good?" I asked.

The cast nodded. Everyone started to stand when Sean called out, "Can everyone hold on for a minute? I'd like to go over my notes now." He motioned for them to sit back down. It was a power play, pure and simple.

"I'm sorry, Sean. But I'm going to have to insist on a break." I made a point of gathering my script. "I'll see you all back here at four." I herded Rosie and Molly toward the door. Diego saw what I was doing and hastened to leave.

"PJ, a word," Sean said.

"For sure. Just give me five." I hurried through the door. Wylie caught up with me on the way to my trailer.

"He's pissed," she said.

"Good. I'm done with his posturing."

I assumed Wylie would continue on to her own trailer. Instead she went inside mine. Teddy and Logan were already there.

"What are you two—"

The door opened again and Rosie joined us. "Hey, boss. Great table read. I'm glad we did that."

"Why are you all in my trailer?" I asked. I knew what they were doing. But I was officially at my limit for interactions with people. I truly did want five minutes to breathe.

Sean let himself into the trailer before they could answer. "It's a fucking party in here."

"Yeah, I was hoping for a minute alone," I said pointedly.

The door opened again and Diego and Molly came in. "I told you they would be in here," Diego said to her.

"Okay, everyone out," I said.

"Yeah, I'd like a minute alone with PJ," Sean said.

"No, you too. Everyone out." I directed Diego and Molly out the door. Logan resisted but Wylie gently pushed him out ahead of her.

Rosie gave Sean a look before crossing her arms and sitting on the couch. "I've got to talk to Addy. It'll only take a minute. I can wait until you're done," she said to Sean.

"You'll have to wait outside," he said. He went to touch her shoulder. She awkwardly leaned to the side so he wouldn't touch her. He noticed the movement and it pissed him off, but he kept the anger restrained.

"It's fine, Rosie." I jumped in before Sean could say anything.

"But—"

"You can wait outside," I said.

"Fine." She stood and let herself out. Before the door closed, I glimpsed everyone I'd just kicked out milling around outside the trailer.

"What's with the goddamn fan club?" Sean asked.

I shrugged and leaned against the counter. "We spent a lot of time together at the start of the shoot. They're all good kids."

Sean grinned. "I don't know, Rosie seems like she has more than a passing interest in you." He leaned against the counter right next to me. His sickly sweet cologne washed over me. A whole trailer and he still managed to crowd me.

I let that pitch go. "What's up? What did you want to discuss without the cast?"

"You, actually. I think you're coddling them too much."

"I disagree. I've gotten great performances out of them so far," I said.

"Why do you always do that?" He didn't raise his voice, but his tone shifted. "It's like you're contradicting me on principle."

"Everything I do isn't about you." I pushed off the counter to grab a water from the cabinet behind us. It gave me just enough distance to maintain control.

"And yet in every conversation we have you find fault with something."

"I'm not trying to debate you. I'm just telling you what I think and what I see. A movie is a collaboration of ideas and opinions," I said.

He smacked his hand on the counter. "Don't lecture me on what a movie is. I've been making them a hell of a lot longer than you have."

"Actually, that's not—"

The toilet flushed. Sean and I turned as a unit and stared at the closed door. A second later, Teddy came out buttoning his jeans with dry hands. My first thought was the popcorn at Jed's.

"Whoa. Hey." He grinned at us. "Jesus, Sean. You trying to maintain body heat or something?" He laughed at his own joke.

Sean took a step back. "I didn't realize you were in here."

Teddy gave him a comically judgmental look. "Shit, dude. This is why people say you're a creeper. Someone tells you about personal space and your first response is to say you thought you were alone." He laughed even harder.

Sean swallowed his irritation and smirked. "At least she's a dyke or I'd really have a problem."

Teddy stopped smiling. "Uhh. Awkward. Look, I know you're the producer and all that, but I'm not really cool with you saying that word. It's not yours, you know?" His reaction was entirely overdone, ridiculous enough to be farcical.

"Okay." Sean drew the word out. "I didn't know the word police were here." He chuckled to hide his discomfort.

"It's cool, man. Just don't say shit like that." Teddy clapped him on the shoulder and started walking toward the door. "Is Logan still around?" he asked me.

"I think he's outside," I said.

"Excellent." Teddy led Sean outside. I stared in awe at the closed door. Maybe this movie wasn't going to be the death of me.

CHAPTER TWENTY-SEVEN

The view was gorgeous. Of course it was. The house the studio had rented for the wrap party was high up in the hills. The ocean sparkled in the distance. Moonlight rendered the water silver and ethereal. The air on the porch was sharp and chilly—the first hints of fall. I could hear the party raging inside, spilling out onto the patio below, but here it was still.

"You did it," Wylie said from behind me.

I turned and leaned against the railing. She was wearing a black suit with a black shirt and a black tie. It made her a shadow that emerged in slivers. First the moonlight on her bright hair, then the glint of her silk tie, then the sharp lines of the cold glass she held out to me.

"No champagne?" I took a sip.

She half-smiled. "I know you better than that."

"You really do."

She rested her forearms on the railing and looked out at the view. "You know you should join the party."

"No. I did my job. This is my reward."

"Silence?" She turned and searched my face.

"My favorite thing." I was kidding, but only just.

"You want me to leave?"

I almost said yes because I didn't want to feel the things Wylie made me feel. But the warmth of her suddenly seemed so much better than the familiarity of my isolation. I shook my head. Wylie reached over and took my drink. I watched her sip from the glass. She set it on the railing and stepped into my space. The scent of citrus was emboldened by the gin on her breath. I touched her jaw with a fingertip and drew a line to her chin. She watched my eyes as I studied her. Her lips were faintly pink. I traced the bottom one. She let me. The air had left the night. My heart climbed into my throat, suffocating me. My hand was trembling as I slid it up her neck into her hair.

When I finally kissed Wylie, she arched into me. I slid my free hand around her waist and pulled her closer. Her lips were so, so familiar and yet, a revelation. We'd kissed a thousand times and this still felt different. She tasted sharp and clean. Her tongue suddenly filled my mouth and I sucked it.

Her fingertips fumbled at the buttons on my jacket. She got the outer one undone only to grumble in frustration when she realized the double-breasted coat was fastened inside as well. I started to laugh but then her hands were on me, tugging my shirt out, sliding underneath to press against my bare stomach.

I shifted and turned so her back was to the railing. I kissed down her neck until I met her stiff collar. I tugged the knot out of her tie and worked the buttons open so I could taste the soft skin at the base of her throat. She ran her fingers through my hair, tugging at the curls. I kissed back up to her mouth, wanting to fall deep into her.

Wy let go of me so she could open her belt. The soft rattle of the buckle made every single one of my nerves stand at attention. She gripped my wrist and pushed my hand down her pants. Damp cotton pressed against the back of my hand. I slid my fingers through slick warmth. Wy's breath caught in my ear and it was sexy as hell.

I knew this was precarious. There were a not insignificant number of people at this party who would have sold a photo of us in a heartbeat. And yet. I didn't think I could have stopped touching her if half my crew had opened the door. Her gentle grip on my forearm, urging me forward told me she felt the same.

The hot, soft skin under my fingertips overwhelmed me. She was tangible in a way I'd forced myself to forget. It was easier to be completely alone than to want this—the rush of her heartbeat, the slick proof of her wanting. She pressed her open mouth against my neck. Her teeth were a hard counterpoint to the thick warmth enveloping me.

The sound of the door opening behind us shocked the hell out of me. I rocked back from Wylie. She tugged her shirt closed.

It was only Hannah. She glanced back into the room she'd just left, then closed the door behind her. "If this is a secret, you two need to not be doing it here." She was very matter-of-fact.

"Fair point." Wylie started doing up her buttons. I didn't remember having undone them all.

"We're not—It's not a thing," I said.

Hannah shook her head. "There are so many levels of me not needing to know."

"It really was just a moment. Sorry we weren't more discreet." Wylie started retying her tie.

"Hey, it wouldn't be a wrap party if I didn't walk into an illicit make out sesh." Hannah grinned. "But Sean is looking for you and it's becoming clear that Wylie is also missing."

"Fuck." I tucked in my shirt and buttoned my jacket. "Am I good to go?"

Hannah stepped closer and looked me up and down. "Clothes are fine. Hair is mussed. And you have a fairly obvious bite mark."

"Shit." Wylie tilted my chin up. She ran her thumb over a tender spot on my neck. Even with Hannah watching, it felt intimate and sexy.

"You gave me a hickey?"

"I'm sorry," Wy said.

"We're in our thirties and you gave me a hickey?" My ire was sort of undermined by her laughing at me.

"You weren't complaining when I did it." She tugged the collar of my jacket up then frowned. "That won't work."

"Here." Hannah opened her purse and pulled out a compact. "This'll cover it long enough for you to make an appearance."

I pulled my shirt collar out and let Hannah dab makeup onto my neck. "You're my hero."

"Aww. You're just saying that because you know I'm not going to tell anyone you were making out with Wylie."

"It was an accident," I said.

Hannah nodded condescendingly. "Yes, I often accidentally undress my colleagues during work functions." She closed the compact. "That's better." Her eyes flicked up to my hair. "Hair is your department."

I ran my fingers through my curls and redirected them. "Lead the way."

Hannah brought me downstairs and out to the lower patio. It was packed. I could see most of my cast. They were all paired up with a cast member of another gender except for Rosie who had her arm tucked into her mother's. I still didn't know if she'd invited her mom because I told her to or because she wanted to call my bluff. Either way, it was one less body to track for the next couple of hours. Teddy intercepted me and Hannah as we walked outside.

"There you are." Teddy grabbed my arm and started to pull me toward the far end of the porch. "We need you here so he can make his dumb speech. Once he does that, I can roofie him and remove him from the party."

I stopped walking. "Please tell me you're kidding."

"Uh, yeah. Of course I'm kidding," Teddy said.

I didn't believe him at all. "Teddy."

"Come on. I'm just fucking around." He laughed and pulled at my arm. "Really. I'm going to get him wasted so he passes out. No roofies will be harmed in the process."

"You swear?"

"Yes." He stopped and faced me. "Really. Logan's going to swap my wine so I can out drink Sean."

"These are the kind of shenanigans that never work out."

"It'll be fine. Let's go. We need to get you over there." He tried to get me walking again.

"Not until you promise not to pull any stupid stunts," I said.

"There she is!" Sean shouted. Everyone who didn't know I was in the crowd turned to look at me. I forced a smile.

"Trust me," Teddy whispered before shoving me forward.

It was an inauspicious beginning to what was sure to be a disastrous evening. Sean held out his hands to welcome me. I managed to sidestep the greeting by shoving my hands in my pockets and turning to stare out at the sea of faces.

"We've finally tracked her down, folks." Sean did a grand wave of his hand. "I'm sure she and Wylie just had to get dressed before joining us."

I settled on a noncommittal smile. Anything else would have given him power. He started a rambling introduction for the cast and crew as if I hadn't spent the last seven and a half weeks with them. After the third of his jokes landed with lukewarm laughter, he gracefully stepped away.

"Thanks." I nodded in his general direction. "You all know I'm not one for speeches. And if you didn't know, now you do. I'll keep this short. Thank you all for putting so much into this picture. I truly couldn't have done it without you. Thanks especially to Simon for finding me unscented lube. We didn't use it and you were two hours late, but your dedication is admirable."

"I love you, Addy," Simon shouted from the back.

"Love you too, bud." I winked at him and he blew me a kiss. I said the right things about the cast and crew. Sean's scowl made brief appearances every time the crew laughed when they were supposed to. It thrilled me enough to speak for five whole minutes. Halfway through I locked eyes with Wylie. She was standing off to the side, back in the shadows. She toasted me with the gin and tonic I'd abandoned. Her presence was enough to make me fumble so I tried to look away, but I couldn't help being drawn back into her.

When I wrapped up, Sean jumped to take my place. Apparently, he was the emcee. The moment I stepped into the crowd, the cast and crew turned away. Some shook my hand, others returned to previously abandoned conversations. Sean quickly realized he'd lost them.

Instead of making my way to Wylie, I found the bartender and got another drink. My convictions seemed to disappear when I was around Wylie. I knew I needed to stop things before they became more. I also knew it would be a whole thing and I just didn't want to do it. This was why I was alone. That way, I only had myself to disappoint.

I took my drink back to my balcony high above the party. Music and voices and laughter drifted up. It was enough to surround me— give me the illusion of people—without actually having to engage with anyone.

"I knew I'd find you up here again," Wylie said from behind me.

I didn't bother turning this time. "You know me, always retreating."

"So are we going to talk about it?" She leaned her forearms on the railing next to me and stared out at the expanse below us.

"Sure."

"Do you even know what we're talking about?" Her tone had shifted. She was looking for a fight. Maybe this would be easier than I thought.

"Us, I assume," I said.

"Actually, I was thinking about your rush to tell Hannah there's nothing here."

I looked at her in question. "You said the same thing."

"Yeah. You're not the only one who has to save face." Her brow furrowed and she shook her head. "Should I have said 'sorry, Hannah, PJ just said something real dismissive and shitty and I'd like to unpack it'?"

"Oh."

"Yeah."

The silence stretched until something had to break. I decided it would be her this time. "I'm sorry. I'm just not good at this. Relationships. This is why I'm not in one."

"Really?"

I shrugged. "I can't be responsible for someone else's emotional state or feelings or whatever."

"Wow. You're serious, aren't you? You really believe this shit?"

"It's not shit. It's honesty. I'm sorry you don't like it." I focused on my drink. It was hitting me hard. I'd finally found a bartender who would pour a strong enough one right when I needed my wits about me.

"No. I mean you're not alone. You've never been. You push people away and then you claim to be a pariah, but that doesn't mean it's real."

"I don't know what you mean." I really didn't.

"I mean that your cast has fully rearranged their sleeping schedules, their performances, their social interactions for the last week and a half so that you could comfortably make a movie. Your mother flew a thousand miles to be with your friend so you wouldn't worry about her." Wylie pushed back off the railing. I made the mistake of following her movements. She was livid. She was also crying. Not sobbing, just crying. Crystalline tears ringed her eyes. "And I—I let you lecture me on building relationships that you find too complicated or imperfect just because I actually acknowledge that I don't like to be alone."

"That's bullshit. I'm sorry."

"What is?"

"You know I don't actually like to be alone," I said.

She blinked at me in what appeared to be disbelief. "Right. So why do you always talk about isolating yourself and liking solitude?"

"Because I like privacy. Everyone expects something from me which is fucking exhausting. So, yeah. It's easier to climb into my cave in the hills where no one will ask me to be whoever it is they want me to be." I thought Wylie knew that. I thought she was the only one who knew that.

"PJ. That's just life."

"Our lives are different than most people's and you know it." I scowled at her. "Every time we step onto a movie set or go out for dinner, we're supposed to be fifteen different people all at once."

"That's the public. That's the press. I'm talking about the real people in your life. Hannah and Teddy and Phil." Wylie pointed at the mass of people below us. "They are all here for you. You don't need a facade with them."

"Yeah, well the last time I let my guard down was when I fell in love with you."

"Fine. Blame me." She leaned over the railing and stared at the blackened sea in the distance. Below us, the party ebbed and flowed with sound and feeling and laughter. Here it was cold and still. "You can retreat into your bungalow for years if you want, but when you emerge, those people will be waiting for you. Not because they're fans of your work or they think you're hot. They'll be waiting because you are so fucking compelling that they can't help but want to be part of your life."

I tried to find her point, but it was lost on me. "That doesn't mean I have to let them in."

She finally turned so she could glare at me. "You are such an ass."

"Okay." That we could agree on.

"The illusion of being alone is a luxury that they grant you. That we all grant you. You can keep the world at a distance because when you're ready to not feel alone or you need something, we are at your beck and call," she said.

"So what? I owe you something for that?"

"No, but we also don't deserve to be dismissed just because you find being loved a burden."

CHAPTER TWENTY-EIGHT

After weeks of twenty-hour days in Phil's backyard editing studio, I was certain the impression of my ass would be permanently etched into his solitary extra chair. Strictly speaking, I didn't need to be there the whole time. The alternative, however, was admitting that I was available. I could not be available. Not to my mother or Taryn or my agent. Certainly not the press. It didn't matter if I was available to Wylie because she was never going to speak to me again. I'd been hoping for something a little less extreme, but according to her, this was what I'd always wanted. Social interactions that I controlled.

My initial anger had bled away and now I was just sad. I didn't want to examine too closely exactly why I was sad because if I did that, I might have to admit that there was a bit of truth in what Wylie had said.

Not surprisingly, spending hours on end for days on end studying video of Wylie wasn't helping. The sway of her hair, the gentle curve of her brows, the arc of her lips were all emblazoned on the back of my eyelids. She was a moving picture I couldn't escape. I felt like Romeo studying Juliet's corpse. She was beautiful and that was all she was. Out of my reach, mocking me with her visage. My isolation was a tomb I had chosen.

Phil was entirely unaware of my black mood. Well, he knew I was brooding, but he didn't bother to ask why. It wasn't that he didn't care—just that he didn't care to ask. Which was one of the reasons I liked Phil.

We were piecing together Xavier's death when Phil cut into my focus. "Check this out." He brought up a video. I was expecting the movie we were editing, but no, it was some gossip site. He hit play and it was Diego outside of some restaurant.

"It was hands down the best set I've ever been on. PJ Addison creates this environment that is just so loving and kind. She's a professional of course, but she also makes you feel like you're part of her family. Or like part of her, you know?" Diego half-smiled in a way that guaranteed anyone watching would immediately share the video. He was a very pretty boy.

"And Sean Murray? What was it like with him on set?" the interviewer asked.

"Who?" Diego was confused by the question.

"Sean Murray. The executive producer. Did he change the dynamic?"

"Oh." Diego shook his head. "No, I guess not. To be honest, I couldn't pick the guy out of a lineup."

Phil triumphantly hit a button to stop the video. "He's great. I think I love him."

"Who? Diego?"

"Yeah. These interviews are just hilarious," he said.

"What interviews?" I asked. Phil looked at me incredulously. "What?"

"The interviews they've been doing," he said.

"Who? What interviews?"

"You seriously haven't seen any of them?" he asked.

"Any of what?"

Phil rolled his eyes. "Just a sec." He typed something into the search bar then hit play on *Five minutes of Diego Jiménez not knowing Sean Murray*.

The video was as described. A supercut of Diego repeating various versions of the previous interview. It always ended with him saying "I couldn't pick the guy out of a lineup." By the end of the video, the editor had cut out all the interview pieces and it was just Diego saying the line. There had to be twenty interviews.

"What is he playing at?" I asked. I wasn't expecting a response from Phil, but he didn't see the question as rhetorical.

"It's not just him." He turned the screen so I could see the other YouTube hits. There were nearly identical videos of Teddy and Logan. The girls were included on the *DSN: Redux cast doesn't know Sean Murray for twenty minutes.* They all said the exact same line.

"How long have they been doing this?" That wasn't rhetorical.

"A week maybe. Probably a bit longer, but the bulk of the interviews have been in the last five days or so," Phil said.

"The studio is going to fucking lose it."

Phil shrugged. "Not really your problem, right? I mean, you can't control the cast."

"No, I can't." As evidenced by this little stunt.

"I assume they didn't tell you they were doing this?"

"No. But they all miraculously stopped sending me messages a week ago. It can't be a coincidence."

"Aww, that's sweet."

"It's not sweet. It's a disaster," I said.

"How?" Phil spun in his chair to face me. "I mean, it's actually kind of brilliant. The studio can't retaliate contractually. Movie is done. The promo is already launched. They can't pull it without looking like assholes."

"Are you kidding? They don't have to do any of that. They can just blacklist the cast." Adrenaline rushed through my body. My scalp got hot and my wrists started to itch. This was going to blow up spectacularly.

"Okay. Let's say you're right. But do me a hypothetical." Phil waited for my nod before continuing. "You're a casting director at another studio. You hear a rumor that Diego Jiménez is a nightmare to work with. He's vain and difficult. You also have seen any one of these interviews—which are getting serious coverage. What is your takeaway?"

I sighed. The man had a point. "It's still a risky move."

"Sure. Of course it is. But it's worth it."

"Why?"

"Hoo boy. You really are kind of a dumbass, aren't you?" He laughed. I did not laugh. "Addy, it's a love letter. To you."

"That's a little dramatic."

"It's not."

"Fine." I didn't want to continue this discussion. It was veering a little too close to what Wylie had said for my comfort. "It's a wonderful grand gesture, but that doesn't mean it's for me. They all really hate Sean."

"They hate him because you hate him, but I won't argue with you." Phil spun back to his bank of monitors and returned to *Redux*. Two minutes later, he was fully back in his zone and I was stuck with a whole mess of feelings and thoughts. It was very inconvenient.

"I'm stepping outside for some air."

"Sure thing," he said without looking away.

Phil's place was small but the one-bedroom Spanish bungalow was more than compensated for by the yard, which took up half the lot. Slabs of tile in green and teal and dark, dark orange made up the patio. I stretched out on one of the chaises and stared up at the sky. A single star was visible. Probably a planet, actually. It was early in the evening still. Only eight or nine. It felt obscene to be this exhausted when only a month before, this was when my day was starting in earnest.

I didn't know what else to do so I called Gerri. She'd be able to get my head on straight. She picked up on the first ring.

"Hello, my sweet P."

"Hey, Ma."

"How are you? How's editing going?"

"It's fine. We should be done next week." I closed my eyes and listened to the gentle lap of Phil's neighbor's pool. The cars in the distance were a low hum.

"How is it? Are you satisfied with how it's turning out?"

"Yeah, actually. Emma gave me an amazing performance. She's the blonde who was in that mystery show you liked," I said.

She chuckled. "Oh, I know Emma. She's just lovely. Excellent mahjong player too."

"What?"

"Mahjong. She took all my money."

I sat up. "When did you play mahjong with Emma?"

"Last week at Taryn's." Her tone suggested that I was completely aware of Emma hanging around Taryn's house with my mother.

"Why was Emma at Taryn's?"

There was a pause as Gerri processed the implications of my question. She answered with laughter. "They're cunning. I'll give them that."

"Mom."

"Your cast. They dropped by Taryn's last week. Spent some time getting to know her. Discussed their approach with Sean to make sure she was comfortable. They were all really wonderful, sweet P. You should be proud of them."

"Which cast members?" I asked.

"All of them, I think. Emma, of course. Rosie. Logan and Diego. Teddy. He's brilliant. I'm sure you know that. Of course, I think Diego might pretend to be a bit dumber than he is. Oh, I also met Molly and that musician she's dating. Kayla?"

"Kayleigh?"

"Yes. Them."

"No Wylie?"

"No, but they all made me think you two knew they were there so she probably doesn't know either. How is Wylie? I haven't spoken to her since she told me about the divorce."

"I don't know. We had a fight," I said.

"I'm sorry, baby. Do you want to talk about it?"

"Not really."

"Okay," she said.

"Ma?"

"Yes."

"I'm very private," I said. She waited. Which was fair since I hadn't actually said anything worthwhile. I didn't know how to ask the question without parroting Wylie. "Like, to the detriment of my personal relationships. Is there something wrong with me?"

"I don't know if I can answer that. I mean, I think you're just perfect in every way. As long as that privacy makes you happy, I don't see the problem." She wasn't being facetious. She really did think I was literal perfection.

"Spoken like a mother," I said.

"Why are you asking? What's got you so twisted up?"

"Wylie." I lay back down and stared at the blank sky. It was darker but no more spots of light had appeared. "She said I treat being loved as a burden." I'd repeated the line so many times in the last few weeks that it had become a sort of gruesome mantra. "And maybe I do. But the last time I opened up to someone, we were both outed and the pressure destroyed us."

"Well." She sighed and sidestepped. "I don't know about all that, but I would like to see you with someone."

My misery slipped into irritation and I fell back into what was comfortable. "What if I'm happier alone?"

"That's entirely possible. I certainly am. And I probably would believe you if I hadn't seen you with Wylie when you were young."

"What if I've changed? I'm not the same person I was when I was with her."

"Of course you've changed." Her tone shifted into annoyance tempered by love. "That doesn't mean she's not part of you still. You two went through a fairly traumatic experience together. It made you grow into each other. When you split, both of you left pieces behind."

"So I should go back to my girlfriend from when I was a kid?"

"That's not what I'm saying," she said.

"What are you saying?"

"I don't know. Just that I've seen you in a relationship where you were deeply happy. I don't want you to miss out on future happiness out of habit. And pushing people away is your habit."

To my great relief, the dark wood and glass door to Phil's studio swung open. "Hey, Addy, you still—" he stopped abruptly when he saw I was on the phone. "When you're done," he whispered.

"Ma, I gotta go. Phil needs me."

"I didn't mean to upset you," she said.

"You didn't. You've given me a lot to think about." So much for her helping uncomplicate my thoughts.

"Okay," she said with hesitation. "I love you. Don't forget to get some rest."

"Will do. Love you, Ma." I hung up.

"You didn't have to do that," Phil said.

"Believe me. I needed to do that."

"I was just wondering if you were cool with me ordering dinner? I'm feeling nachos."

"Nachos are absolutely what I need right now."

"Good because I already ordered. Also, I need to know which take you want for the end of Xavier's death. Come look."

I followed him back into the studio. He had two shots queued up that were identical when frozen. He played the first and Xavier was slowly dragged out of the frame. The blood that he'd coughed up as he died left a grisly line in the dirt. Phil stopped the video and started the next one. This shot followed his blank face as he was dragged away. His eyes were glassy in death.

"I like the first. It leaves the audience behind. We don't know where he's being taken and the second shot prompts that question."

"Excellent."

He slotted in the right take and we watched the final version of Xavier's death. It started with him in the woods wearing only his little underwear, calling out for Ava. It was dusk and his laughter quickly turned to frustration. When he found the pile of clothes she'd dropped but no sign of his girlfriend, his frustration became fear. He stumbled into his jeans and sneakers. The rest of their clothing, he gathered before running through the woods.

When he ran into Black Hat, he fought valiantly, all the while accusing him of killing Ava. They engaged in some classic fisticuffs before Black Hat pulled out that obscenely long Bowie knife and rammed it into the beautiful muscle of Xavier's bare chest. He twisted and pulled. The arc of blood spatter glistened in the fading light. Xavier dropped to his knees. Black Hat stabbed him twice more and Xavier fell back to the ground. His body was dragged out of frame.

We compared notes and found the scene perfect. By the time we'd finished, our dinner had arrived. Phil grabbed a couple of beers from the small studio fridge. We took our very healthy meal outside.

"So you going to give your own little 'couldn't pick the guy out of a lineup' interview?" Phil grinned and took a long pull from his beer.

"No, I don't think I will." It sounded prim, but dammit, I felt prim about the whole thing.

"Come on. It'll be way more hilarious coming from you."

I shook my head and fought an eye roll. "I don't think it'll do anyone any favors. Besides, until I know what their whole plan is, I'm not wading into those waters."

"I'm pretty sure we've seen the whole plan."

"No, I somehow doubt that," I said.

"Either way, it'll give them a thrill to have you jump in."

"I'm not that exciting."

"For sure." He leaned back and waved a hand dismissively. "You're just the director they're fawning over in all these interviews. Totally forgettable."

"Don't do that. I can't take any more of this PJ on a pedestal shit." I stood and marched to the other side of the yard. Of course, there was nowhere to go after that so I just circled back.

Phil was sitting there watching me and laughing. "Touched a nerve did I? Is it so hard being wealthy and charming and attractive?"

"Yeah, whatever. People like Hollywood stars. We're all very charming and attractive." I sat and returned my attention to my nachos.

Phil stopped laughing. "You think you're well liked because you're a movie star?"

"Yeah."

"Hmm." Phil ate a chip and studied me. It was disconcerting. He ate another chip. "You remember our second Sundance?"

I frowned at the seeming non sequitur. "When we were there with *The Night we Lost Bucharest*?"

"Yes, that one. You were just hitting your stride as a director, but still riding your own acting coattails. And everyone wanted you. You brought me to every single debauched party. That producer gave me that whiskey." He stopped to sigh in reminiscence of the whiskey.

"Hollywood parties are big and expensive and they have good whiskey. Is there some point here?" I thought I knew where he was going. I didn't want to go there, but if we were going, I wanted to get there faster.

"The point is you left a party because Huston Samuels thought he was having a heart attack." And there it was.

"Yeah, I'm not a complete asshole," I said.

"He was twenty-two and had no history of heart problems. And he was not having a heart attack."

"But he didn't know that."

"Right. So instead of talking to an executive who you'd been dying to talk to, you spent the night in the ER with one of your young actors who, as it turned out, was having a panic attack," Phil said. I opened my mouth to protest, but he cut me off. "There were ten assistants who could have taken him to the hospital, but you insisted on going with him. You held his hand the whole time. You kept the press away. And you flew out his girlfriend the next morning because you knew she'd keep him grounded for the rest of his events."

"I know you're trying to say I'm nice or some shit. And like fine, whatever. But I don't think it's fair to compare me to a bunch of greedy, amoral execs and say that makes me a good person."

"I'm not saying you're nice." The way he said "nice" made it clear Phil could think of no higher offense. "I'm saying you notice people. You listen to them. What they say and what they don't say. You remember things about them and who they are. It makes them feel seen. Really, truly seen," he said. My frown got more frowny and my pout got more pouty. "That's why people like you. In the Dark Ages, you'd inspire armies to follow you. Instead, you have a bunch of very dedicated, very talented, very pretty people who put you on a pedestal."

CHAPTER TWENTY-NINE

I woke up on the couch in Phil's studio. It was becoming a not uncommon occurrence. There was a cup of coffee on the small table next to me. It was steaming slightly in the morning air. I sat up and stretched. I was suddenly very aware of my own physicality and not in a good way.

"Good, you're up." Phil walked through the studio door. "Have you checked your phone yet?"

I rubbed my face. "No. Why? What travesty do you have for me?" I looked around. "Where is my phone?"

Phil looked around the studio. "Here." He grabbed my phone off the charger on his desk. "You want a banana?"

"Yeah, sure. Thanks." My phone screen was just texts from Diego. I read them in reverse, which made very little sense so I opened my messages. Doing so didn't offer any clarification.

Let me in

Come on

You're not actually mad right??

I brought coffee

Addy. Bro.

Let me in

Don't be mad. I can explain

I checked the time stamps. They were all from the last ten minutes. I tapped his name to call him. He immediately picked up.

"Addy. Hey. You're not for real mad at me, right?"

"It's not even eight in the morning. What could I possibly be mad about?" I asked. I really should have asked Phil for a follow-up before I let him go back in the house.

"The interviews. The whole Sean offensive we launched," Diego said.

"Oh. That." I took a sip of coffee, and it did what sitting up and rubbing my eyes hadn't. "No. I'm not mad. I have questions. I'm worried about you all. But I'm not mad."

"Shit." He blew out a loud, long breath. "You had me worried. Let me in, okay?"

"Are you at my house?"

"Yeah. Who else would ring your doorbell like this?" he asked. His question was punctuated by a faint rhythmic ringing.

"I'm not home."

"Oh. Oh, shit. My bad. Where are you?"

"Phil's. I crashed here again last night."

"That's so sad for you. You need to get a life," he said.

"Well, this has been a lovely talk. Can I go eat breakfast now?"

"No, wait. I need to talk to you."

"About what?"

"The next phase." That sounded ominous.

Phil walked in and handed me a banana. He frowned when he saw I was on the phone, then sat at the desk.

"I have a feeling I'm not going to like the next phase," I said.

"No. Listen. You're going to love it. But we need your opinion or whatever. When are you coming home?"

My wrists started to itch. This boy was going to kill me. "I don't know. We're almost done editing so I'll probably be here for a few more days."

"I get it. That works. We can't be seen in public together anyway. Can I bring you guys lunch?"

"I guess."

"Excellent. I'll text details. Love you, boss. Bye." He hung up before I could respond.

Phil turned to stare at me. "What was that?"

I opened my banana and took a bite. "Diego. Isn't that why you made me check my phone?"

He shook his head. "No. The Wylie split. Didn't you check the news?"

I was way too tired for this. "No. I just looked at my messages and figured that was what you were talking about. I assume the divorce was announced?"

"Damn. She's getting divorced? That's rough."

"See? This is why you should be on set. Or at least set adjacent. They broke up halfway through the shoot," I said. Phil opened his mouth. "And if you say a single fucking thing that blames me for it, I will strangle you."

"I would never." He pressed his lips together.

"Dick."

"I guess this isn't news for you then?"

"No. The studio is working with her agent to roll out the announcements. This is probably a redirection attempt in response to Diego's little stunt."

Phil laughed. "Probably."

"You're going to get to meet him, by the way."

"Yeah, I assumed I would at some point."

"No. Today. He's coming over to bring us lunch and discuss, quote, the next phase of the plan, unquote."

Phil fought a grin. "And you're not happy about this, right?"

"Not remotely."

"Well, I'm delighted."

"Of course you are."

"We better get to work. I want to give Diego my full attention." He turned back to his monitors.

❖

"Phase six," Diego said.

"The premiere," Teddy said. They sketched out the title in the air together like they were in the worst pitch meeting I'd ever seen.

"I'm going to stop you right there, boys," I said. Phase six. They were trying to give me a stroke.

"You can't stop us yet. We haven't even told you the plan." Diego looked at Phil for help.

"He's right. Hear them out before you shut them down," Phil said.

I thought I was already being pretty benevolent letting them stay. I'd expected Diego and lunch. Instead I got Tweedledee and Tweedledum ramping each other up in a rehearsed scene from my nightmares.

"Sure. Why not?" I crossed my arms and waited.

"Okay. Well, your body language isn't very conducive to my process. I feel like you're not being very open," Diego said.

"Diego," I said.

He rolled his eyes. "We don't have to actually attend the premiere."

"Yes, we do," I said.

"No, we don't," Teddy said.

"Yes—" I started.

"Shut up. Just listen," Diego snapped. "Seriously. I know you're looking out for us and the rest of the cast. And we get that you've been in the business since before Jesus was born, but you can listen, right? Like you can do us that basic courtesy?" His eyes got all deep and dark and serious as he spoke. It was like a switch flipped. This wasn't vapid Diego. This was a new Diego.

"Sorry. Yes, I can listen."

"Thank you." He took a deep breath. "Okay. We don't have to attend the screening. There's no Q&A afterward so the only thing we're required to attend is the red carpet."

"Right," I said.

"So that's all we're going to do," Teddy said.

"Yeah, the whole cast will go. Solidarity and all that," Diego said.

Teddy nodded along with him. "We'll follow along with everything expected of us. We'll wear nice outfits and smile for the cameras and play nice with reporters."

"Okay." I glanced over at Phil. He also seemed to be missing what exactly was subversive about this plan.

"But then," Diego said grandly.

"Then we're going to leave and have our own afterparty," Teddy said.

"We will take one thousand photos. We will post them immediately. We will go Live. We will absolutely flaunt that the cast is united. And as a cast we opted to peace out as soon as we possibly could," Diego said.

"Got it. So you're trying to piss off the studio?" I asked rhetorically.

"Yes, exactly." Diego nodded, delighted that I'd followed along.

"Hold up. You're intentionally pissing off the studio?"

"No. We are intentionally distancing ourselves from the studio. Doing so will have the accidental but entirely delightful consequence of pissing off the studio," Teddy said.

"To what end?" I asked.

Diego leaned in. "Phase seven."

"And what's phase seven?" I asked. Like a dipshit.

"We can't get into phase seven today." Diego's tone was firm with just a hint of regret. Teddy shook his head.

"Can I ask a question?" Phil politely put up his hand.

"Yeah, sure," Diego said.

"What were phases one through five?"

Diego shook his head. "I'm sorry. That's a lot of ground to cover."

"Right. Of course." Phil sat back with a shit-eating grin. He was enjoying this far too much.

"Why are you guys telling me about phase—what was it? Seven?" I asked.

"The premiere is six," Diego said.

"Neat. Cool. Six. Why are you telling me about phase six?"

"Because we want your opinion." Diego made it sound exceedingly believable that they actually did want my opinion, but I was still wary of their motivation. "When we escape, what sort of venue will say that we obviously planned ahead, but also has plausible deniability? Like it's possible we just decided to all leave together, but everyone knows we really didn't."

"I don't understand why you're asking me."

Teddy seemed to have anticipated that question. "You know how the studio guys think. Also, we want your buy-in. This doesn't work without your buy-in."

"But you won't actually tell me what you're planning?" I asked.

"No," Teddy said.

"How am I supposed to blindly follow that?" I asked. Both their faces softened. Their initial seriousness had eased into banter, but now they were trying very hard to project a blend of kindness and pity. It looked particularly odd on Diego.

"We all spent two months learning to trust each other. I don't know about you, but for me, that's not normal. Not for a set and not for, you know, life," Diego said.

I sighed. He had a point. "Okay. You're right. I trust you."

"Good." He grinned like he'd been expecting it. Which was fair. "So venue?"

Phil had been intently watching us. He was only missing popcorn. Now that the drama had faded, he sat forward. "What about a club?"

"That would be good for the spontaneous narrative. That said, you can't control the environment," I said. A nightclub was volatile. Guaranteed press, but too many other variables. We needed a location the public didn't have access to.

"You could get a penthouse, throw a private party," Phil said.

"We did consider that. But it would require reservations. There's an obvious trail there. Fucks with our whole plausible deniability thing," Diego said.

"Yeah, but private party is definitely the way to go. What about someone's home? No reservations. Party could have been spontaneous. Make sure it's catered and set up enough to have been planned," I said.

They both liked that idea. Their eyes got big and they started nodding.

"Yes. That. Get some sexy lighting. Plenty of booze. Could have been just thrown together," Diego said to Teddy.

Teddy nodded. "I like it."

Phil figured out where we were headed a moment before I did. And then I did the math. "None of you guys have a house in LA that fits the requirements," I said. Phil started laughing.

"Wylie does." Diego winced.

"Is she on board for phase twenty-three?"

"Phase twenty-three isn't for another month and a half," Diego said dismissively.

"If there's a phase twenty-three at any point, then phase twenty-four will be me killing you," I said.

He laughed. "There's no phase twenty-three. We haven't gone to talk to Wylie yet. We wanted you on board first."

"Okay, well. Wylie is about to file for divorce so I'm thinking her house isn't the best place to throw a fake impromptu party."

"So you're volunteering to host? Great. Thanks." Diego stood. Teddy rushed to follow. "Good talking with you. Gotta go."

"Hey. Sit."

They sat back down and laughed at me. "Okay, fine. Will you host a party for us?" Diego asked.

"Sure."

"Nice." Diego bumped Teddy with his shoulder.

"And Addy's house is distinctive. So it'll kind of imply that she's behind this. Keep them guessing," Teddy said.

"You two aren't trying to pin this whole insurrection on me, are you?" I asked.

They laughed. "No," Diego said. At my look he sobered. "Really, no."

I only believed them because it seemed nefarious. They were very annoying but they weren't malicious. "Okay, what do you need from me?"

They exchanged a look and a silent conversation. "Nothing," Teddy said.

"Yeah. We'll just text details to Russ," Diego said.

"Send them to me for now. Russ is in Iowa," I said.

"Why would you banish Russ to Iowa?" Diego looked horrified at the thought.

"I didn't send her there. She chose it."

"No one chooses Iowa," Teddy said.

"She's visiting her mother. Her mother lives in Iowa."

Diego shrugged. "I assume she'll be back before the premiere?"

"You don't trust me to throw a party without Russ?" I asked.

"Not at all."

Teddy shook his head. "Nope."

Phil laughed.

"She'll be back next week. Assholes."

"Okay. We'll wait until then. Respectfully," Diego said.

"You know adding 'respectfully' to an obnoxious statement doesn't make it less obnoxious, right?"

"I disagree. Respectfully." Diego grinned.

CHAPTER THIRTY

Wylie slid her hand into mine as we walked onto the carpet. We'd spent more time pretending to be together or letting people believe we were together than we'd ever actually dated. So it was fitting to be at the premiere of the latest *DSN*, lying. But what had once been comfortable grated in a new way. The pain of being in love with Wylie and knowing she wasn't willing to love me had faded to a dull ache in the last decade—but this, knowing she did actually want me and that I was the coward? That was the sort of wound that couldn't heal no matter much how time passed.

Of course that cowardice was what had landed me here. When Danny called and told me the studio wanted me to attend the premiere with Wylie, I'd put up the most token of resistance. I'd managed to lie convincingly when he asked me what Diego and the rest of the principal cast were playing at. But when he demanded Wylie and I play up our relationship on the red carpet, I'd capitulated. Like I always did. Privately, I could rail against the bastards all day. Publicly, I fell in line every fucking time. And I hated myself for it.

So I was here. I'd spent the whole day being scrubbed and polished and pressed into a beautiful suit. It was my usual style— navy open-collared shirt, deep green double-breasted suit, shined Chelsea boots. Usually, it would feel like armor. Good tailoring had that effect. Instead it felt like another straight jacket.

A wall of photographers faced us. All of them were shouting our names, trying to get the right shot of us looking directly at them. It all felt silly and pointless. None of the photos would be any different from the rest. But it wasn't my job to critique the process. My job was to step and repeat.

Wylie leaned close and wrapped my arm around her waist. She was wearing heels that put her right at my height. She was also wearing some sort of crop top situation under an open suit jacket and the expanse of skin was sexy as fuck. She waved with her free hand at someone. Her smile was big, infectious, but it had lost some of its warmth. She was playing at having fun.

She turned that fake smile on me. "Do you think you could give me something to work with here?"

I smiled back, equally strained. "What are you talking about?"

"You're being more reluctant than usual," she said softly. Anyone watching would think she was whispering sweet, sexy things to me.

A flash went off very close to us. I leaned close and pressed my lips to her ear. "I'm not sure what you mean."

"Addy! Parsons!" was our only warning before Diego was hugging us like he hadn't seen us since we wrapped—which we were pretending was true. He squeezed between us and smiled for another round of flashes. Then he turned to me. "Christ, bro. What's up with you? You look like you just got diagnosed with a rare oozing disease and she gave it to you."

"That's...graphic?" I said.

"Told you." Wylie softly smiled and gave my chin a shake. "Remember you're supposed to like me."

"Wow. Okay. Too volatile. I'm out." Diego released us and went to rejoin Teddy and Logan.

"The issue isn't me liking you." I drew her in close. I was all too aware of the multitude of cameras around us. If there was any video, some enterprising Gen Z queer was sure to teach themselves lip reading so they could re-create what we were saying with devastating accuracy. And there was certainly video.

"Then why are you acting so reserved?" she asked through a smile.

"You mean aside from you telling me I treated being loved as a burden?" I waved at Molly and Kayleigh. They were twenty feet down the line doing a much better impression of liking each other than we were.

Wylie kissed my cheek for cover as she said, "We can't discuss this here."

I broke all the rules and turned my back to the press. "No. But there's nothing to talk about. You were right. I'm an asshole. And I'm painfully in love with you, which makes pretending to love you for entertainment far more devastating." I spun back to the press with a smile without waiting for a response.

Rosie and Emma appeared to my left. They were a lifeline. If I made eye contact with Wylie, I was sure to kiss her or cry or both. I turned away instead. Rosie hugged me in greeting. Emma took my hand and draped my arm over her shoulder. We posed for the cameras. Wylie watched us for a moment then went to join Teddy.

After the initial gauntlet of constant flashes and shouted names, we had brief interviews. They all felt the same.

"In this film, Taylor really leans into adulthood. We've watched her grow up over the last decade, but here we finally get to see the results of some of those life lessons." I smiled and nodded to another question I wasn't really hearing.

Wylie joined my interview and I grinned at her like she was the only person in the world. She kissed my cheek and strained to listen to the next question. "I think the audience will really enjoy the development of Grace and Taylor's relationship in *Redux*. They've definitely moved from the teen protagonists to a married couple," she said.

"Yes." I nodded like I hadn't heard or said six versions of the same thing in the last twenty minutes. "We—" I laughed at my Freudian slip. "They are functioning as a unit in ways we haven't seen in previous films."

Wylie leaned her head on my shoulder. "The script this time really allowed us to lean into that dynamic and the results felt really authentic."

We were ushered along the line to the next interview. This asshole veered from the script all journalists were supposed to stick to.

"Wylie, could you comment on your recent split? Last month, you and Jocelyn released joint statements saying you were working on yourselves separately but still committed to your marriage. But yesterday, you filed for divorce. What changed?"

Wylie nodded politely until he was done speaking. "We're here to discuss this movie. I don't have any comment on anything else."

He flinched like he'd been expecting more of a rebuttal. When he realized she wasn't going to lambast him, he pressed on. "What about you, PJ? The rumors of your ongoing relationship have been circulating for years. Any truth to the rumor that you're the reason behind this recent split?"

"No comment."

"The timing is suggestive," he said.

"No comment," I said more assertively. "Thank you for coming out." I dragged Wylie down to the next reporter. Wylie squeezed my hand and it felt like a lifeline. There was no telling what she felt about us and my accidental confession of love, but here, surrounded by reporters, we were united.

"You two have acted together, but, PJ, you've never directed yourself. And, Wylie, you've never had PJ direct you. What was that experience like?" The reporter was looking at Wylie, clearly hoping for a sound bite from her.

I cut in. "It was certainly a challenge, but we had an amazingly supportive crew who really made the experience positive."

The reporter nodded and launched into a slightly different line of questions. Not long after, we were rescued by a publicist for group photos. Which sounded like a good idea until I saw Claude, Nelson, and Eddie. Well, they were fine, but that meant Sean was lurking somewhere.

Diego and Teddy hugged Claude and Nelson. Teddy slapped Eddie on the back and shook his hand. Diego grabbed Eddie and hugged him too. Nelson and Eddie seemed, frankly, surprised by the show of affection. It wasn't until Sean appeared by Claude and Teddy looked right through him that I realized what they were doing.

Reporters pressed close to get their shots and shout their questions. The boys didn't overplay their hand though. Instead they just surrounded themselves with their cast mates and posed for a few dozen photos. They all remained completely unaware of the strange man they had allegedly never seen, standing at the edge of the group.

Sean, of course, wasn't having any of that. He moved to the center back of the group. I smelled the sweetness of his cologne behind me before I saw him. He put a hand on my shoulder. Suddenly, Diego was behind me, pulling Wylie and me close.

"How are my two favorite costars?" Diego asked.

"Having the time of my life, thanks," I said.

"Yep, stuff that dreams are made of here," Wylie said.

"Wonderful. I know you're being sarcastic, but I'll take it because I love you both deeply." He squeezed us even closer, then kissed Wylie's cheek followed by mine. It was an obnoxiously loud smack in my ear. I fought my annoyance and kept smiling. Only twenty more minutes and we could leave this oppressively loud, bright place with the specter of Sean Murray. Of course, that meant Wylie might actually want to talk to me. Or at me. Maybe the red carpet was the safer bet.

❖

In a stroke of genius, I managed to ditch Wylie as we all made our escape. She was stuck talking to Rosie so I slid away and climbed in the waiting limo. We were all going to the same place. She could ride with anyone but me.

The limo was blissfully quiet. Faint lights were placed to keep drinks from being spilled, but otherwise it was dark. The divider was up so I was alone. I breathed exactly one deep, calming breath before the door opened and Wylie climbed in.

"Asshole," she said. She closed the door and we started to drive.

"Why am I an asshole?" I asked. And then I answered my own question. "Oh, that."

"What? I'm exceedingly curious why you think you're an asshole."

"Because I blurted out that I was in love with you on the red carpet and then ran away. And also because of all the stuff you said at the wrap party about me pushing people away." I realized I was slowly pushing myself back into the corner of the seat. I didn't stop the movement, but I at least acknowledged how pathetic it was to myself.

This was why I liked my usual car with my usual rotating featureless drivers. They didn't talk to me. I didn't talk to them. We were silenced by the rules of propriety. But no. Russ insisted I'd want a limo for the premiere. She said it was retro. And now I had an actual privacy screen and a pissed off Wylie who was going to make me have a real conversation. The whole thing was distasteful.

Wylie nodded. "Yeah. All of that makes you a spectacular asshole. But I was actually talking about you ditching me just now."

"I didn't ditch you."

"You did. If I hadn't bribed our driver, he would have left without me." She had me there.

"Okay. Yeah. I'm an asshole for that reason too."

"Stop doing that," she said.

"What?"

"Agreeing with me. You already look stupid hot. When you agree with me, it makes it harder to be mad at you."

"I look stupid hot?" I pointedly looked up and down the length of her. She had her feet stretched out and was turned sort of sideways to talk to me. Her arm was up on the seat back, which pulled her suit jacket open. "You're wearing that. And sitting like that. And getting mad at me for looking hot?"

"Fuck this." She leaned over and kissed me. Nothing delicate about it either. She just stuck her tongue in my mouth and crawled into my lap.

I grabbed her ass and pulled her closer. She unbuttoned my shirt and pulled it out of my pants. Her hands were warm on my cool skin. I shoved her jacket off her shoulders. I was wrestling with the crop top when she grabbed my hands and pressed them to the seat.

"What are you doing?" I asked, suddenly stymied.

"Last time you left me high and well, not dry."

I rolled my eyes. "That was a very bad line."

"Do you want this? Me?" Her fingers twitched against the top of my hands. She was asking about a hell of a lot more than sex.

"Very much," I said.

I kissed the corner of her mouth, her cheek, her lips. She released my hands. I brushed my thumb across her cheek, watched her pupils shift. She let me study her face. Then I kissed her again slowly, thoroughly. I wrapped an arm around her waist and shifted so she was lying beneath me on the long seat. She scraped her fingers through my hair and pressed my face to her neck. She tasted like salt. I bit her shoulder and thrilled at the soft flesh between my teeth. I wanted to swallow her, to consume her.

Wy groaned and tilted her hips up. I rushed to open her pants. She pushed them down and got them low enough to give me relatively unimpeded access. I was already high on the night. The stress and fear had ramped me up, and the moment I touched her, that adrenaline shifted to trembling want. I slid inside her and I could feel her everywhere. Surrounding me, filling me. Wylie gripped my neck and pulled me up to kiss her again. Her mouth was warm, her lips smooth and soft.

She wrapped her hand around the back of my arm. "Please, PJ."

I slowed my movements, shifted to a subtle twitch of my fingers. "What?"

"Fuck me. God, you're a fucking tease."

I grinned even as I readjusted so I could fuck her hard and fast the way I knew she wanted it. When I pressed inside her again, she threw her head back and cried out. Once, twice and she was gone.

"I forgot how easy you are," I said.

"You are such an ass."

I laughed. "You like me."

"I'll like you more if you do that a few more times."

"This?" I curled my fingers forward and her hips jumped.

"God, yes."

She pulled me down to kiss her again. Her hands pulled at my hair. I could judge from the urgency and the pressure when she was about to come again. I slowed and let her ride against my hand. Her movement was inhibited by my weight against her. She groaned in frustration. I lifted my hips enough to let her move. She rode my hand hard. Her heel dug into my leg as she arched back and came again. I collapsed against her chest and listened to her heart pound.

When I slowly pulled out, she frowned. "I'm not done with you."

I glanced out the window. The swerves in the road had become all too familiar. "Want me to have the driver circle the neighborhood a few times?"

She laughed and smacked my shoulder. "No. Later."

I kissed her again, pressed my tongue past her lips, imprinted the feel of her all around me. "Fine. But I'm going to hold you to that."

CHAPTER THIRTY-ONE

I stretched out my feet, sipped my drink, and watched a few generations of *Dangerous Summer Nights* cast members laugh in my backyard. The guys hadn't told me anything about the party itself—even though I was apparently hosting it. They had entirely cut me out of it actually. Russ sent me invoices and I paid them. That was my contribution. It was absolutely worth it. The yard was littered with candles. Everything was in full bloom—though on closer inspection, it appeared that Russ had brought in a bunch of new tropical flowers that were now spilling fragrance from their pots. Even the sky had decided to participate, blanketing us with a rich navy sky and a slender split of moon.

Jeffrey was ensconced with Gwen, the woman who'd been the lead of the third movie only to be killed in the opening of the fourth. Kaleb and Florian were with the first sequel killer—a devastatingly gorgeous woman who had gone on to helm some prestige television show that won handfuls of awards. And unless I was mistaken, Taryn and Diego were flirting so hard that she was in danger of pregnancy just from eye contact. Which was an interesting development.

A manicured hand with short, dark painted nails slid down my shoulder. Wylie cupped my chin and turned my face up so she could kiss me.

"Hi," she said.

"Hi." I grinned like an idiot.

"Is it my imagination or are Taryn and Diego making serious eyes at each other?"

"Hundred percent. I already got a wedding invitation," I said.

Wylie laughed softly. The yard around us suddenly erupted in applause. Wylie pulled back so we could see what had caused the ruckus. But of course they were all just staring at us.

"You idiots finally work it out?" Jeffrey called.

"That's none of your business, sir," I said.

"Babe, this is absolutely our business." Taryn pointed at us and made a little circle in the air. "This launched half of our careers."

"She has a point," Wylie whispered.

"Fine. Yes. Whatever." I grabbed Wylie and pulled her down to kiss me again.

They all started laughing and shouting at us.

"Can I launch this on Insta?" Diego asked.

Wylie and I stopped kissing to shout at him. "No."

He had crossed the yard during the applause and was now hovering and holding out his phone. "Look at the photos first. You two are hot."

"Absolutely not," I said.

He rolled his eyes. "Fine." He sat on the arm of my chair that Wylie wasn't leaning over. "Hey, listen." He glanced behind him, then lowered his voice. "Do you think Taryn would go out with a younger guy?"

"Aren't you like twenty-seven?" I asked.

"No." He frowned. "Not until next month."

"You're only like five years younger than her," Wylie said.

"Yeah, but she's way more respected and established in the business. That creates, you know, a power discrepancy. I wouldn't want to cross a line."

"You would be the one with less power," Wylie said.

"I know. But what if she feels like it's inappropriate?"

"Diego, buddy," I said.

"Yeah?"

"The fact that you're having this conversation means you're already aware of her boundaries and yours. So just ask her out and keep making it clear that you're open to discussion."

"Right. Okay. Thanks, guys." He hustled back to where Taryn was watching the lights over the city.

"So did he tell you what the next phase in the plan is?" Wylie asked.

"Isn't this it?"

She shook her head. "I don't think so."

"I assumed he was kidding about it going beyond tonight."

Wylie hmmed and surveyed the yard. "Logan. He'll be our weak link." She nodded to where Logan was sitting at the bar with Rosie and Charlie, the girl who starred in the fourth movie.

"Should we separate him from the girls?"

"Get him alone for the kill? Heck yeah." Wylie touched my shoulder. "Okay, I'll go get rid of Rosie and Charlie. You interrogate."

"Deal."

Wylie went to the bar and got a drink. She and Rosie chatted a bit, then Charlie got in on it. Wy pointed to something across the yard. The girls both stood and they all went to study some flower. I moved in and sat next to Logan.

"Hey, bud."

"Addy!" He hugged me. "What do you think?" He gestured at the packed party. "Did we do good?"

"You did so good. How did you get all these former cast members?" I asked.

"Well, a handful of them were already going to the premiere. We just reached out to them. Taryn and Jeffrey were super cool about helping us contact the right people."

"Yeah, they're pretty great."

"They are. When we started talking to the cast from the other movies, Jeffrey was all over recruiting." He drank his beer and nodded enthusiastically. This kid was adorable.

"So when is Diego launching the next step?" I asked.

"I'm not sure. I think he wants to see how this news cycle goes with like the party and the premiere." Dammit. Wylie was right.

"Got it. I guess that makes sense."

"Yeah. Because we want to establish how at odds you and Sean are in real life, you know, so it will cement how removed you are from the studio." Logan was entirely unaware of the motivation behind my questions. Which was good. Except I had no clue what we were talking about.

"Do you think that'll work? Will this be enough?" I was grasping, but he really wasn't giving me much to work with.

"Oh, it'll work. I mean, the texts are pretty fucked up."

"I've heard," I said. We had subject matter. Progress.

"Diego didn't make you read them? Shit. Of course not. There are just so many." He drank more beer, then leaned in. "I'm trying to convince him to only release like half the conversations, but he thinks it's important to show the full picture."

"Yeah, that's definitely a conundrum." It was pretty hard to weigh in since I still didn't know what we were discussing. "I assume you've talked about this with the girls too. What do they think? What about Teddy?"

Logan nodded sagely. "Yeah, Emma thinks we've got to do the whole thing. Teddy is with me. Rosie and Molly are somewhere between, I guess. They say there's a balance between too much info and providing nuance or something."

"Maybe I can weigh in?"

"Shit. Yeah. That would help. Diego really respects your opinion." Logan grabbed his beer and stood. "Come on."

I followed him, worried we were going to Diego. He would immediately shut this shit down. But maybe I could glean some information before he made them close ranks.

"Babe," Taryn said when we stopped by her and Diego.

"Babe."

Logan gripped Diego's shoulder. "Bro, I need your iPad. Addy said she'd help us decide how much to release."

Diego looked at Logan, then me, then back at Logan. "You dumbass."

"What? Why?" Logan's eyes got big.

"She played you." Diego nodded at me. I smirked. "How much did you tell her?"

"No. She already knew." Logan looked at me in slow-growing horror. "Right? You knew." He gasped and clutched Diego. It was all very dramatic. "No."

I pressed my lips together to keep from smiling too hard. "So how did you get Sean's text messages?"

"Goddammit, bro." Diego smacked Logan's shoulder. "I wanted her to be able to honestly say she didn't know about it. I was protecting her."

"Fuck." Logan's eyes shot back and forth between me and Diego. "I didn't know. Why didn't you tell me? I wouldn't have said shit."

"I thought you knew."

"Boys," I said. "I'm perfectly comfortable lying and saying I didn't know any of this. Now tell me what's going on."

Taryn put her hands up. "Wait. I'm out. Diego said I don't want to know this part." She left, but I saw the quick brush of hands between her and Diego.

"So how did you get the texts? And are you sure the source is legitimate?" I asked.

Diego sighed and frowned at me. "It was at the wrap party. Teddy wanted to make sure Sean didn't have any evidence of their relationship."

"Yeah. We were just going to delete any photos of them being buddies and also their text messages," Logan said.

"But when we were in there, we got a little curious."

Logan nodded very sincerely. "Curiosity is very healthy."

"It was too much to read right then so we just took all his messages," Diego said. "Did you know Sean has never deleted a text thread?"

"Yeah. They go back like fifteen years. There are like messages from his pool guy in 2010 talking about cleaning the tiles. So much boring shit." Logan rolled his eyes.

Diego glanced around us, then leaned in. "There's also a lot of not boring, horrifying shit. Damning shit."

"Hey." Wylie's hand slid across my back. It was warm and comforting where Diego's tone had made me break out in a cold sweat. "Did you get them to spill?"

"Of course I did." I turned and grinned at her. "They took Sean's phone at the wrap party and liberated fifteen years of text messages."

"Fuck." Wy nodded at them, impressed. "How did you get his phone?"

Diego was offended by the very question. "We roofied him. Teddy told you we were going to make sure he couldn't get handsy at the party."

"Teddy promised me you wouldn't roofie him," I said.

"He lied." Diego shrugged.

"Doesn't that seem problematic to you?"

"Nope," Diego said.

Wylie laughed. "So you roofied him and helped yourselves to his phone?"

"And then spent the entire party reading some of the most disgusting, hateful things I've ever read about women," Diego said.

"That doesn't sound fun," I said.

"It was not."

"Nope." Logan shook his head.

"And what's your plan now?" Wylie asked.

Diego gave Logan an utterly withering look. Logan panicked. "I'm sorry. I didn't know I wasn't supposed to tell her."

"Yeah, bro. That's on me." Diego gripped Logan's shoulder and Logan relaxed. Diego turned to us. "We're going to release the entire package to a bunch of media outlets and send it to the DA's offices in New York and Los Angeles. Anonymously, of course."

"Why? To what end?" I asked.

"Because I will never recover from my revulsion of having looked that man in the eye and shaken his hand and I want to make sure everyone else is as disgusted." Diego shrugged. "It'll destroy his reputation. If he ends up in jail, fucking great. If he just ends up alone and the punchline of every Woody Allen/Roman Polanski type joke online, also fucking great."

"I'm hoping for a gutting op-ed that dominates popular culture for weeks," Logan said.

"Yeah, he put a lot of money on that one," Diego said matter-of-factly.

"Diego went with documentary in seven to ten years. And also podcast series," Logan said.

Diego stopped Logan. "No, Emma went with podcast series. I predicted devastating memes."

"Right. Right." Logan nodded.

"I'm sorry. What?" Wylie asked.

"Yeah, you didn't actually put money on this?" If they had, I was going to smack all of them.

"Why not?" Logan asked.

I was pissed off. "Because you're still treating the whole Sean thing like a joke. He damaged real people. The women he talked about in those messages are going to have to read about their own assaults. It's not a lighthearted romp."

"Whoa. Hey." Diego put his hands up. "Slow down. We know. The bets are our way of dealing with the trauma of reading the texts. It's about us managing our own feelings."

"Okay?"

"And we've spoken with as many of the women we could identify, which was only like a handful, but still." Logan was outright embarrassed by the fact that they hadn't found more of the women. "We outlined the broad strokes and asked what they were comfortable with. All but one said to go for it."

"And she just wanted to read the texts to prepare herself. Once she did, she gave us the green light," Diego said.

"Then why did Taryn just bow out?" I asked.

"She wants to be able to claim as little knowledge as possible. We're respecting that. Duh."

Once again, I was forced to admit that Diego and his cohort had actually given thought to their actions and potential consequences. Which was inconvenient for the picture I'd prematurely constructed of them.

"And this is why you wanted to throw an exclusive party?" I gestured with my drink at the overfilled patio.

"Sort of." Diego flinched. "The thing is, you chose to work with him. I mean, we all did. But you two did repeatedly." He put up his hands. "And I get why. You were reluctant and all that, but every time they swore up and down that he wouldn't be on set the days you were there. And then he would show up anyway."

"Yeah. But that doesn't excuse it." Wylie glanced at me. "We should have known better."

"Wait. How did you know that?" I asked Diego.

He grinned. "Sean and Danny talked about it. A lot. It doesn't totally let you off the hook, but the messages make it pretty clear that you two were fed up with Sean's behavior."

"So you're doing all this to make sure our reputations don't go down with Oath?" I asked.

I never got the answer to that because Jeffery tapped his glass to get everyone's attention. We turned in the direction of the sound.

"Hey, everyone. This isn't my party, but I wanted to offer a few words. To the *Redux* cast, my sincere thanks and congratulations." Jeffrey raised his glass in the direction of Diego and Logan, then Rosie and Emma. Molly and Kayleigh saluted him with their own glasses. Teddy, standing next to Jeffrey, rounded out the circle with a handshake. "You all managed to resolve something that my costars and I fumbled ten years ago. A blight on Hollywood. And that blight is the breakup of PJ Addison and Wylie Parsons." He had to shout the last bit because the yard erupted in laughter. "So thank you for getting these two back together and erasing our collective shame."

"I think we're going to have to kill him," I said to Wylie.

She nodded slowly, wisely. "Maybe twice."

CHAPTER THIRTY-TWO

When we fell asleep that night—naked, pressed chest to chest, my fingers entwined in Wylie's hair, hers drawing patterns over my spine—it all was worth it. Wylie drifted in and out of sleep. Her bare thigh between my legs kept me on the edge with every movement. Her skin was soft and smelled bright and sweet. I didn't care if I'd be erroneously lambasted in the press for destroying her marriage. I didn't care if the rags scrutinized our every movement for the last year or the next. If I could have this, I could survive it all.

I finally slept and it was the best sleep I'd gotten in a decade. This was the real problem with love. Once you'd had it, everything after was washed out and weak. Even sleeping was a chore.

The next morning, I reached out and found the bed empty. My heart raced. I got up and searched for my robe. When I realized why I couldn't find it—that Wylie was wearing it—I slowed and grabbed a different one. I found her sprawled on the couch. She had the shawl collar crowded up around her ears and half the windows open, which seemed counterintuitive and also perfectly Wylie.

"Morning." I tipped her chin up and kissed her. I slid my hand down her side.

"Well, good morning to you." She looked pointedly at my wandering hand.

"Get over yourself." I pulled my glasses out of the pocket of the robe she was wearing and put them on.

"You're lucky you look cute with your glasses and your hair all rumpled."

"Babe, I'm always cute." I kissed her again.

She smiled. "There's coffee. And I sure wish I had more." She looked longingly at her nearly empty coffee cup.

I rolled my eyes and took her cup and saucer back to the kitchen. I filled my own thin china cup. When I brought the mugs back to Wylie, she had shifted enough to give me a whole eighteen inches of couch at her feet. I handed her one of the saucers and sat. She lifted her feet to rest in my lap.

"Hi." She smiled at me.

"Hi."

We spent a luxurious few minutes staring at each other and grinning like idiots. Wylie broke first. She set her coffee down and picked up my iPad from the table.

"You know, you should probably change your passcode," she said as she unlocked it.

I shrugged. "You and Russ are the only ones who know it."

She shook her head at me. "Everyone who matters is talking about our little party last night."

She handed over the iPad open on an article about the premiere. I glanced through it. A good chunk of the article was about the main cast, director, screenwriters, and various producers leaving the red carpet together. Another paragraph was dedicated to the who's who of *DSN* alumni at our party. The end was rife with speculation about the behind-the-scenes drama at Oath Entertainment. An anonymous source had provided a quote about how a high ranking person on set had warned the actors to stay away from a certain other high ranking person on set. It was purposefully vague and had Diego's fingerprints all over it.

"Are they all like this?" I asked.

"This is one of the better ones. Most of them are either too conservative and refuse to speculate on the meaning or they're pure speculation. Those are entertaining but have little provable accuracy," she said.

"How many include Diego's quote?"

"All of them. But he swears it didn't come from him," she said. I gave her a look of disbelief. "I know. I accused Teddy and he fumbled so I'm thinking it's him."

"That's cute."

"Very."

"You know what else is cute?" I asked.

"What's that?"

"You in my robe. Big fan." I set my coffee and the iPad down so I could stretch out on top of her and kiss her.

"Oh, yeah?"

I nodded and kissed her again. She gripped my bare toes with her longer ones. "Stop that," I said.

"You like it."

"I do not. You're going to pinch me." I'd forgotten until right then that she used to do that. It annoyed the hell out of me. I'd missed it desperately.

She immediately pinched my leg. "Oops."

"You're a freak with freakish toes, you know that?"

"Yeah. But that's okay. Because you think I'm cute in your robe." She smiled with more vim than she had a right to.

I kissed her again. "It's true."

"Bet you can't guess what's underneath it," she said.

"I'm thinking it's nothing." I leaned up and slid a finger under one side to peek under the thick cotton. "Is it nothing?"

She clapped her hand over mine. "Excuse me, sir."

"What? I'm just trying to follow up on a rumor I heard." I wiggled my fingers but she had them trapped.

"Yeah? What rumor?"

"That you're naked under here," I said.

"You're the one who started the rumor."

"That doesn't mean it isn't true."

She laughed and pulled me down into a kiss. Her lip slid between mine. It was soft and warm and exquisite. The tip of her tongue played over my bottom lip. I opened my mouth to let her in. She tasted like rich coffee—full and sweet and bitter. Her hands slid into my hair and held me still while she explored my mouth. I tilted my hips to make her groan.

"I take it you're up since coffee is started. Have you—fuck," Russ said.

I pushed up off Wylie as if that would hide what we were doing or that she had very clearly slept over.

"I'm sorry. I didn't realize." Russ was bright red. She backed out of the room.

"It's fine. Come back," I called, laughing.

Wylie pulled her robe closed and sat up. "Russ, get back here."

Russ slowly came back. She sat in a chair across the room, her eyes very carefully on the floor. "I'm so sorry."

"Hey, it's fine." I checked to make sure my robe was tied. "You want coffee?"

"Please."

When I returned with another cup of coffee, Russ was a normal color and she was making eye contact with Wylie.

"Doing okay there, pal?" I asked.

Russ took the coffee and nodded. "Sorry. I don't think I've ever known you to have an overnight guest."

"Never?" Wylie asked.

"There's no cool way for you to answer that so please don't," I said.

Russ bit back a smile and drank her coffee. "I came because your phone is off and you've got a meeting with Paulie at noon. And the execs over at Oath won't stop calling about last night. They'd like to see you this afternoon."

I groaned. "That really cuts into my plans for the day."

Wylie leaned over and whispered loudly, "Are they naked plans?"

"Very naked."

Russ said nothing.

"Can we put them off for a few days?" I asked.

"Probably. But we should at least respond so they stop calling," Russ said.

"Russ, can you give us a minute?" Wylie asked.

"Sure." She stood and left the room.

Wylie took my hand. "This is all going to be a shitshow."

"Yeah."

"I mean Oath. And Diego's Sean bomb. Not to mention when the paparazzi realize we're together."

"Are we?" I asked without thinking. And then I was terrified of her answer.

Wylie smiled slowly. "Oh, yes."

"Even though I'm a self-involved asshole?"

"Tragically, I find your assholery charming."

"Really?"

"I love you, PJ. I've always loved you. To the detriment of every adult relationship I've ever had."

I grinned. "Jeffrey is going to be insufferable."

"Yes. That. He might be worse than the media when it goes public."

"Are you going somewhere with this?" I asked.

"Let's not be here."

"What do you mean?"

"Run away with me. Just for a couple of weeks. And then Russ and Paulie will be able to respond to every media and meeting request with 'Sorry, she's out of the country and cannot comment.' I'm sure we can find somewhere without cell service."

"Are you serious?" There was a certain genius to the idea.

"Yeah. I mean, the circus will be here when we get back. But hopefully it will have died down a little. Plus, we can make out without people taking photos of us."

"You're not going to propose are you?"

A look of irritation went across her face. But it was more amusement than offense. "You think so little of me?"

I shrugged. "You have a habit of getting married."

"I do not."

"Babe," I said.

"Asshole," she said.

"I'd love to run away with you."

"Yeah?" A grin spread across her face.

"It's a damn good idea."

"Full disclosure, it wasn't mine." She picked up her coffee and settled back into the corner of the couch. "Diego and Taryn are running off to Mexico. They flew out this morning."

"Seriously? When did you find this out?"

She nodded. "Last night. Taryn said she was going on a wellness retreat. Diego is going to visit his grandfather. Taryn's retreat just happens to be on a beach in Oaxaca. You'll never believe where

Diego's family estate is." She raised her eyebrows suggestively. "They denied they were going together, but they happen to have the same flight."

"Good for them."

"Yeah. It's fucking adorable."

"Russ," I called.

A minute later, she walked back into the room. "Yeah?"

"Can you book us to go somewhere out of the country without cell service?"

She sighed in amusement and irritation. "Sure. When do you want to leave?"

"Today," I said.

The amusement became overshadowed by the irritation. "Of course. Any preferences on location?"

Wylie and I looked at each other and shrugged. "A beach," Wy said.

"You're not going to propose are you?" Russ asked her.

"I strongly dislike both of you," Wy said.

❖

Three hours later, Wylie and I were lounging on the bamboo sofa, staring at the palms overhead swaying in a light breeze. I had my feet up on the table. Wylie's head was in my lap and her feet hung over the arm of the couch. Her assistant would arrive within the hour with a packed bag and Wylie's passport. In ninety minutes, a car was taking us to LAX. I hadn't bothered to ask where we were going.

"I wasn't fair to you, you know?" Wylie played with my hand, tracing the outline of each joint and line.

"How's that?" I asked.

"At the wrap party. I was just pissed at you."

"What you said was fair." I threaded my fingers through hers.

"Yeah, but I took my anger at myself out on you."

I frowned. "Why were you mad at yourself?"

"Because I didn't have your conviction. You chose loneliness over a lie. You've always been more principled than me. Even when we were young."

"Don't confuse stubbornness for conviction," I said.

She shrugged and went back to drawing patterns on the back of my hand.

"Wylie." I freed my hand so I could tilt her chin toward me. "I love you. It's always been you. I loved you when I was so angry at you that I couldn't see. I loved you when I watched you marry someone else. I loved you when I was with someone else and when I was alone." Her eyes started to fill. Just a little. "You at least tried for happiness. I just gave up. I'm never doing that again. It's you and me from here on out."

She gave me a small smile that grew as she sat up to kiss me. "Your convictions are hot."

"You're only saying that because they're directed at you."

"Yes, obviously. I'm an actor, babe. Always have to be the center of attention."

I laughed as she lay back on my lap. We spent an hour and a half flirting and discussing nothing. At some point, Wylie's assistant came by. When the car came to take us, we held hands and stared into each other's eyes and ignored everyone and everything around us. None of it mattered. Or at least, none of it mattered as much as she did.

About the Author

Award-winning author Ashley Bartlett was born and raised in California. Her life consists of reading, writing, and editing. Most of the time Ashley engages in these pursuits while sitting in front of a coffee shop with her wife.

It's a glamorous life.

She is an obnoxious, sarcastic punk-ass, but her friends don't hold that against her. She lives in Sacramento, but you can find her at ashbartlett.com.

Books Available from Bold Strokes Books

A Case for Discretion by Ashley Moore. Will Gwen, a prominent Atlanta attorney, choose Etta, the law student she's clandestinely dating, or is her political future too important to sacrifice? (978-1-63679-617-8)

Aubrey McFadden Is Never Getting Married by Georgia Beers. Aubrey McFadden is never getting married, but she does have five weddings to attend, and she'll be avoiding Monica Wallace, the woman who ruined her happily ever after, at every single one. (978-1-63679-613-0)

Flowers for Dead Girls by Abigail Collins. Isla might be just the right kind of girl to bring Astra out of her shell—and maybe more. The only problem? She's dead. (978-1-63679-584-3)

Good Bones by Aurora Rey. Designer and contractor Logan Barrow can give Kathleen Kenney the house of her dreams, but can she convince the cynical romance writer to take a chance on love? (978-1-63679-589-8)

Leather, Lace, and Locs by Anne Shade. Three friends, each on their own path in life, with one obstacle…finding room in their busy lives for a love that will give them their happily ever afters. (978-1-63679-529-4)

Rainbow Overalls by Maggie Fortuna. Arriving in Vermont for her first year of college, an introverted bookworm forms a friendship with an outgoing artist and finds what comes after the classic coming out story: a being out story. (978-1-63679-606-2)

Revisiting Summer Nights by Ashley Bartlett. PJ Addison and Wylie Parsons have been called back to film the most recent Dangerous Summer Nights installment. Only this time they're not in love and it's going to stay that way. (978-1-63679-551-5)

The Broken Lines of Us by Shia Woods. Charlie Dawson returns to the city she left behind and she meets an unexpected stranger on her first night back, discovering that coming home might not be as hard as she thought. (978-1-63679-585-0)

Triad Magic by 'Nathan Burgoine. Face-to-face against forces set in motion hundreds of years ago, Luc, Anders, and Curtis—vampire, demon, and wizard—must draw on the power of blood, soul, and magic to stop a killer. (978-1-63679-505-8)

All This Time by Sage Donnell. Erin and Jodi share a complicated past, but a very different present. Will they ever be able to make a future together work? (978-1-63679-622-2)

Crossing Bridges by Chelsey Lynford. When a one-night stand between a snowboard instructor and a business executive becomes more, one has to overcome her past, while the other must let go of her planned future. (978-1-63679-646-8)

Dancing Toward Stardust by Julia Underwood. Age has nothing to do with becoming the person you were meant to be, taking a chance, and finding love. (978-1-63679-588-1)

Evacuation to Love by CA Popovich. As a hurricane rips through Florida, so too are Joanne and Shanna's lives upended. It'll take a force of nature to show them the love it takes to rebuild. (978-1-63679-493-8)

Lean in to Love by Catherine Lane. Will badly behaving celebrities, erotic sex tapes, and steamy scandals prevent Rory and Ellis from leaning in to love? (978-1-63679-582-9)

Searching for Someday by Renee Roman. For loner Rayne Thomas, her only goal for working out is to build her confidence, but Maggie Flanders has another idea, and neither are prepared for the outcome. (978-1-63679-568-3)

The Romance Lovers Book Club by MA Binfield and Toni Logan. After their book club reads a romance about an American tourist falling in love with an English princess, Harper and her best friend, Alice, book an impulsive trip to London hoping they'll each fall for the women of their dreams. (978-1-63679-501-0)

Truly Home by J.J. Hale. Ruth and Olivia discover home is more than a four-letter word. (978-1-63679-579-9)

View from the Top by Morgan Adams. When it comes to love, sometimes the higher you climb, the harder you fall. (978-1-63679-604-8)

Blood Rage by Ileandra Young. A stolen artifact, a family in the dark, an entire city on edge. Can SPEAR agent Danika Karson juggle all three over a weekend with the "in-laws," while an unknown, malevolent entity lies in wait upon her very skin? (978-1-63679-539-3)

Ghost Town by R.E. Ward. Blair Wyndon and Leif Henderson are set to prove ghosts exist when the mystery suddenly turns deadly. Someone or something else is in Masonville, and if they don't find a way to escape, they might never leave. (978-1-63679-523-2)

Good Christian Girls by Elizabeth Bradshaw. In this heartfelt coming of age lesbian romance, Lacey and Jo help each other untangle who they are from who everyone says they're supposed to be. (978-1-63679-555-3)

Guide Us Home by CF Frizzell and Jesse J. Thoma. When acquisition of an abandoned lighthouse pits ambitious competitors Nancy and Sam against each other, it takes a WWII tale of two brave women to make them see the light. (978-1-63679-533-1)

Lost Harbor by Kimberly Cooper Griffin. For Alice and Bridget's love to survive, they must find a way to reconcile the most important passions in their lives—devotion to the church and each other. (978-1-63679-463-1)

Never a Bridesmaid by Spencer Greene. As her sister's wedding gets closer, Jessica finds that her hatred for the maid of honor is a bit more complicated than she thought. Could it be something more than hatred? (978-1-63679-559-1)

The Rewind by Nicole Stiling. For police detective Cami Lyons and crime reporter Alicia Flynn, some choices break hearts. Others leave a body count. (978-1-63679-572-0)

Turning Point by Cathy Dunnell. When Asha and her former high school bully Jody struggle to deny their growing attraction, can they move forward without going back? (978-1-63679-549-2)

When Tomorrow Comes by D. Jackson Leigh. Teague Maxwell, convinced she will die before she turns 41, hires animal rescue owner Baye Cobb to rehome her extensive menagerie. (978-1-63679-557-7)

You Had Me at Merlot by Melissa Brayden. Leighton and Jamie have all the ingredients to turn their attraction into love, but it's a recipe for disaster. (978-1-63679-543-0)

All Things Beautiful by Alaina Erdell. Casey Norford only planned to learn to paint like her mentor, Leighton Vaughn, not sleep with her. (978-1-63679-479-2)

Appalachian Awakening by Nance Sparks. The more Amber's and Leslie's paths cross, the more this hike of a lifetime begins to look like a love of a lifetime. (978-1-63679-527-0)

Dreamer by Kris Bryant. When life seems to be too good to be true and love is within reach, Sawyer and Macey discover the truth about the town of Ladybug Junction, and the cold light of reality tests the hearts of these dreamers. (978-1-63679-378-8)

Eyes on Her by Eden Darry. When increasingly violent acts of sabotage threaten to derail the opening of her glamping business, Callie Pope is sure her ex, Jules, has something to do with it. But Jules is dead…isn't she? (978-1-63679-214-9)

Head Over Heelflip by Sander Santiago. To secure the biggest prizes at the Colorado Amateur Street Sports Tour, Thomas Jefferson will do almost anything, even marrying his best friend and crush—Arturo "Uno" Ortiz. (978-1-63679-489-1)

Letters from Sarah by Joy Argento. A simple mistake brought them together, but Sarah must release past love to create a future with Lindsey she never dreamed possible. (978-1-63679-509-6)

Lost in the Wild by Kadyan. When their plane crash-lands, Allison and Mike face hunger, cold, a terrifying encounter with a bear, and feelings for each other neither expects. (978-1-63679-545-4)

Not Just Friends by Jordan Meadows. A tragedy leaves Jen struggling to figure out who she is and what is important to her. (978-1-63679-517-1)

Of Auras and Shadows by Jennifer Karter. Eryn and Rina's unexpected love may be exactly what the Community needs to heal the rot that comes not from the fetid Dark Lands that surround the Community but from within. (978-1-63679-541-6)

The Secret Duchess by Jane Walsh. A determined widow defies a duke and falls in love with a fashionable spinster in a fight for her rightful home. (978-1-63679-519-5)

Winter's Spell by Ursula Klein. When former college roommates reunite at a wedding in Provincetown, sparks fly, but can they find true love when evil sirens and trickster mermaids get in the way? (978-1-63679-503-4)